W9-AUD-138

DEVIL IN THE DARK

CHRIS LINDBERG

Copyright © 2016 Chris Lindberg
All rights reserved.
ISBN: 1539796248
ISBN 13: 9781539796244
Library of Congress Control Number: 2016918280
CreateSpace Independent Publishing Platform
North Charleston, South Carolina

DEVIL in the DARK is the follow-up to Chris Lindberg's debut thriller *CODE of DARKNESS*.

CODE of DARKNESS introduces Rage to the thriller genre and is available at Amazon, BarnesandNoble.com, and many other fine online retailers in both paperback and e-book format.

ACKNOWLEDGEMENTS

To my good friends Katie Telser and Ed Braun, both of whom once again did the heavy lifting in editing the book cover to cover. To my father-in-law John McKiernan, who helped me understand the workings of both sea-faring ships as well as Naval missions. To Tony Stewart, who designed a cover to which the contents of this book aspire to live up. To mom and Sandy, for reading the story only because of who'd written it. To Jenny, Luke, and Emma, who inspire all that I do.

And of course, to you, the reader, for taking a chance on this book. I hope you enjoy reading it as much as I did writing it.

For Mom and Dad

PROLOGUE

He had no recollection of the days anymore.

He'd stopped counting them when hunger had taken over his every waking thought. His stomach growled incessantly; his ribs pressed outward against his skin.

In his time here, he'd been reduced to a shell of his former self. A beggar waiting for his next meal.

And there would be no escape, he knew; he would die in this Godforsaken place, if not from starvation, then disease, or torture.

The night watchman had begun his rounds of the prison camp. The sound of his footsteps could be heard in the deathly still hallways outside.

He had no idea how many others were here, American or otherwise. The only things he saw were the concrete walls that surrounded him, the dirt floor beneath him, the sliver of light that came through the meager opening that passed for a window, the white bucket in the corner, and the boots of the night watchman who brought him his one meal and jug of water each day.

Anything else happened only under the black hood.

His stomach rumbled loudly; his mouth began to water. His lone meal of the day was only moments away. Cold beans, one uncooked potato, one dented metal jug of water. Every day the same.

He heard the sound of boots outside his door. Instinctively, he crawled to the tiny opening just in time to see the familiar, dirt-caked brown boots of the night watchman who slid his meal through.

Then he saw a second pair of boots appear. Black. Unfamiliar.

SNAP.

Before he could understand what was happening, the night watchman's face appeared in the opening as he crumpled straight to the floor, the man's wide, expressionless eyes staring back into the tiny cell, before being dragged from view. The steel doorknob rattled with another snap, this time the sound of metal, and the knob fell to the floor as he realized it had somehow been broken off from the other side.

As the door swung open, he moved back instinctively, ready to give them a fight as he'd always done before they pulled the black hood over his head.

But as the figure came into view, he realized it was not one of his captors. Rather, a lone man stood before him, almost a foot shorter than he was. The man wore what looked like black fatigues, but ones that bore no markings, military or otherwise. He didn't appear to be carrying a weapon, either. The dim light that crept in from the hallway outside revealed the blackest eyes he'd ever seen in a man.

"Sergeant First Class Otis Charles Brown, USMC?" the man addressed him in a deep, raspy, almost angry voice.

"Yes sir," he replied, willing himself up to stand at attention.

"Come with me," the man said. "We're getting you out of here."

1

The U.S.-Mexican border checkpoint at South Fitchburg, Texas had become among the busiest in the entire country, rivaling the likes of Tijuana, El Paso, and Nogales.

Enrique Castillo had been traversing this checkpoint for over a year now. In that time, what used to take him fifteen minutes to commute to his job had swelled to over an hour. He'd even been late a few times, which meant docked pay. And with his mother ailing and now in the hospital, lost wages were one thing he could not afford.

It was Friday morning. As he drew near the crawling pileup of cars, vans, and trucks lined up to go through the checkpoint, a sense of unease came over him. He'd been working legally at the Broadway Chicken Farms processing plant this past year, on an employer-issued visa. Enrique had once saved a young tourist boy who'd run in front of a bus in Mexico City. The boy's father had turned out to be the manager at the Broadway plant and had pulled a few strings to get Enrique the visa. The man had since left the company, but they'd kept Enrique on, even promoting him to line supervisor.

But last night, in his hometown of Ciudad Juarez, the visa had been stolen, picked from his pocket somewhere along the market boulevard where he shopped for his mother and young sister.

In desperation, he'd turned to a local counterfeiter, who charged him $250 to create a replica passport and ID made from an Idaho driver's license.

The counterfeiter had suggested a far-off state like Idaho, since U.S. Customs and Border Protection officers would likely spot a fake for border states like Texas or Arizona, but not one from a northern state they rarely encountered. Both the passport and the ID included a picture of Enrique, and they looked professional enough to justify the hefty price tag, which had all but depleted Enrique's savings.

Now it only had to hold up long enough for him to apply for a replacement visa through his employer.

As he crept along in his rusty 1989 Oldsmobile, a bead of sweat formed on his forehead. He prayed that this would work.

It was a few minutes after nine o'clock in the morning, and U.S. Customs and Border Protection officer Otis Brown had already detained two different groups trying to smuggle illegal substances through the border crossing, as well as two more trying to get themselves through using suspicious IDs. He had a feeling it was going to be a record day. He usually worked the evening shift; but in need of some overtime, he had elected to add a morning shift to his schedule for this week.

It had been four months since he'd been brought back stateside, since his rescue from the Taliban prison camp in Afghanistan. His wounds had healed, his body had recovered from starvation, his physical condition was back in a prime state, and his state of mind was well enough to pass all the PTSD recovery benchmarks. He was ready for his next tour and had put in the paperwork to re-join his battalion. Now the waiting game had begun.

Jobs were hard to come by in this stretch of the country, so Otis's father Silas, longtime Sheriff of Broward County, had made a few calls. Otis didn't like accepting his father's help, but it seemed to be the only way he could get a job, and he knew this was only a temporary stop on his way back to deployment.

At least with this job, he felt he was doing something while he waited: in the month since he'd been hired on as a CBP officer at the South Fitchburg border crossing, he'd taken part in deporting over six hundred illegals and stopping over $10 million in narcotic drug shipments from entering the country through his beloved home state.

The April morning sun was already baking the barren Texas landscape. This early in the season the climate usually offered one last reprieve from the months of relentless heat ahead of them. Otis had learned to deal with the desert heat all his life, but it had been three straight days of one-hundred plus degree temperatures. The slow-moving stream of cars lined up to pass through the checkpoint stations idled uneasily. The K-9 units were panting as they were led from vehicle to vehicle. Otis wiped a bead of sweat from his brow, then took a long swig from his bottle of Dasani.

Otis waved the next car forward. The lone passenger inside was a young man. He was Hispanic, maybe twenty, and looked extremely nervous. The old car he was in sputtered a bit, as if echoing the young man's apprehension.

"May I please see your ID, Sir?" Otis said, coming up to the driver's side window. As he did so, Alexa, the K-9 unit lead, began leading one of the sniffer dogs around the young man's car.

"Yes, sure," the young man replied. He handed his passport and driver's license to Otis.

"Castillo," Otis first examined the passport, glancing up at the young man before moving on to the license. "Enrique Castillo. Resident of ... Twin Falls, Idaho. What brings you all the way down here?"

"My mother, Sir," the man said. "She's very ill and in the hospital. I try to come down once a month, when I can."

"All right," Otis replied. The passport seemed to check out. He hadn't yet seen an Idaho license while on post, but current and past IDs from all fifty states were on the board inside for him to compare this one to. If they were fakes, they were good ones.

Alexa and the dog finished circling the man's car and moved on to the next one in line, a red sports car.

Just as much as the ID, it was the man's demeanor, and his situation, that raised Otis's suspicions. While something about the man seemed genuine, it was not his job to give people the benefit of the doubt. Before going inside to examine the license, he wanted to ask the man a few more questions.

"So, Mr. Castillo," he began, "it's a pretty far ride from Twin Falls down to the border here. How well does this thing make the trip?" Otis gestured to the car.

"I'm sorry," the man said, seemingly alarmed by Otis's observation. "What do you mean?"

"Well, I mean no offense by sayin' this," Otis began, "but this is what, a twenty-year-old car. And not in the best shape, judging by how it's soundin' right now. Now if I'm thinkin' right, comin' from Idaho, you've got to cross at least the Rockies, and dependin' which way you go, either the Tetons or the Sawtooths. Then you got another thousand or so miles after that. So I'm just wonderin' – how do you pull that ride off in this thing, 'specially every month?"

Otis glanced out of the corner of his eye to see that the dog had moved on from the sports car to a rusted minivan.

Otis noticed that the young man's demeanor had gone from nervous to desperate: his breathing had accelerated, and sweat was now pouring freely down his left temple. Even so, he managed to give Otis a response: "Sir, please, I do the best I can," he said. "I can't afford to fly. I can't afford a new car. I just try to see my mother. She is sick. How can I not see her? I have to try."

Otis gave the man a long look. He'd been told a lot of lies in his life, from his days as a bouncer back in college, to questioning suspected terrorists he'd captured while in Afghanistan. Again this man's story seemed to ring true, but Otis's instincts told him otherwise. He'd have to detain the man while he gave the license a better look.

"Would you exit the vehicle, please, Sir?" Otis took a step back, motioning for the man to open the door.

The man's expression became frantic, and he glanced around briefly, as if weighing the idea of making a run for it. He clutched the top of the steering wheel, resting his forehead on it. Finally, he let out a defeated sigh and opened the door, his eyes staying on the ground as he did so.

As was procedure, Otis instructed the young man to turn around and face the vehicle. As he began the standard pat down, he glanced over to see that the sniffer dog had moved to the first car in the line next to his, a rusted, old black Ford SUV. He immediately noticed the dog's demeanor: it had found something, without a doubt. But in his months of watching sniffer dogs' behavior, both in this post and back on tour, he recognized that this wasn't the dogs' usual response from finding a stash of narcotics. Instead, the dog seemed agitated, erratic, even fearful.

As if something much worse was inside the vehicle.

He looked up briefly toward the hill on the Mexican side of the border, and saw the men with RPGs.

In that instant, instinct took over.

Ambush.

He didn't have time to get to Alexa or anyone else.

"DOWN!" he screamed. He grabbed the young man and dove behind the concrete barrier next to them.

As he landed on top of the young man he was about to detain, explosions rang out, fire showered down all around them, and everything went black.

2

Twenty seconds earlier, Enrique's heart pounded as the Customs and Border Protection agent asked him to step out of his car.

He was going to be detained, and his passport and license would be proven as forged. He was going to be arrested. Without any form of proof to keep him in America, he would be deported back to Mexico, without getting a chance to obtain a new visa.

Mexico, where there was no opportunity to earn a good living.

Where he had no chance to make enough money to support his mother and sister.

Where he would watch his mother die and his sister be taken by the drug gangs.

But there was nothing he could do to change the situation he was in.

He could not run.

He would have to face it like a man ... and hope to be given another chance somehow.

Taking a deep breath, he opened the door, and rose out of the car.

The officer was a big man, at least six inches taller than Enrique, maybe six foot five, with a burly chest, light features, and a crew cut of thinning blond hair.

The officer asked Enrique to turn around and began patting him down. As he did so, Enrique could hear a dog making noises behind them. Growling and whimpering.

Suddenly, the officer screamed out, "DOWN!"

A powerful arm scooped Enrique up across his midsection and threw him over a concrete barrier. He crashed down on the pavement, hitting his head as he landed. The officer landed on top of him, knocking the breath from his lungs.

The explosions seemed to ring out all around them. A powerful burst of hot wind hit Enrique's face, again slamming the back of his head against the ground. The officer suddenly went limp on top of him. He opened his eyes, only for a split second, and saw the entire world on fire around him, before the heat forced him to shut them again.

Minutes passed. Maybe longer. He realized his hearing had been taken from him. Every breath he took seared his lungs. The officer lay on top of him, his large frame pressing Enrique into the ground, his sheer mass keeping him from being able to breathe. Yet Enrique knew this man was the only reason he was still alive, putting the concrete barrier between him and the explosions, and now his body sheltering him from the heat and chaos that had ensued.

Enrique prayed that the man was only unconscious, and not dead.

Enrique did not know how long it was before the heat began to subside. The noises of the outside world started to ring in his ears once again. Screaming. Yelling. Crashing. Sirens.

His head was pounding, like someone had started up a jackhammer inside his skull. He opened his eyes and tried to look around him, but his vision wouldn't focus.

The feeling in his limbs had begun to return, so he decided to try moving his arms and legs. His body ached all over, but none of his bones felt broken.

He was able to wrench his right arm free from under the officer's chest. He couldn't tell if the man was alive, so he needed to check for a pulse. He placed two fingers against the man's thick neck and pressed as hard as he could, but sensation hadn't yet returned to his fingertips.

Or the man who had saved his life was dead.

Not accepting that possibility, Enrique began pushing upward with all his strength against the large man's mass, working to get himself free, but being as careful as possible in case the officer had suffered any broken bones. Once he was free he would check the man's pulse again and get help for him.

There was still a great deal of heat around them; Enrique could see fires burning out of all corners of his eyes. And despite the ringing in his ears that wouldn't seem to subside, the screaming and yelling and the sounds of fires could be heard from all directions.

He realized he hadn't even begun to wonder what had happened. Had someone's fuel tank gone up? Or was it some kind of bomber? Or something else entirely?

Seconds later, he had freed himself. As he rose to one knee, he caught a glimpse of the carnage around him: burning cars, smoke everywhere, people standing back in shock, crying, screaming, ambulances and fire trucks arriving.

Then he saw the buildings.

The South Fitchburg crossing had three main buildings: two checkpoint stations and the main structure, all one story tall, all made of brick.

And now all three of them lay in ruins: their brick walls blown wide open, their roofs collapsed, black smoke pouring upward from the many breaches torn into the edifices.

Anyone who'd been inside had surely not survived.

Snapping back into focus, Enrique quickly bent down and checked for a heartbeat again, this time putting his ear against the officer's massive chest and pressing the side of his head against the man's breastbone. Though he couldn't hear it, he could feel the heartbeat thumping against his ear. The man was alive. Enrique thanked God for saving the man who had saved *him*. But there could be broken bones, internal bleeding, organ damage -- Enrique didn't know.

He stood and looked around for help. Seeing two paramedics searching for victims amid the rubble, he began waving his arms and called out: "Help! Help! Over here! Please!"

One of them, a young woman with cropped brown hair, heard Enrique's cries and turned in his direction. Tapping her partner on the arm, she pointed toward where Enrique was standing, and the two began running toward him, lugging their medical equipment with them.

Enrique knelt down once again and noticed that the officer was starting to come to. His eyes flitted open; grunts issued from his mouth.

"Try not to move," Enrique told him. "Help is on the way."

The man opened his eyes and looked at Enrique. He struggled to say something but clearly was not coherent enough to form the words.

At that moment the two paramedics arrived. The man quickly began setting up the equipment while the woman began tending to the officer. Their focus had immediately shifted to the injured man, barely giving Enrique any notice.

It was then that Enrique realized this might be his only chance to cross the border.

He looked around him uncertainly. Could he just leave the man who had saved his life?

He then looked over at his car. Despite the explosions, it looked as if it might still be drivable.

He glanced back at the officer. The man was in the right hands now. If he was going to survive, it was up to the paramedics. There was nothing Enrique could do for him.

He then heard the sirens and saw the police cars approaching the scene.

Police.

They would want to question anyone … witnesses, survivors.

He had been given a second chance, the chance he had hoped for just moments ago, a chance to make it across the border, a chance to keep his job, to keep supporting his family, even if the circumstances that were enabling him to do so had been most dire.

And with the police now arriving, his window was closing.

All he could think of were his mother and sister. They needed him.

He made his decision.

Stepping back from the paramedics, Enrique began moving toward his car.

Seconds later he was opening the door, his fingers searing as they touched the still-hot metal and warped plastic of the door handle. He had left the keys in the ignition, and the old car started right up. Without hesitating he shifted the car into Drive and pulled forward, through the blasted gate, over smoldering debris and rubble, away from the police cars and fire trucks that were now arriving on the scene.

Seconds later, he could see more emergency vehicles approaching from the northwest, so he quickly made a turn to the right, heading east. Within moments, he was gone, away from the scene, away from the carnage, in hopes of somehow salvaging his family's future after this terrible event.

3

At 9:45 A.M., General Jack Dunlap swiped his card to enter the National Security briefing center in the Pentagon.

The President had already been informed of the events that had occurred forty-one minutes ago at a CBP checkpoint in southwest Texas: three car bombs had gone off right as they were about to pass the border checkpoint, destroying all three CBP buildings and killing everyone inside. Remote "spotter" cameras had also captured five men armed with rocket-propelled grenade launchers on a hilltop, who also fired upon the structures.

Early counts confirmed thirty-one CBP officers and twenty-two civilians dead, with another twelve missing.

It was an orchestrated, perfectly-timed, all-out assault on a U.S. border crossing.

And a devastatingly effective one.

It wasn't his duty to determine why, or how ... he would leave that to the FBI.

His duty was to punish whoever was responsible for this atrocity.

He swiped his card a second time to enter the War Room and opened the door. Inside were all the familiar faces he'd expected to see: the Director of Homeland Security and his top advisers, the President's National Security Advisers, FBI leadership, senior officials from both the NSA and CIA, Secretary of Defense Aaron Collins, and of course, Edward Armstrong,

Dunlap's long-time colleague, who had recently been promoted to Deputy Defense Secretary.

Dunlap took his seat toward the end of the table, next to Armstrong.

"Edward," Dunlap greeted him in a low voice.

"Jack," Armstrong nodded back to him.

"This going to be the usual show," Dunlap said under his breath.

"Of course," Armstrong whispered. "Here we'll discuss our official position on the attack; what will be shared with the press. Inner circle will be in about an hour."

"I know what you're thinking," Dunlap said. "Collins wants to send *him* in, doesn't he."

"I think you already know the answer to that," Armstrong said wryly. "Now let's listen in; the meeting's about to start."

4

Under cover of night, the Marauder stealth watercraft cut through the choppy waters of the Strait of Hormuz, closing in on its newfound target.

Hours earlier, the Covert Ops Division had received intel that a band of Somali pirates had seized command of the *Al-Habra*, an Egyptian freighter, shortly after it had departed from port. Given that the cargo included sensitive materials that could affect national security if in the wrong hands, a private American security firm had been contracted to protect the vessel. But the aggressors quickly overwhelmed them, assuming control within thirty minutes of first contact. The captain was able to issue a distress signal before the ship was overtaken, providing the Division with the details they had now.

According to intel gathered thus far, this particular group of invaders had been much larger, more heavily armed, and better organized than any band of pirates would be, suggesting that they had ties to some other organization or terrorist group.

The mission was to regain control of the vessel, with minimal to no loss of life among the hostages, and to capture at least two of the pirates alive for interrogation.

Suited up in his black, unmarked fatigues, Rage sat strapped into his jump seat, deep in thought.

It had been just over a year since he'd joined the Covert Ops Division, or as his superiors always put it, had been "taken in" by them. In that time, he had traveled with them to the most dangerous corners of the world, running point on the most perilous missions, the odds stacked against their success each and every time.

And yet, with few exceptions, they succeeded time and again. Their success was due not only to the skill of the soldiers around him, but also to his gift: the unique abilities embedded within his DNA that enabled him to command speed, quickness, and strength like no other living being. On top of this, his body could rapidly regenerate cells, repairing itself from even major wounds and injuries in a matter of moments. These abilities allowed him to punch holes in enemy defenses, move quickly to a target point, and retrieve or eliminate the target before the enemy could even react.

But within his gift lurked a darkness: the violent actions needed to complete his missions would activate an urge within him; one that propelled him to thirst for even more violence, unleashing a beast even he could not control. It was something that had plagued him all the way back to his days as an orphan, when the other children gave him his namesake as a result of his dark nature.

But the Division had created a remedy for these urges: a medication that could quell his violent tendencies, enabling him to master them, and maintain control during missions.

And, in the end, he knew he was doing good for the world. While most missions entailed a great deal of bloodletting - for which his medication had made him develop a distaste - he knew his role was to do the dirty work that few others would ... and no others could.

He was a weapon of justice, as sanctioned by the Division, by the Pentagon, by his Commander-in-Chief. As a private citizen he would never be able to do the things he did, see the things he saw, right the wrongs he'd righted.

The ship was now within fifty yards. The Marauder maneuvered directly behind it, cutting forward through the vessel's wake. The SEALs around him made their final preparations, readying the powerful harpoon guns that were to be aimed at the stern of the ship. Each harpoon gun was equipped to fire a long, tightly-wound rope, at the head of which was an oversized knot called a monkey's fist, designed to wrap around the stern's railing with very little noise.

The SEAL Commander gave the signal. It was time.

The four harpoon guns fired, sending the long ropes twisting skyward, all four of the massive knots wrapping around the stern's railing.

Winters, Larson, Pikulas, and Hurley were the four SEALs accompanying him on this mission. Each of them secured his rope to the Marauder, hooked himself onto the rope at the waist, then began climbing the rope toward the ship.

Rage watched the four SEALs board the vessel. He pulled on his black gloves, grabbed hold of the rope nearest him, and began climbing himself.

Once aboard, he moved to the rendezvous point behind the bridge. Winters pulled up the motion-tracking device, which identified all heat signatures within a twenty-meter radius.

The bridge itself was three stories tall. The device picked up two signatures on the first level, four on the second level, and ten on the flying bridge. Winters was also able to lock onto a large number of signatures just below deck, almost immediately beneath the spot where they stood.

The hostages. They were all being kept in an enormous room, most likely the galley. Winters noted that the majority of the signatures, it looked like at least thirty, maybe forty, indicated that the hostages were seated on the floor in the center of the space, while six additional signatures suggested figures walking around them.

They would secure the hostages first, then re-take the bridge.

The team deftly descended the stairwell that led to the galley, Winters leading the way with the motion-tracker, then Pikulas, Larson, and Hurley behind him with their night-vision scopes. Each of the SEALs would take out his target within line of sight, while Rage would eliminate the two on either side of the entry point.

Pikulas gave the signal. Without hesitation, the team moved quickly into the space. Rage heard the four silencer rounds go off, saw the four targets in view immediately drop. His turn. He leapt onto the target to his left and quickly turned the man's neck, then back-flipped toward the second target, who had begun to run.

It was all over in seconds.

Pikulas identified himself to the hostages, then ordered them to stay put while the team finished the job.

He signaled upward. The bridge was next.

The two signatures on the deck level of the bridge showed figures sitting at a table; the door to the bridge was propped open. They would need to keep each engagement as quiet as possible to maintain the element of surprise — no easy task, given that the metal decks provided no insulation or soundproofing.

Pikulas ordered Larson and Hurley to the doorway. Both took their positions, took aim, and took out the two targets. The only sound was of the two mens' heads hitting the wooden table as they fell forward.

They climbed the stairs to the bridge's second level. As they neared the top, Winters pulled out the motion tracker once again.

The screen revealed a figure heading straight toward the hatch above them.

Pikulas motioned to Rage, who didn't wait for the order. He leapt straight up through the opening and was on the target, immediately breaking his neck. He then

hurled himself at the other three. As he turned the first one's neck, silencer rounds found homes in the other two, dropping them to the floor in twin heaps.

"We have them trapped on the flying bridge," Pikulas whispered. "But element of surprise is likely gone. They may try to escape through the top hatch and down the emergency ladder. We need to know how many are up there, and if there are hostages."

"Sir," Winters said, staring down at the motion-tracker. "Still ten signatures on the bridge. Two at the controls, the others taking positions. No one's made his way toward the hatch yet. We can't count on that not changing, though."

They circled up and formed the plan. Rage, Pikulas, Hurley, and Winters would take the stairwell to the bridge. Larson would pull the flank, climbing the emergency ladder and waiting for anyone atop the tower who might use the hatch to escape.

They couldn't just deploy smoke grenades; the Strait of Hormuz was difficult enough to navigate — even though all ships had a second location to steer the ship, the last thing they needed was a blinded command center. And it was likely the pirates had taken out the crew in the second steering location.

Standard grenades wouldn't do either: the shrapnel and concussion effect would cripple many of the delicate instruments on the bridge.

And a firefight would be no different. There were too many of them; as many as a hundred rounds could be fired before it was over, and that didn't even account for the ricocheting effects. Any hostages would be killed, and the bridge would be destroyed. Any of these options would effectively turn the ship into a floating battering ram, without anything to control its progress.

Rage was their only chance. He knew this.

He nodded to Pikulas. "I'm going in. Stay out of sight; wait for my signal."

And before Pikulas could issue a protest, Rage was gone.

He climbed to the top landing, then showed himself in the doorway to the flying bridge, arms raised high above his head.

He quickly assessed the room: eight gunmen, all but one of whom had their guns pointed at him. Their faces were wrapped in tight black masks: he couldn't get a good look at any of them to see if they might be Somali, Iranian, or otherwise. They all had AK-47 rifles, not some patchwork of different rifles like most bandits he'd encountered. Their clothing and gear were uniform: they were clearly well-organized and well-funded.

These were not just pirates.

"Lower your weapons," he called to them. "We are here to offer you a deal."

The ship's captain and first mate remained at the controls, both covered by the lone gunman who was not pointing his rifle at Rage. Each took a nervous glance back toward him.

"I am unarmed," Rage said, keeping his hands above his head.

A powerfully-built man only a few inches taller than Rage barked something in Arabic to one of the others, a tall, thin man, who in turn spoke to Rage.

"You. Come forward."

Rage took a step toward them, entering the room. He stopped in a spot that put him exactly at the center of the circle of gunmen surrounding him, not one of them more than six feet from him in any direction. All kept their guns trained on him.

"Drop to knees," the lanky pirate ordered him.

"Lower your weapons first," Rage said flatly. "Then you can hear my offer. It's your only way to get off this boat alive."

The lead pirate said something to the others. All but two lowered their rifles.

"That'll have to do," Rage muttered to himself.

In a blinding motion, he lunged at the pirate whose gun was trained on the hostages, ripping the rifle from his hands before knocking him cold. He immediately leapt toward the nearest two gunmen, smashing their heads together, cracking both mens' skulls. From the corner of his eye, he saw Pikulas, Hurley, and Winters pop into the room and begin firing, each taking out one of the pirates with a shot to the head.

That left only the leader and his translator, neither of whom had time to react before Rage tore both men's guns from their grip. He tossed both firearms to the floor in Pikulas' general direction.

Rage grabbed the leader by the collar so that they were face to face. He tore off the man's mask, snarling into the man's wide, suddenly terrified eyes.

"Enough," he heard Pikulas call out from behind. "We needed two survivors, we got three. I'd rather keep it there."

Rage turned on Pikulas, the heavy-set pirate swinging with him, caught up in Rage's firm grip. The urge had returned, he could feel it, sparked by the violence of the past few moments. It was hitting its crescendo now: he found himself wanting to give in to it; to beat both masked gunmen to a pulp.

He needed to stop it. Now.

He grunted in disgust, throwing the pirate to the deck. He opened a pouch in his belt, removing a small vial from it, then dropped a tiny red pill into his palm. He quickly popped the pill into his mouth.

"Easy," Pikulas said evenly. His eyes moved from Rage's face to the small vial that Rage was replacing in the pouch. "We're all on the same side here."

"I'm aware," Rage grunted, turning his back on Pikulas and walking away.

Even though Pikulas was his C.O. for official record, it was common knowledge that on all missions, the C.O. was little more than a chaperone for Rage, setting strategy and tactics, but mostly making sure he got in and out alive. If Rage wanted to break from the plan, the C.O. would need to go with Rage's instincts.

On all but one occasion, this approach had paid off.

He shook his head, not allowing that memory to enter his mind.

He took a deep breath, then exhaled. The urge had subsided. The medication's effects were instant, as they'd always been.

He snapped back into the moment just as Pikulas received a call from Division command on his comm/GPS unit. Rage half-paid attention as he answered it.

Until the C.O. addressed him directly.

"You're needed stateside, immediately," Pikulas told him. "A transport is en route to airlift you directly from the deck at 0200."

5

Under the burning mid-day sun, Enrique pulled the Oldsmobile into the parking lot at Broadway Chicken Farms. Without closing the car door, he ran for the main entrance.

The usual twenty-minute drive up to the plant had turned into almost a two-hour ordeal. The main roads were littered with police cars, so he decided to use out-of-the-way side roads. And it became clear that his car wasn't nearly in as good shape as he'd thought: it had sputtered and died several times. And his phone had been smashed when he'd been thrown over that concrete barrier, so he could not call his manager to explain why he would be so late.

His face and clothes were bloodied and covered with dirt and soot. He kept a spare shirt in his trunk, but he needed to clean himself up. So he had stopped at a gas station to wash off.

He was now at least presentable for work, but because he was so late for his shift, he would have to wait until his lunch break to speak with his manager about the visa.

He ran inside and punched in. His line was already in full swing, with a sub line supervisor overseeing the group. He nodded to the sub, a sweet, fifty-something pug-faced woman named Esmelda, and went up to her to relieve her.

"Gracias," he told her, nodding as he placed his yellow safety helmet over his head. "Sorry I'm late."

"Enrique. El jefe wants to see you in his office," she replied.

"What?" Enrique said, surprised. "Why?"

"No se," she said, shrugging. "He just told me to send you to him if you showed. That's all I know."

"Okay," Enrique said, unsure. "Gracias."

"Good luck," she called out after him.

Enrique approached the door, which was slightly ajar, and went in.

"You wanted to see me, Sir?" Enrique asked.

Ronaldo Cruz looked up from his computer screen and arose from his chair. Ronaldo, or Donald as he liked to be called, was a short, stubby man with dark olive skin, long-outdated, gold-rimmed glasses, and a tightly-trimmed ring of gray hair that circled around a perfectly bald head. He had been Enrique's manager since the day he'd started. He moved about quickly for such a stout little man, a never-ending supply of energy. He always had a smile on his face, and he greeted each of his workers with a thick-fingered handshake every morning as they came in for their shift.

"Enrique," he said urgently in his gruff little voice. There was no smile today. "Por favor. Come in. Close the door."

Enrique, immediately thrown by his manager's demeanor, came in and did as Donald asked, closing the door behind him.

"Sit down, please," Donald gestured to the nearest chair. "I tried to call you, but your phone didn't pick up. I'm afraid we might not have much time."

"What is it, Sir?" Enrique said timidly, taking a seat. He was beginning to panic.

"Enrique," he began, "the checkpoint you pass through to come here was attacked this morning. You were there when it happened?"

Enrique froze. "Uh ... yes, yes, Sir," he replied, not sure how Donald knew this.

"Do you know anything about it?" Donald asked, his eyebrows raised.

"Que?" Enrique replied, startled by the pointed question. "No, no, Sir, nothing. I swear."

Donald stared at him for what seemed like long moments. "I believe you," he finally exhaled. "Of course I believe you."

"Sir, why did you ask me this?"

"Enrique," Donald said, his voice heavy. "What happened at the check-point is all over the news. They have pictures."

As he said this, he turned his computer monitor on his desk around so that Enrique could see the headline story on the screen. Next to the headline was a picture of the border crossing's smoldering buildings. Just below it was a picture of a car, with a clear shot of the license plate.

"They are saying a car fled the scene after it happened," Donald explained. He pointed to the picture. "A car with a Mexican license plate. This is your car, Enrique."

Fear filled Enrique as the magnitude of what Donald was sharing with him took hold. "No, no. Do – do they think I had something to do with this?" he exclaimed.

"I don't know," Donald shook his head. "But they have released this to the press, which means they are looking for you. Enrique, you are a good boy; a good worker. I would open my home to you. But I can't protect you."

"But - but what do I do?"

"You need to run, Enrique," Donald implored. "Leave your car here. They are looking for it. I am going to call the authorities after you leave, say I tried to detain you. But you ran. I couldn't stop you."

"Where will I go?" Enrique exclaimed. "I don't know anyone else here!"

"There is a tunnel that I know of," Donald said as he took out a pencil and sheet of paper, then drew some directions. "Just past town, an abandoned barn off of Navarro Road. Go to the far side of the barn, to the bottom door. If it's locked, find a way to break the latch. It will take you back to Juarez; it's no longer safe for you here. It's the only way I know of. But you have to leave now."

"But - but I —"

"GO!" Donald ordered him, pointing to the door. "There is no time. Go out the back door, the loading dock. And run, Enrique. Stay out of sight until you see that barn. May God be with you, my boy."

Enrique opened the door, only to see four uniformed men at his station, talking to Esmelda. He saw her turn and point toward Donald's office.

Enrique closed the door. "They are here!"

The look of surprise on Donald's face quickly turned to one of determination. He picked up the metal chair across from his desk, and with all his might, threw it through the window, shattering it. He then purposefully fell backward to the floor.

"GO!" he shouted at Enrique.

Enrique paused for a second and then moved to the window. He understood what Donald was doing: staging Enrique's escape, as well as his own attempt to stop him.

"Thank you," Enrique said gratefully.

Then, he jumped out of the first-story window and ran like the wind.

6

The scent of hospital-brewed coffee was the first thing that stirred Otis from his sleep.

As his eyes flitted open, he realized he'd been moved to a different room; the décor was slightly different, the TV in a different location, and there was no other bed in this room, as there had been in the one where he'd last awoken to find his mother, Annie, and his father, Silas, waiting by his bedside.

Now he was alone in this new room with nothing but the bright rays of sunshine poking through the half-drawn, off-white blinds of the far window, and the fragrance of the coffee wafting in from the hallways of St. Eduardo Hospital.

Luckily, his injuries had turned out to be far less serious than the on-scene paramedics had assessed: just a concussion, a few cracked ribs, and some bruises. They'd kept him in the hospital as a precaution, but he had been told that he would be released about twenty-four hours after being admitted. Within a matter of days he'd be mostly back to normal and could get back to work.

Back to normal ...

He was kidding himself, he knew; nothing would be back to normal. The attack had killed sixty-two people. Thirty-one of them had been his fellow CBP officers; some of them friends, acquaintances - all of them fathers, mothers, husbands, wives, sons, daughters.

Sixty-two dead.

His stomach began to turn.

He had seen a lot of death since going on his first tour.

But never had he seen this much death in one place, at one time.

The world would go on without sixty-two of its men, women, and children who had *not* been fighting a war ... but rather had been in the wrong place at the wrong time.

He closed his eyes and fought back tears.

Several moments passed. He looked at the clock on the wall. Noon.

He'd been here more than twenty-four hours now. One of the doctors would be in any moment to send him on his way. When he heard footsteps in the hall he tried to sit up, but the intense pain that shot through his body reminded him that he wasn't quite yet ready for any sudden movements. He grimaced in pain and sank back into the bed.

He heard the footsteps cease just outside his door, followed by the sound of two male voices. He anticipated the sight of doctors in scrubs or white lab coats to come in. Instead, two men in dark suits entered the room. And it quickly dawned on him as to why he'd been moved to a private room.

"Sergeant Otis Brown, good morning," the first man addressed him. "I'm Special Agent Buck, and this is Special Agent Dossey, with the Dallas Bureau of the FBI. I see you're doing a bit better this morning."

"Um," Otis said, surveying the two men. "Better'n yesterday, I s'pose."

"Glad to hear it," Special Agent Buck said. "We're going to need to ask you some questions about what happened yesterday morning."

"'Course," Otis replied.

"First," Special Agent Buck began, pulling up a chair and taking out a laptop computer, "can you tell us what you saw and heard leading up to the attack?"

"Yeah, sure," Otis said. "I'd just started shift. I was processin' a crosser, young Mexican fella with what looked like a falsified driver's license. I was about to detain him when I heard one of our dogs reactin' to a vehicle, but not the normal reaction to narcotics or hidden passengers. Much more panicked. Then I looked toward the hills across the border and saw men with grenade-launchers. Four, maybe five of 'em. I grabbed the fella I was processin' and we dove behind a barrier. No time to grab anyone else. Then everything blew up around us. That's all I remember."

"Can you describe the man you were processing?" Special Agent Buck asked.

"Short fella," Otis recalled. "Maybe five-foot-eight or so. 'Round twenty, I'd guess. Like I said, Mexican, dark hair, olive skin. Wearin' a button-down shirt and jeans, I think. Was in an older car, like a Pontiac or somethin'."

"Can you describe his demeanor?" Special Agent Dossey asked as he took notes.

"Nervous, on edge," Otis recalled. "'Course half the people I see're like that."

"Why do you think he in particular was acting this way?" Buck asked.

"Well, if I were to give him the benefit of the doubt," Otis said, "I'd say it was because he said he had a sick mother in the hospital. But since it ain't my business to do that, I'd think it was because he had a suspect ID."

Buck and Dossey said nothing, just glanced at each other, then back at Otis.

"I mean, he's okay, right?" Otis asked. "I ain't been awake long enough to catch up on the news. Tell me he ain't dead."

"He fled the scene," Special Agent Buck said, leaning forward.

"Hmmph," Otis muttered, looking down at his lap and thinking it over. "Fled?"

"Got in his car and drove through the gate," Buck confirmed.

"So, what're you thinkin'," Otis said. "That he's suspect or somethin'?"

"A person of interest, at the very least," Buck said.

"I don't know," Otis admitted, rubbing the back of his head. "Somethin' don't add up with that."

"Why do you say that?" Dossey asked.

"Well, I mean, why would he put himself in the line o' fire?" Otis thought aloud. "T'be a distraction for just one CBP officer when there were a bunch o'us on duty? An' why would he keep goin' across the border? Why not turn around?"

"All good questions," Buck replied. "There were also what were likely suicide bombers with car bombs present, so the 'line of fire' argument goes out the window. As to why he crossed the border, he could have had a shipment that still needed to get across. We don't really know."

"On top of that," Dossey chimed in, "he fled a crime scene."

"'Course he did," Otis said. "C'mon, he was prob'ly scared. Almost got killed. Prob'ly was in a panic; wasn't thinkin' straight.

"And somethin' don't seem right about the suicide bomber notion, either," Otis added. "I been exposed to plenty o'them. Suicide bombers do it for some extreme cause, usually religious. This's strictly business. And when've you ever heard of a Mexican suicide bomber?"

"There's a first time for everything," Buck commented.

"I s'pose," Otis said, "but it still doesn't add up in my book."

"Do you recall anything else you might be able to share with us?" Buck asked.

Otis thought about it for a moment, trying to recall any other details.

"No," he finally said. "Nothin' that comes to mind, at least."

"Well, we appreciate your insight, since you're really our only witness," Dossey said. "We can't share any other details since it's an ongoing investigation, but if you can think of anything else, here's my card."

"Yes, thank you, Sergeant Brown," Buck added. "We'll be in touch."

And with that, the two men stood from their chairs and left the room, leaving Otis alone with his thoughts once again.

7

The streets of Ciudad Juarez were quiet on this early Saturday evening, save for the occasional gunfire echoing off the one- and two-story stone buildings.

At just before six o'clock P.M., Enrique stepped off the street bus and walked quickly toward Santa Angela hospital. Only yesterday, he'd survived a deadly attack at the U.S. border crossing just outside South Fitchburg, learned that the U.S. authorities were searching for him, and escaped back to Mexico using a hidden tunnel.

His mother, Consuelo, had been admitted to Santa Angela six days ago after taking a turn for the worse in her long illness. Until yesterday, Enrique had visited her every night after his shift ended.

The hospital itself was an old, white stone structure with a grimy interior. Enrique took the stairwell to the second floor; his mother's was the room toward the end of the hall. As he rounded the corner, he noticed two armed men standing outside his mother's door. He could see inside the room, where he saw a tall man in a long black leather coat standing at the foot of the bed. Enrique immediately recognized him.

Javier Escondido Oropeza; known throughout Mexico as *el Chacal*, or the Jackal.

The leader of the largest drug cartel in Mexico, known as the *Diablos del Rio*.

Murderer of countless rival cartel members, gang leaders, police officers, government officials, journalists, and many more.

The most powerful man in all of northern Mexico ... some would argue, in all of Mexico itself.

Beyond the man's towering figure, Enrique could see his mother asleep on the bed.

Cautiously, Enrique stepped toward the two men. The one nearest to him held up a hand. He was slightly taller than Enrique, with a short goatee, black leather vest, and black leather wristbands with silver studs on them, like someone from a biker gang. But compared to the other henchman next to him, who was covered in tattoos and a heavy beard, the man looked almost clean cut.

"Jefe," the man called into the room. "Visitor."

Oropeza turned toward the door, and a look of recognition washed over his face.

The henchman walked Enrique into the room at gunpoint. Oropeza put a hand on the man's weapon, lowering it.

"Hernandez," he said flatly, "leave us. Close the door."

The goateed man turned and walked out the door, closing it behind him.

"Enrique, my boy," his uncle regarded him, speaking in their native Spanish tongue. His dark, deep inset eyes examined Enrique. "It's been a while. After hearing about her condition, I thought I would pay my dear sister a visit. Please, come in."

Enrique walked in, unsure of what to say.

Javier walked back to the bed, standing over Enrique's mother.

"She looks so peaceful, doesn't she," Javier said quietly, keeping his eyes on her for a long moment.

"Yes," Enrique said.

"She always was an angel."

Enrique nodded silently.

"It must be quite a burden on you, having to care for her like this," Javier observed. "Not to mention your young sister back at home. How are you faring?"

"I - I do what I can, sir," Enrique said simply.

Javier stared into him as if pondering something, then spoke.

"Enrique," he began, "a man doesn't get into the position that I am in by playing games. So I'll be honest with you, and in return I ask that you be honest with me."

"O-okay," Enrique said, taken aback by his uncle's statement. "Yes, of course."

"I know you are hiding," Javier told him. "I see the news. I know you were there when the border crossing was bombed. And I know you are a suspect."

Enrique said nothing.

"So this means you cannot go back to the U.S. for work. The Americans want a villain; they always want a villain. And in this case, it must be a Mexican. You were there and you fled, so you are what they have.

"But you have another problem," he went over and gently placed a hand on Consuelo's shoulder. "Your dear mother; my dear sister. She is ill and needs care. But you cannot go back to your job, and there is no work to be had here, so there is no money to pay her bills. So, we must figure something out."

Enrique remained silent. He began to understand what his uncle was getting at, and a stream of fear washed down his entire body like ice water. Javier Oropeza had more money than anyone in the region and could easily buy the entire hospital if it suited him. But Enrique knew his uncle, and he knew he would never give anything without wanting something in return.

"What - what would you have me do?" Enrique finally said.

A smile spread across Javier's lips.

"Enrique," he said. "You have always been a smart boy. Very smart, with good instincts. Which is why I have this proposition for you."

8

The sun had begun to set when Sheriff Silas Brown returned home for the evening. Long shadows stretched across the dusty Texas landscape.

It had been over a week since the attack on the border crossing. Since then, smuggler activity had spread out among several surrounding ranches. Crossers had become emboldened by the disarray along the border, and they seemed to be getting more aggressive by the day, even killing ranchers' dogs as they crossed their property.

Silas's son, Otis, had been out of the hospital for five days now but had not yet been cleared to return to work. Silas felt the boy was about to teeter over the edge any minute now out of sheer restlessness.

The day's activities had prompted him to call it a day much earlier than he usually did on a Sunday. He rubbed the exhaustion out of his eyes as he opened the front door, but he was immediately pulled from his stupor as his nostrils were greeted by the juicy smell of Annie's cooking. The griddle, he decided. Something with beef, onions. Just what the doctor ordered, after a day like this.

"Annie? M'home!" he called out as he closed the door behind him.

"Silas, you're home early," Annie's head appeared in the kitchen doorway. "Well, good. Dinner's just about on. Now go see if you can get that son of yours out of the back garage."

"Lemme guess," Silas mused as he hung his keys on the wall hook. "Workin' on the Jeep again?"

"What else?" she said, throwing her arms up before going back to stirring something in a large pot.

"Yep, figgered," Silas said. "I'll go yank 'im outta there."

Silas took off his belt and holster, then lumbered to the back garage. Just an oversized shed on an outcropping of Silas' property, the structure stood twenty feet behind the main garage, with a dirt driveway that led out to a side road. Silas had mostly used it for storage until a few months back, when Otis had bought an old but sturdy Jeep CJ after returning from his third tour in Afghanistan.

Silas pushed open the wooden door. "Evenin' Otis," he said.

"Hey Pa," Otis returned, his legs jutting out from under the Jeep, which was up on lifters. "You're home early for a Sunday."

"I'm aware," Silas said, heading to the fridge for a can of beer. He cracked it open. "Just about dinner time. Mama's fixin' up one o'her beef concoctions she gets from the cookin' show on the TV. You ready?"

"Sure. 'Bout the same time you're done with that beer. Why you home s'early?"

"Long day," Silas exhaled. "Busy. 'Nuther dog shootin' at a border ranch. This time it was old lady Mabel's."

"Shoot. 'Nuther one? She okay?"

"Yep. Just a might scared is all. But she's a tough old woman."

"Smugglers?"

"Looks like it."

"And what're you gonna do about it?"

"Got Border Patrol involved. They're gonna step up night patrols around the border ranches."

"That's it? I ain't gotten a call yet."

"That's *it*? What else you got in mind? And you're still on leave, remember?"

"Pa, this is the third one in like a week. Don't you see a pattern here?"

"Fourth, if you count the Johnson's a week ago. And 'course I see a pattern. But the county only has twenty officers, Otis. Half of 'em part time. What d'you think we're gonna be able to do with twenty troopers?"

"I don't know. But you can't rely on just Border Patrol t'help you. Not while our numbers're down from that attack. And half those that are left're as corrupt as they come. I been watchin' some of 'em at my checkpoint. At least three of 'em are on the take with the cartels, I know it."

"Well, not for long, least in these parts," Silas said. "That new chief come in, few weeks before the attack? Your new boss, you met her. Ellroy, I think. She's out to clean this thing up. Since you been out and the checkpoint's been closed, she's been combin' the surroundin' countryside, lookin' for weak spots. Past three days they've sealed up four major smugglin' routes, includin' a tunnel. S'why the smugglers're comin' through here now."

"So they've made it our problem."

"*My* problem," Silas corrected him. "Not anybody else's."

"If they're comin' through our county, our *town*, it's everybody's problem, Pa."

"Listen," Silas said, leaning against the tool stand as he took another swig of beer. "This is one o'those things where it's shared jurisdiction. It's my county, yes, but it's the Feds' *border*. And like I said, this new chief seems to be crackin' down on the activity. Turns out, she's the one who cleaned up that stretch o'land in western Arizona few months back. So after your old boss got caught dealin' with the cartels, the Feds moved her over here fast as they could to fix it."

"Still," Otis argued. "I don't care how different you think things'll be. There's no way they're throwin' enough CBP at this rural stretch o' country to cover all the ranches all the time. No way."

Silas crossed his arms and frowned. "So what're you sayin', Son?"

"I'm sayin'," Otis pulled up from under the Jeep to look at his father. "That you need help. CBP needs help. The *people* got to do somethin'."

"Let me get this straight," Silas said, beginning to pace slowly. "You think a bunch o' untrained civilians should try to take on heavily armed drug smugglers? Am I gettin' that right?"

"No," Otis clarified. "Not everyone. Just those that can do somethin' about it. Those that are trained to be *able* to do somethin' about it."

Silas stopped pacing and stared at his son. "I know what you're thinkin', and the answer is no."

"What if I wasn't askin'."

"The answer is still no. I know you're a grown man now, so I can't tell you no because I'm your father. But I'm still Sheriff. And the answer is no."

"You don't even know what I'm thinkin'."

"I know exactly what you're thinkin', and I know why," Silas said sternly. "But this ain't overseas. This ain't a war zone and you ain't doin' a tour. This is home, and you know we got laws here. And takin' the law in your own hands is *against* the law."

"Pa, you forget what the hell happened to me a week ago? It *is* a war zone! And we don't do somethin' about it now, it's gonna get even worse!"

At that moment, Annie opened the door. "Only war zone 'round here's gonna be in the kitchen, if you two don't get in the house. Now come on. And keep y'voices down. I c'n hear you all the way in the house. Come on, now. Let's go."

"You heard your mother," Silas said to Otis. "Let's stop this now and get some grub."

"Fine," Otis said. "But I ain't done with this."

"Far's I'm concerned, you *both* are," Annie said. "Now not another word from either of you."

After eating dinner mostly in silence, Otis returned to the garage, while Silas and Annie went upstairs to prepare for bed.

"Silas," she said, beginning to apply night cream to her face. "What exactly happened out there with Otis, in the garage?"

Silas sighed. "I'd say nuthin', but you wouldn't believe me, would ya."

"No, I don't think I would. That boy doesn't upset easily."

"No, he doesn't," Silas agreed. "An' it's not just about him nearly gettin' killed at the crossing. It's about everything that's been goin' on since. He wants to do somethin' about it."

"Like what?"

"He didn't say, exactly. But I didn't really let him because I figured on what he was *gonna* say."

"And what was he gonna say?"

"He wants to go after 'em."

"The smugglers?"

"Yep. And I can't say I'm surprised."

"You know our boy," Annie said. "Anytime somethin' happens he's the first to get involved. Well, I'm glad you talked him out of it."

"Who says I did?"

"Well, you did, didn't you?"

"I jus' told him no, was all. Annie, he's twenty-seven years old; he's his own man, now. C'n do what he wants."

"Well, you're surely not gonna let 'im, are you?"

"As Sheriff, I told him no. As his father, I couldn't tell him no."

"Silas, you need to talk to him again. Make sure he's not gonna do some-thin' stupid. He could get himself killed!"

"Darlin', he's been in the Marines six years, now. There's not much he can't handle."

"That sounds like the Marine talkin' in *you*, Silas." Annie said crossly.

"Maybe. But I'm more worried about what he might do that I'd have to lock 'im up for, more'n gettin' himself hurt or killed."

9

Rage had finished his fifth day of training when his ultimate commanding officer, General Jack Dunlap, finally paid him a visit.

The Covert Ops Division's training facility was completely hidden from any public eyes, miles into a cordoned-off federal zone, in a clearing surrounded by acres of thick forest. The sole point of entry, a simple iron gate and two-man booth, stood one hundred yards into a gravel drive off a rural Virginia county road. Only government vehicles with special badging could pass through.

The lone structure on the grounds was a two-story building that housed meeting rooms and a mess hall on the first level. On the second level were Rage's private living quarters.

Behind the structure was an outdoor training ground that Division brass called "the Set." The Set, over eight acres in size, was a completely changeable and inter-changeable landscape that enabled Division structural engineers to create massive staging grounds, replicating the exact setting of the next mission. Giant earth movers and construction equipment sat silently in the hangar at the back of the staging ground, while building materials lay waiting in the massive warehouse adjacent to the hangar.

Rage emerged from the shower and began to towel himself off. The four SEALs assigned to accompany him on the mission had departed the facility about thirty minutes prior, leaving him alone in the facility.

When he'd returned home from the Strait of Hormuz eight days ago, he didn't have to wait until the briefing to hear what the next mission would be: it had been all over the news. An attack on a U.S. border crossing, involving suicide car-bombers and rocket-propelled grenades. His mission would be to go after whoever had been responsible.

When the intercom announced that Dunlap had arrived on the grounds, he knew they'd found the culprit, and phase two of his training would begin. The Set would be transformed into an exact replica of wherever they would be carrying out the mission, and his team would begin running exercises specific to the task at hand, instead of general combat exercises, as they had been doing for the past week.

Rage threw on a quick change of clothes and headed downstairs. As he reached the bottom landing, he saw Dunlap in the main lobby speaking quietly to a second man in a dark suit whom Rage didn't recognize.

Dunlap glanced up, saw Rage approaching, and quickly wrapped up the conversation. Both men began to walk toward Rage.

"Why don't we have a seat." Dunlap got right down to business, gesturing to the round table and chairs near the corner.

Rage followed them to the table, looking out the window as he did so. He could see construction crews were already on the grounds, groups of hardhats in trucks headed toward the storage facilities near the back of the clearing.

"Don't waste much time, do you," Rage said, sitting down.

Dunlap glanced out the window himself, nodding. "Not when there's little time to waste. As you've probably guessed, our investigation into the Texas border attack has concluded. We have a target."

"And who's the suit," Rage asked, tilting his head toward the second man.

"Ferguson Millett," the man in the suit said, extending a hand across the table. "Assistant Director, National Security Administration."

When Rage didn't return the gesture, the man withdrew his hand.

"Together with the CIA and the FBI," Millett continued, opening the briefcase, "we've assembled the details on how the attack was executed, who was behind it, and where they're located."

"Your mission," Dunlap interjected, "will be to run point with the SEAL squad you've been training with for the past five days. You will go in and re-trieve the target, dead or alive, along with his top lieutenants, and make way for the two CIA agents who will accompany you to confiscate any and all intel they can find on this individual's network."

"Who's the target and where," Rage said.

Millett produced a tablet screen with an image of a middle-aged Hispanic man, black-haired with a ponytail and graying goatee, and eyes almost as dark as Rage's own. "Javier Escondido Oropeza," Millett said. "Known throughout Mexico as the Jackal. Leader of the *Diablos del Rio* cartel, the largest drug ring in Mexico."

"A drug lord," Rage grunted, surprised. "*That's* who did this."

"Correct," Millett confirmed. "And he's not to be underestimated. In the past ten years, Oropeza has all but wiped out all rival cartels in his region, essentially claiming ownership of our southern border all to himself. The FBI estimates that *Diablos del Rio* shipments into the U.S. last year exceeded $150 billion."

"So if business is booming," Rage asked, "why attack? Seems stupid to jeopardize all that."

"And, if he's as smart as he seems to be," Dunlap added, "he's got to assume there will be retaliation. He'll know that we'll figure out that he was behind this and come after him. Which means only one thing." He nodded to Millett to continue.

"Escalation," Millett answered. "Beginning with a bit of retaliation of his own. As it turns out, the FBI discovered that the vast majority of Oropeza's shipments these past two years came through the South Fitchburg, Texas station. The very same border crossing that was attacked."

"So again," Rage asked, "why attack it?"

"For the past two years," Millett said, "the South Fitchburg station had been run by a leadership team suspected of turning a blind eye to smuggling activity. Any seized shipments were always by the same small number of CBP officers; the vast majority of officers had no shipments seized, or a very small number. When an investigation of the station concluded, the captain was arrested, along with a few senior officers, and there was a change in leadership. Within the first few days of this change, over $12 million in shipments was seized, almost the entire haul of the past year. The cartel had been channeling so much through South Fitchburg, knowing which lines to get into to avoid inspection, that virtually everything was low-hanging fruit. The new captain made a name for herself immediately."

"And just as fast, became a target of the cartel," Rage concluded.

"Along with the entire station," Millett added.

"So she got wiped out when the checkpoint got hit?" Rage asked.

"No," Dunlap answered. "By an odd stroke of luck, she was at an offsite meeting in El Paso that morning."

"So in retaliation for losing a couple of shipments," Rage asked, "they wipe out the station?"

"And as a statement, too, we think," Millett added. "That *they* own the border, not us. That they set the rules, and when South Fitchburg changed the rules, they had to be made an example of."

"And where is this Jackal located," Rage asked.

Millett laid out a large map of the border region. "Here," he pointed to a spot on the map. "A multi-acre compound outside of Juarez, Mexico. Just a few miles across the border. Reinforced, high walls, all you'd expect."

Rage looked up at them both skeptically. "And the Mexican government is just gonna let us fly right in there and raise hell, right?"

"In a word, yes," Dunlap answered. "In exchange for additional aid along with concessions on some current matters, the Mexican government is co-operating. Though they'd rather do it themselves, ultimately they want the Jackal gone as much as we do."

"All right," Rage said. "So when do we go in."

"One week from tonight," Dunlap said. "You'll train at night; that's when we'll do the insertion. Get some rest; phase two training begins at 0100."

10

Enrique had wanted to stay with his mother longer that evening, but Juanita needed help with her homework, so he had to get back home before she went to bed.

As he pushed through the creaky, rusted metal front door to the tiny apartment building they'd lived in for the past twelve years, his mind wandered yet again back to the offer his uncle had made him a week ago. Many would have accepted right away, perhaps even called it an honor, to become one of his uncle's coyotes: it paid very well, that was well known. But normally one had to have been a mule for at least a year or two before being considered worthy of becoming a coyote. So this was unprecedented.

The mules were the carriers; the coyotes were the leaders, the navigators, the brains behind each shipment. And they were always the priority: mules were a dime a dozen, his uncle had always said; he could get any poor young fool to carry a heavy pack full of product across any terrain into harm's way. But not everyone had the brains to be a coyote, to understand the terrain, to sniff out possible problems, to find the good hiding places when the Americans did their fly-overs or rode by on ATVs or horses. Coyotes were the only ones trusted with key information: where the shipment was from, to whom it was being delivered, and how to get it there. The mules just followed. And if there was ever trouble, a coyote's instructions were always to flee immediately; their job was to avoid questioning by the Americans, to leave the shipment, and to get back to safety to fight another day. The mules were never so lucky.

His uncle's offer not only included employment and generous pay; it also meant that his mother would get access to the best doctors available: his uncle's connections across the region would make certain of that.

So when Enrique refused the proposition, it not only surprised his uncle, it surprised Enrique as well.

Even with all that his uncle had offered, Enrique found himself unable to resort to a trade that had destroyed more lives than he cared to count.

And it was also a terrible risk. Right now, he was desperate, but at least he was alive. If he were to be killed while doing his uncle's dirty work, his mother and sister would be all alone.

No. There had to be another way.

He climbed the stairs up to the third floor. Approaching the old wooden door to their apartment, he stopped for a moment and rubbed his eyes, wiping the exhaustion from them, putting on a brave, happy face for his baby sister. From the hallway he could hear Juanita inside the tiny main room, singing along to her favorite music on the tinny radio that sat on the kitchen counter. Closing his eyes, he could picture her in there, smiling, happy, not a care in the world that a twelve year-old girl shouldn't have.

He opened the door and walked in, a big smile on his face.

"Juanita!" he said happily as he came up to hug her.

"Enrique!" she ran up to him. "How is Mama?"

"Good, she is good," he forced himself to lie to her. "She will be home again in just a few days. Now, is your homework all done for tomorrow?"

"No, I've been waiting for you to help me!"

"I thought so," he said. "What do we have for tonight?"

"Algebra and history," she said with a sigh.

"Well," he said, setting his bag down and pointing to the kitchen table. "That just happens to be my specialty. Let's get to work, okay?"

Hours later, after her homework was finished and Juanita had gone to bed, Enrique found himself unable to get to sleep. For the past hour he'd been poring over the sparse job listings section in the weekend's newspaper, certain he'd missed something – anything – that could possibly be a fit for him.

But there was nothing.

He could no longer go back to America for work. And he was too far from anyplace in his own country that could offer him employment. Mexico City, the tourist cities along the coasts, were all several hundred miles away; he couldn't uproot his family in the state his mother was in.

No; whatever he was going to do, he would have to do it in Juarez.

At that moment, his cell phone rang. Glancing about, he saw the clock – it was just after eleven. Who would be calling this late? He grabbed the phone and opened it.

"Hello?" he answered quietly.

"Senor Castillo?" the female voice came from the other end.

"Si, this is he," Enrique replied pensively.

"This is Nurse Gonzalez calling from the hospital. I'm afraid your mother has taken a turn and needs emergency surgery. We ask that you come down immediately."

11

The tiny town square of South Fitchburg was a testament to the spiraling economic conditions that had plagued this lonely stretch of Texas border towns for decades.

Austin Avenue, the main drag through town, once boasted several proud storefronts, including four restaurants, five watering holes, two antique shops, a grocery market, pharmacy, clinic, dentist's office, bookstore, even a tiny accounting practice. A fifteen-foot-high bronze statue of Sam Houston had stood tall at the center of the town's central square, overlooking a lush patch of maintained green grass and neatly-coiffed floral gardens. The town had mostly been supported by the four manufacturing plants at the Fitchburg industrial park just north of town, along with the railroad that came through town.

Now the railroad was gone, the Sante Fe Railway having re-routed its southernmost line through the central part of the state twenty years ago, and inside of the following ten years, with it went three of the factories that had employed almost half of Broward County's eighteen thousand residents. Now, back in town, of the many businesses that had once populated South Fitchburg's main strip, only three remained: Wendy's Diner, The Blue Cat Bar and Grill, and the clinic, now down to only one practitioner, Dr. Holloway. Sam Houston still stood proudly in the square, now overlooking sparse patches of brown weeds among dried dirt and sand. The remainder of the two- and three-story buildings that remained on the sand-swept stretch of road now displayed boarded windows and broken signs, a sullen reminder of the region's decline.

The lone plant still humming was Broadway Chicken Farms, a regional supplier to many brand-name chicken products sold to grocers and restaurant chains throughout the southwest. It was almost lunchtime on Monday, which meant an influx of plant workers would soon be coming into Wendy's Diner for their usual mid-day grub.

Otis had been up late working on the Jeep the night before and had over-slept. He was about to make himself a sandwich in the kitchen when he realized he hadn't been out since he'd gotten out of the hospital – over a week now. He decided to head into town to grab a bite to eat, and to get a little change of scenery.

On his way into town, he thought about the conversation he'd had with his father the night before. To him, the smuggling activity was nothing short of an invasion. His country, through his proud home state of Texas and now even his hometown, was being poisoned by an enemy that snaked through holes in its protected border.

But he knew there was nothing real he could do about it: even with all his military training, he would never be able to assemble any kind of sizable group to make a difference. There simply weren't enough trained men. After risking his life for his country on the other side of the world these past six years, he felt angered and powerless about what was happening to it in his own back yard.

Otis walked into the diner, taking a seat at the counter. He ordered his usual, a chicken salad on rye with extra mustard and pickles, and a Coke. "Comin' right up," Alyson, the young waitress behind the counter, smiled back at him. "Always nice to have you back in town, Otis."

"Thanks," Otis said, taking off his ball cap, then looking to his right to see a folded-up edition of the day's *Broward County Gazette* on the counter next to him.

He began looking for the sports page, then noticed the front page story on Old Mabel's ranch smuggling case. The headline read, "Fourth Border Ranch Dog Killing Stumps Local Authorities." His brow furrowed at the headline, but he began perusing the story:

> *Local police and Border Protection officials continue to pursue leads on the fourth incident of smuggling across a border ranch in the past week. Mabel Williams, a widowed rancher just outside of South Fitchburg, called police when she noticed her two ranch dogs had been shot to death. Local police*

and Border Patrol agents searched the area to find evidence of smuggling activity on the ranch. Evidence was found in a wooded area at the edge of the ranch, where ...

He was so involved in the story that he hadn't noticed the man who had sat down on the stool next to his.

"Unbelievable, ain't it," said the deep, gruff voice coming from his right. "Guess it was only a matter o'time, though, wudn't it."

"'Scuse me?" Otis said, glancing up from the paper to look at the man next to him. The man, very large and broad-shouldered, was wearing a red, plaid flannel shirt and jeans. He had deep set-in eyes, almost hidden below a protruding brow, thick gray hair mostly slicked back except for a few wisps that hovered in front of his forehead, and a full gray beard.

"Just sayin'," the man continued, undeterred. "Them smugglers. They been doin' it in surroundin' areas so long, at some point they's gonna try here, too. Gotta switch thangs up. Ranches, no Border Patrol there. I'm s'prised they didn't think of it earlier."

"Yeah, I s'pose," Otis said, turning his attention back to the story.

"Name's Wayne Voorhees," the man cut in again. Otis turned once more to see the man had extended a large hand.

"Otis Brown," Otis returned, shaking the man's hand pensively. Alyson returned with the Coke. Otis nodded to her in thanks and picked it up, taking a sip.

"I heard tell the new Border Patrol Cap'n is expected to crack down on this purty quick," Voorhees said. "But I have my doubts. You ask me, that little lady runnin' things over there got no idea what she's in fer."

"That right," Otis asked. "Makes you think that?"

"Too much in-bred corruption in her group. Whatever she tries, she got moles in her bid'ness. Moles tell the cartels what she gonna do afore she does it, the cartels stay one step ahead o'her. As a ree-sult, *their* bid'ness keeps a'hummin'."

"An' what if she weeds the moles out?"

"That ain't go'happen, son," Voorhees said. "Too many moles. Money's too big for there not to be. Even if she gets rid o'all the existin' moles — which she won't —there'll be more. And they'll always find a way to keep her from gettin' the big score. No, she ain't go'fix nuthin' round here."

"Thanks for the upliftin' news," Otis said, taking another drink of Coke. Alyson arrived with his sandwich and chips. Otis took up a chip and tossed it in his mouth. "So what all are you exactly gettin' at, anyway?"

"Point is, son, Border Patrol ain't the answer. Cops ain't the answer, either. Not enough of 'em, and not enough firepower. So, there's gotta be a third option."

"And what option is that?"

"Well, y'see," Voorhees began, "I happen t'lead a little organization down the road a bit. Y'might've heard o'the TIFF?"

"Texas Independent Freedom Fighters," Otis nodded. "Course I have. The militia. Down in Clark Junction. Who *hasn't* heard of 'em 'round here?"

"You got it," Voorhees answered. "Now over a hunnert-seventy-five strong, and growin' leaps n'bounds every day. Betcha we got two hundr'd able-bodied men by summer."

"And so I'm guessin' that's why you're talkin' to me," Otis surmised.

"You'd be guessin' right," Voorhees smiled. "I heard tell 'bout you, son. Heard you's havin' trouble bein' redeployed. Heard 'bout what happened to you at the crossin'. Guessin' that mighta pissed you off some. Hearin' bout you and now lookin' at you, you strike me as someone who'd wanna do somethin' about what's goin' on."

Otis rubbed his chin. "I don't know," he said. "Militia's ain't exactly my cup o'tea. Thanks, but no thanks."

"But you ain't heard all I got t'say yet," Voorhees leaned in, speaking quietly. "We got some plans. Big plans. We wanna give your daddy a bit o'help."

Otis paused. "What do you know about my daddy?" he asked.

"Come on, son," Voorhees smiled. "We know who y'are. Know you's the Sheriff's boy. Know he's gettin' in knee-deep and it's only gonna get deeper on 'im. And like I said, he don't have the men or the firepower to keep up with what's happenin'. And like I also said, Border Patrol gonna just trip over they's own feet."

Otis just looked at Voorhees, waiting for him to continue.

"So we plan on offerin' him a little help. Unofficial help, o'course. We got the men, we got the firepower, we got the resources, and we got the training. Fifty-six of our men are ex-military. Think about all that afore you say no."

"And what exactly are you gonna do," Otis asked suspiciously.

"That," Voorhees said, placing a giant hand on Otis's shoulder, "will have to wait 'til after you say yes. Now we's got another meetin' t'night, over at the VA hall down in Steppeville. Back meetin' room, can't miss it. Seven o'clock. I'm hopin' I see you there."

At that he pushed back the stool and stood up. "Now I best be runnin' on," he said. "I hope you'll 'least extend me the courtesy of not tellin' your daddy 'bout our little talk. You have a good afternoon, son."

Otis watched as Voorhees made his way out of the diner, got in an old pickup truck, and drove down the street, out of view.

12

H ours earlier, the soft, milky light of pre-dawn began to sift its way
through the dusty windows of Santa Angela Hospital.

Enrique lay stretched across three plastic chairs in the waiting room, trying to
get a wink of sleep while his mother was in surgery. He had not been successful. He'd been here since around midnight, when he rushed to the hospital
after getting the call. He was not able to see his mother before she went into
the operating room, so he had been waiting with baited breath every second
she'd been in there.

It was just after five o'clock in the morning. He'd left Juanita sleeping in
her bed, but she would be waking up in the next hour for school. In hindsight
he should have at least left her a note, but he wasn't thinking clearly when he'd
left – all he could think of was getting to his mother.

At that moment the doctor emerged through the waiting room doors. He
was tall, with a bald head and gray mustache; his blue scrubs had slight traces
of blood on them, the blood of his mother. Enrique tried to read the man's
expression but could not.

"Senor Castillo," the doctor said, "I am Dr. Santoyo. I wanted to let you
know that your mother has pulled through surgery; she's in the recovery room
right now."

"Oh, thank God," Enrique said. "Is she awake? When can I see her?"

"She's resting now. She'll probably be asleep for another few hours."

"Okay," Enrique said. He would have to go get Juanita ready for school. "I will be back," he said, starting to head for the door.

"Senor Castillo," Santoyo said, "wait a moment."

"Si?" Enrique said, stopping and turning back to face the doctor.

"I want you to understand what your mother is up against," he said. "This will not be an easy road. What she just went through took a lot out of her, so she needs to be stabilized. She will need to remain in the hospital for a few days. From there, she'll need constant care over the next several weeks. Do you understand this?"

"Yes, Doctor," Enrique said anxiously.

"We will do all we can for her," the doctor finished, checking his watch. "But beyond that, it will be up to you."

"Yes Doctor," Enrique said. "Thank you, Doctor."

On the bus ride back home, the gravity of all that Dr. Santoyo shared with him began to sink in: a longer hospital stay, constant care for when she returned home … Enrique had no idea how he was even going to pay for what she'd just gone through, much less everything that lay ahead.

There was only one thing to do. There was no other way.

He picked up his phone and dialed the number for his uncle.

13

I t was just after five o'clock in the evening. Otis pulled himself out from under the Jeep to fetch a drink of water when his cell phone rang.

Half-debating whether to answer it, he ambled over and looked at the tiny screen to see who was calling. It was Kyle Farnston, a local kid with whom he'd done a tour in Iraq several years back. Kyle had been one of the best soldiers Otis had ever served with, until he suffered a serious head injury on his last tour that prevented him from seeing clearly out of his right eye. Like Otis, he was appealing to be placed back on active duty. Unlike Otis, due to his limited vision, his chances were slim to none.

Otis picked up. "Hello?"

"Otis Brown," the familiar voice came. "It's Kyle. Kyle Farnston, from tour. Remember me?"

"Kyle," Otis returned. "Course I remember you. Been awhile, though. How're things? Any movement on bein' redeployed?"

"Heh, none," Kyle huffed bitterly. "Sucks, don't it. How 'bout you?"

"Same," Otis admitted. "Hopefully sometime soon."

"Hey, I heard you was keepin' busy at the Fitchburg border station til somebody hit it," Kyle said. "You back to work yet?"

"Not yet," Otis said. "Was nothin' that's gonna keep me down. Station's wrecked, though. So what brings the pleasure o' your call, Kyle?"

"Well, I was gettin' to that," Kyle said. "I hear you ran into the leader of the TIFF this mornin' over at the diner."

"Yeah? You hear that from the leader o' the TIFF himself?"

"I s'pose I did," Kyle admitted.

"And what'd he want you to talk to me about?"

"Now, I'm actually callin' on behalf of myself, Otis," Kyle said.

"Okay, then," Otis said. "Then what'd *you* want to talk to me about?"

"Wanted to make sure you was comin' over to the meetin' tonight," Kyle replied.

"Then I'll tell you what I told him," Otis said. "Thanks, but no thanks."

"Now, Otis, sounds like you're pre-judgin'," Kyle said. "You ain't got no idea who all's involved. What kind o'things we got planned."

"No, and I don't care to," Otis said flatly. "And Kyle, you best be careful yourself. You know well as I that any fightin' force is only as strong as its weakest link. S'why we weed 'em out in the Corps. I'm bettin' you the TIFF has plenty o'em."

"Well, we got plenty o' *strong* links, too. Lotsa guys like you an' me."

"An' what're y'all *really* gonna do, Kyle," Otis said skeptically. "Wait around 'long the border til trouble comes your way? Then what? You really gonna *shoot* somebody on American soil?"

"No," Kyle said. "It ain't gonna be like any o'that. Most these smugglin' groups is small an' unarmed, or lightly armed at the most. I ain't gonna give up the leadership's plan, mostly 'cause I don't know the details yet, but we's just gonna round 'em up, not shoot anybody."

"Can you speak fer everyone on that, Kyle?" Otis asked.

"I c'n speak for the TIFF and its leadership," Kyle answered. "An' that's good enough fer me."

"Well, then, I guess that'll do for ya," Otis said. "But not me."

"Otis, listen ta me," Kyle said. "Why don'tcha just come on out, hear what the leadership has to say. We got a lotta good men there, wantin' to do the right thing. I know that's what you wanna do, too. Ain't no one's plan to get anybody hurt or killed. We's just go' turn them over to the police, is all. Deter 'em from comin' cross our land anymore. If'n for nuthin' else, do it for a fellow jarhead. What do ya say."

"I'll think about it," Otis said after a pause. "But I wouldn't get my hopes up."

"Well, that's better than a no, I guess," Kyle sighed. "I hope y'join us."

"Okay, Kyle," Otis said, and hung up.

Twenty minutes passed, and Otis closed up shop for the day and headed into the house to clean up for dinner. As he walked through the back patio door into the living room, he saw Silas come in through the kitchen.

"Pa," he said, nodding to Silas as he closed the sliding glass door.

"Otis," Silas exhaled heavily back at his son. He lumbered over to the fridge, opened the door listlessly, and pulled a can of beer off the top shelf. He then set the beer down and leaned forward on the counter, cupping both hands back over the edge, just staring down at the countertop.

"Pa," he said quietly. "What is it?"

Silas exhaled heavily again, keeping his eyes down. "We lost a man today," was all he was finally able to say.

"Who?"

"Paul Reynolds," Silas said.

"Officer Reynolds?" Otis said, recalling one of his father's part-time officers.

"You know 'im. Family man. Wife, three sons."

"What happened?"

"Still tryin' to figger it out," Silas sighed. "Looked like he'd been patrollin' one o' the border ranches last night — on his own time — and got shot up."

"Shot up?"

"Rancher found him early this afternoon along his fence," Silas said grimly. "Coroner counted over twenty bullet holes across his head and torso."

"Holy mother," was all Otis could bring himself to say.

"Fifteen years on the force, never even got a nick," Silas said. "Now one unlucky night, wrong place wrong time, and he's gone.

"He was in even in uniform," Silas went on after a pause. "Probably wanted to look official, scare any of 'em off."

"An' they killed him instead," Otis concluded.

Silas could only nod in reply.

Otis sat down at the kitchen table to think things through. He was right when he'd said it to his father the other day: it was a war zone now. Smugglers first killing ranch dogs, now uniformed police officers? Bombing a border checkpoint? They were doing things that had never been done before. Bold, brazen things. Ruthless things.

Things that could not go unpunished.

At that moment, Annie came in through the mud room door, carrying some bags from the market. She set them down and rushed to Silas, embracing him tightly.

"Silas, I just heard the news on the radio," she said. "I — I'm so sorry."

Silas didn't say a word, just held her against him, as tightly as he could.

Otis looked over at his mother and father embracing. He had always seen his father as infallible; bulletproof. As someone who could take anything, lead men safely through any situation, whether it was back in his days as a Marine, or as Sheriff now. And even though Otis had grown into his own man, he always felt that his father would be there to look out for him, to protect him.

But in that moment, his father looked older, more vulnerable, almost fragile. As if he was the one who needed to be looked out for now.

And if the cartels were now killing police officers, how long until they began targeting them? Or even organizing attacks against all authorities in the region? This thought suddenly made his father's vulnerability very real.

He stood up from the table. "I'm gonna go out for a bit," he said. "Don't wait on me for dinner — I'll be back later this evenin'."

14

After eleven hours of drills and training had carried into the noon hour, Rage had slept until early evening.

The compound that the Division had recreated for the training reminded him of terrorist compounds they'd raided back in Syria and Yemen: plenty of hiding places to stage an ambush, along with maze-like hallways designed to confuse any invading forces. All designed to safeguard their precious leaders.

From what he'd learned so far, the target's intelligence and cunning was head and shoulders above that of most previous targets. Javier Oropeza, the man known as the Jackal, was an educated man who'd seen success in many ventures before going into the illegal drug trade. He was also a product of the military, earning Mexico's highest honors as a soldier and marksman earlier in life. The man alone would probably give even a few of the SEALs a run for their money. Add on a number of loyal, trained fighters and a compound that would be hard to navigate, and the mission became much more dangerous.

Rage looked at the clock; ten minutes until the first debrief of the day. He switched on the evening news. It was a national report on a Texas border town police officer murdered while patrolling a ranch:

"… the officer, a father of three, was believed to be patrolling a small group of border ranches near his home while off-duty last night, when he encountered his attackers. His body was found along the fence of the Kilpatrick family ranch just outside South Fitchburg, Texas, only four miles east of last week's deadly attack on the South Fitchburg Customs and Border Patrol station. Local authorities won't comment on the matter, but many in town believe that last night's killing is related to that attack, as well as the string of shootings of ranch dogs in recent weeks. Authorities have no official suspects as of yet, but say, and I quote, it is 'very likely' that one of the cartels from across the border is responsible. Dwight, back to you …"

He changed the station until he found something that was not news, a game show. He set down the remote and walked to the large window overlooking the Set. There had been something in the briefing about the shooting of ranch dogs in the area that may or may not have been connected to the attack on the station, but the killing of a police officer seemed to be the glue that tied it all together.

None of it should have mattered to him; his only concern should be executing the mission. Taking out the target. Nothing beyond that.

But in his mind, he knew differently: he needed these other details, these other reasons, to fuel his fire for the mission. Orders sent him on each mission. But discovering reason behind each mission was what motivated him, what gave him purpose, to do what needed to be done.

To bring out the beast lurking inside him.

It used to be that the beast *was* the motivation. But his medication had changed that. It had given him a severe distaste for violence, for killing, even if those he was sent to kill presented a dire threat to the world. The chemicals he ingested into his body had reversed the inner urges within him, had enabled him to banish them completely – so that he was always in control.

But that control quelled his fire to execute the missions at hand; it even sometimes made him question why he was doing what he did. Killing was a messy business, he knew; both inside and out of one's head.

So finding reason, finding true purpose behind each mission had become essential to his ability to go on doing them. The senseless killing of sixty-two civilians and Border Patrol officers had been enough. But the murder of an outgunned police officer had somehow made it more personal.

At that moment, the buzzer announced that someone was at the front gate of the compound. Rage switched the remote to show the array of video feeds along the grounds, and he saw the Humvee pulling up the main drive. He glanced at the clock again; the squad was here early.

He quickly donned his fatigues and headed down the stairwell. When he arrived at the base of the stairs, he saw only one man in the entryway: Captain Dale Stevenson, leader of second squad, the backup unit to the one he'd been training with.

Rage opened the door and walked toward Stevenson, who turned to face him.

"You're probably wondering why I'm here," Stevenson began, his upper East Coast accent ringing clear in Rage's ears.

Rage didn't reply; he just kept his eyes on Stevenson.

"Heh," he snickered at Rage's lack of response. "I'll lay it out, then. This morning, one of the men on Captain Johns's squad had a bit of a freak accident. Broke his arm. Now, you know the drill: if one man on a SEAL squad goes down, the entire unit gets swapped out, and second squad is brought in. So that makes me your new C.O."

Rage stared at him for a moment. "Why wasn't I informed of this by Dunlap."

"You know why," Stevenson said flatly. "It's always the duty of the C.O. to inform his men of changes. So that's what I'm doing now."

Rage said nothing. He stared at Stevenson in stunned silence, letting this change of events sink in. Captain Carter "Chuck" Johns had been Rage's C.O. on many of his most important missions and was one of the best officers he knew. To go from Johns to someone like Stevenson was nothing short of a worst-case scenario.

"So now that you're in the know," Stevenson continued, "let's be clear on something. You and I share a history, we both know it. And it doesn't take a genius to figure out that you don't like me any more than I like you. We don't need to get into why, do we?"

Rage did not reply.

"Didn't think so," Stevenson shook his head. "Yet, somehow, the Division saw fit to pair us up again. So, we need to set some ground rules. Because the last time we were together, things didn't go so well."

"You weren't the C.O. then," Rage said quietly.

"But I am this time around," Stevenson said, puffing out his chest a bit. "So we need to do this, in order to prevent history repeating itself."

"That was one incident," Rage said.

"During the *one* time we were on a mission together," Stevenson retorted. "God knows how many other 'incidents' you've been responsible for, that Johns and your other C.O.s chose to sweep under the rug."

"None," Rage snarled.

"Of course not," Stevenson returned sardonically. "In any event, this is *my* mission now, and you will fall in line this time. There will be no undermining my authority while in the field. We need to have this understanding right now."

"Or what," Rage challenged.

"Or I'll file a request to have you taken off the mission," Stevenson said flatly.

"Don't think that's gonna happen," Rage said.

Stevenson smiled. "I know you're a special case. I know all about your record. But I also know other things, aside from what happened during our mission. You have friends, I have friends. I know about your history – your ... imbalances, let's call them. You could wind up being a danger to the mission, to my men. Like before."

Rage glared at Stevenson, not saying a word.

"You're gifted, there's no question," Stevenson spoke quietly, leaning into Rage a bit. "But the truth of the matter is, you don't have the experience, or the mindset, to command a team. You are a specialist. We do our job, you do yours. When a decision needs to be made that will affect the lives of the soldiers under my command, it is *my* call, and you need to fall in line. Am I making myself clear, soldier?"

Rage felt his anger begin to boil over inside him. "You're a real brave man standing this close to me and talking like that," he managed to say through gritted teeth. "Either that, or real stupid."

"Threats, now?" Stevenson cocked his head, eyes wide. "I'm thinking *you* must be the stupid one. How about I call General Dunlap right this moment and have him sort this out, after I inform him of your behavior toward your C.O.?"

Rage swallowed hard, suppressing the urge to respond to Stevenson's threat. He knew that the chain of command governed all conflicts, whether inside or outside of military ranks. Even with Rage's stature within the Division, Dunlap would have no choice but to defer to the rules, which put Stevenson's authority before Rage.

He would be cut out of the mission ... and to him, being part of the mission was far more important than any disagreement he had with Stevenson.

"When it comes to the lives of your men," Rage said quietly, holding back a snarl, "it's your call."

Stevenson stood up straight and crossed his arms. "All right," he said.

"But when it comes to my actions affecting my life alone," Rage held up a finger, "that'll be my call. And no one else's. Understood?"

"Personally, I could give a rat's ass what happens to you," Stevenson said flatly. "But if you get your head blown off while under my command, it'll be on me. I'll give the orders. If you choose to disobey them, I'll make sure everyone understands you acted on your own."

"I'm glad we understand each other, then," Rage said.

Stevenson smiled thinly at Rage. "So long as you understand me, I don't really need to understand you," he said. "Briefing begins in thirty minutes. Meet back here then."

Without a word, Rage turned and walked back to the stairwell.

15

Enrique was helping Juanita with her homework when she finally spoke up about his evening plans.

"Who's coming to pick you up again?" she asked, looking up from her math workbook.

"Some ... friends," he said, checking the window again. "They are going to help me get a new job."

"Where?"

"In Juarez," he replied. "But sometimes I'll be in America, too."

"What will you be doing?"

Enrique exhaled; he hated not being able to tell Juanita everything. He didn't want to lie to her, so he tried to be as vague as he could.

"I'll helping to ship things to America and back," he said. "They call it exporting. I'll be one of the bosses."

"What kind of things?"

"I – I don't know yet," he said, rubbing his forehead. "The important thing is, I'll be working again. Much as I love staying here with you, of course." He smiled.

"All right," Juanita said. "Just sounds fishy, is all."

"No, not at all," Enrique began, then he looked out the window again. A black Humvee had pulled up. He ran over to hug her. "They're here! I have to go. I'll see you later, okay?"

"Okay," she said quietly, returning his embrace.

Enrique kissed her on the forehead and made his way for the door. He dropped the keys as he turned the knob, and he realized his hands were trembling. He wondered if Juanita had noticed.

"Adios," he said, forcing a smile.

As he pulled the door closed, he remembered seeing her sitting at the table, her young face showing no real expression, just looking at him, not saying a word.

He readied himself for the men he was about to engage with. He knew they were his uncle's employees, but they were dangerous men. They were the kind of men who had probably done terrible things, things Enrique would have trouble imagining people doing.

He emerged from his building and walked across the dusty dirt road toward the large SUV. As he approached, the rear passenger-side door opened. Enrique climbed in.

He immediately noticed the man to his left, a lean but muscular man with a shaved head. The man was wearing a black t-shirt with some script on the front, and his arms and neck were covered in tattoos. Then he saw the enormous machine gun resting between the man's legs, the butt end on the floor, the nozzle leaning to the right, pointed menacingly in Enrique's direction.

As the vehicle lurched forward and began down the dirt road, Enrique instinctively glanced back up toward his apartment building. In the window he saw the silhouette of Juanita's head, looking on as they drove away.

16

As sunset stretched across the western horizon, Otis pulled into the parking lot of the Steppeville VA hall.

He pushed through the front doors of the VA hall and looked around. Though the parking lot was mostly full, the front bar was all but empty: just two old men sat a few seats apart at the bar, watching the TV; two more sat hunched over in one of the worn booths across the dimly-lit room. A pool table and two dart boards stood deserted under slightly brighter lights to his left. An old Hank Williams song quietly twanged out of old speakers that hung from the ceiling, surrounding the bar area.

He walked up to the bar and nodded to the bartender, a seventy-something man wearing a mesh baseball cap with a Navy ship emblem sewn onto the front, and red suspenders stretched over a stained, off-white button-down shirt.

"What c'n I getcha, tiny?" he said, looking up at Otis with a ragged smile.

"I'm good, thanks much, sir," Otis returned. "Actually I'm—"

"Lookin' fer the meetin'?" the bartender cut in. "Right back'air, through them doors." He pointed toward the double doors just beyond the bar.

"Much obliged," Otis said, touching the bill of his Texas Rangers cap in thanks.

"Here, Son," the main said, pulling a glass off the shelf behind him and pouring it full of ice and water. "Gets a might warm back in'air. Y'might need this."

"Again," Otis took the glass and again touched the bill of his cap. "Much appreciated."

Otis stepped through the doors and into a short, darkened hallway. Doors lined both sides as well as the far wall. On the left were the restrooms; on the right, the door to the kitchen. On the far wall was a door that had a large placard on it that read: "PRIVATE MEETINGS ONLY – KEEP OUT."

Must be the place, he thought.

As he walked through the last set of doors, he was greeted with a heavy mix of smells; among the few that stood out the most were cigarette and cigar smoke, body odor, and stale, cheap beer. A thick haze of smoke permeated the air before him, settling at its thickest at the eight-foot-high hung-tile ceiling that was already patterned with brown smoke stains from over the years.

Through the haze, Otis could see an enormous room spread before him; in the room were rows upon rows of metal folding chairs, all but a few of them occupied. Otis figured there had to be at least a hundred men in the room, maybe even a hundred and fifty. He gazed to the left to see a long table near the wall. At that table were two men, one of them tapping away at a laptop computer, the second setting up an overhead projector. Another man casually lumbered over to the table. Wayne Voorhees.

Otis decided to keep a low profile. He hunted for a seat in the far back.

As he scanned the room, he saw Kyle Farnston near the front, engaged in conversation with two other men, though every few seconds he appeared to glance around the room. He also recognized Ty Wallace, a kid two years behind him in high school who had joined the National Guard but was quickly discharged for what Otis had heard were several instances of "erratic and dangerous conduct."

Wallace turned to scan the room, his familiar wild, twitchy eyes squinting to see through the haze. Otis pulled his Rangers cap down a bit further on his forehead.

Otis's eyes then swept a bit to the right and saw two men he absolutely didn't expect to see: Coy Allerton and Mike McTeague, two of his father's part-time officers.

If Silas were to find out they were here …

Hell, if Silas were to find out *he* was here …

A crackle of static kicked out from the microphone. Voorhees was about to address the group.

"Ahem, all right," his gruff voice issued from too close to the microphone. "Can y'all hear me in the back?"

"Loud n'clear, sir!" shouted an eager voice from behind Otis.

"A'ight, good, then," Voorhees replied. "Glad you wuz all able to make it t'night. We got some serious bid'ness to cover in the next hour, and some d'tails 'bout y'all's first assignment. Thangs gonna git purty int'restin' soon. In a good way, I might add.

"But first let's pledge our 'llegiance," he said, setting down the microphone and placing a giant paw over his wide chest. He turned toward the large American flag that was pinned to the wall to his left.

Every man in the room rose from his seat and followed suit, and Voorhees led them through the Pledge of Allegiance. The room recited the pledge word for word in unison and remained standing when it was done.

Voorhees picked up the microphone and continued on his own. "We *don't* pledge our 'llegiance to no government, an' to no voice of au-thority other than the Almighty hisself. We stand *ag'inst* any man or org'n'zation that tries to undo those freedoms an' liberties this country was built on, and we will be victorious in our battle against any such perp'trators. Am I right?"

"Right, Sir!" the voices around Otis cried in unison.

"Will we defeat those who mean to defile our freedoms?" he shouted.

"Yes, Sir!" the crowd shouted.

"A'right, then," Voorhees said. "Now let's get down to bid'ness."

Voorhees stepped to one side of the table as the projector screen lit up behind him, displaying a map of the region.

"T'night's the night y'all've been waitin' fer," he began. "As many o'y'all know, we been plannin' this fer months. We known about the trouble's been brewin' on the other side o'the border. We know they's been movin' product through our lands. But recent events have forced our hand. When they started killin' dogs on our ranches, when they bombed our border crossin', killin' sixty-some people ... and I hear the bastards just murdered an officer o'the law. All a' this has caused us to rethink our timin.'"

He pointed to the map on the screen. "These are our lands," he said. "An' we're gonna protect 'em, man fer man, like we been trainin' ourselves to do. Our friends in the po-lice department have provided us with some intel that's gonna help us do that."

Otis figured that Voorhees had to be referring to Allerton and McTeague.

Voorhees gestured to the man sitting behind the computer, and the screen changed to show a series of red and green lines going up and down along the map.

"Now these here are smugglin' routes," Voorhees explained. "The red lines're ones that ain't been used lately, the green lines're ones that have been. From what we know, some o' these routes is pretty damn dang'rous. Hell, we hear the smugglers even give some o'em *names.* So we know the less dang'rous ones is gonna be the ones they'll be usin' more often."

Voorhees nodded to the man behind the computer, and the screen changed again to show clusters of dark blue dots along the border, concentrated most heavily along the green lines.

"Y'wanna stop the flow o'water, ya gotta plug thangs up," he said. "We's gonna be that plug. We's gonna outnumber 'em, we's gonna outsmart 'em, and we's gonna outgun 'em. We's gonna stop 'em in their tracks, take 'em into custody, and gift-wrap 'em for the au-thor'ties, shipments an'all. An' if'n they wanna put up a fight, then we's gonna give 'em a fight. More than they bargained for, in fact. We's gonna intimidate 'em outta usin' our lands for their steppin' stones. An' if they esc'late, we's gonna esc'late, too. We's gonna teach 'em a lesson. An' what lesson is that?"

"DON'T MESS WITH TEXAS!" shouted more men than Otis expected to hear, many of them throwing their fists into the air.

"Tha's right," Voorhees nodded proudly. "Let 'em take it to Cal'forn-i-ay or any other o' them lib'rul states want their bid'ness. We don't want none o' it here.

"S'here's a-what we're gonna do," Voorhees went on, "three nights a week, startin' tomorrah night. We's gonna put each and ever'one a'you along our stretch o'that border, in groups small and large, for couple hour shifts. Line up the big groups with th' smugglin' routes, with spotters and stop-gaps in a'tween for good measure. Each group gonna be about a half-mile apart. So we won't have no line-o-sight, but ever'one'll be close enough to one another t'be able to get t'each other if'n another group needs help. Roy over here's set us up with a commun'cations network that'll enable ever'one to hear each oth-er. If someone sees somethin', ya'll just gotta say so, and help'll be on the way."

Voorhees ambled over to the table, picked up a small walkie-talkie, and held it up in front of the assembly. "We's gonna be usin' these as our commun'cation dee-vices," he said. "Got approx'mately twenny o'em here, donated by a local bid'nessman who'll remain nameless per his askin'. Each team leader's gonna git one a'these. Another person in each team's gonna get a pair o'binoculars an' keep watch o'the landscape. Ya see somethin', you tell your team leader, and we'll git backup thair for ya.

"Now," Voorhees crossed his arms and regarded the crowd, "who here dudn't own a gun?"

Otis scanned the room; not one man raised his hand. Otis figured most of them owned guns, and the few that didn't weren't about to admit to it, at least to this crowd.

"A'ight, then," Voorhees nodded. "B'cause we're all gonna be needin' 'em. I ain't expectin' nobody to go firin' anythang off, but y'all's got t'be prepared."

The slide advanced to show a photo of what appeared to be a group of smugglers being loaded into a CBP van. Otis recognized one of the officers prodding them in.

"Nah as y'all know, this's how they travel," Voorhees explained. "Always a group o'tween four an' six o'em. Most o'em 're mules, who do all the carry-in'. Then ya got the coyote. The mules don't know nuthin' – the coyote does. Smugglin' routes, where they's goin', where they came from, ever'thang. CBP used to jes' throw 'em back over the border when they caught 'em. Catch n' release. But what's happened lately, I got it on good knowledge that ever' smuggler they's catchin', they's keepin' and interrogatin'. So you get the coy-ote, you get the prize.

"So tha's the plan," Voorhees clapped his two giant hands together and rubbed his palms against one another. "We plug the border, we keep a look-out, we commun'cate with one 'nuther, and we catch the bad guys and bring 'em in. Simple as that. Ever'body on board?"

"Yes, sir!" said the throng of men around Otis.

"Nah, we gots a coupla rules o'engagement we still gots to cover," Voorhees said, walking over to the table and gesturing to the computer man to advance the slide, which he did, to show a picture of a rifle. "First is how we deal with th' enemy, the second is how we deal with the law.

"First, th' enemy," he gestured to the slide. "Nah, some o'you might be thinkin' we's goin' inta a war zone, where ever'thang's free for the shootin'. Well, we ain't. That ain't our objective here. If'n we never fire one bullet, that'd be fine with me. We are here to catch 'em and bring 'em in to the au-thor'ties, and ult'mately dee-ter 'em from comin' back. Find 'nuther place to brang thair product, jes' not our lands."

Otis leaned back in his chair at this, letting out a small sigh of relief. He'd wondered what Voorhees' intentions were since their encounter at the diner that morning, and what it might mean for Silas and the CBP. Neither was prepared for a bloodbath.

"But we's also gots to be prepared," he warned, putting a finger in the air. "If'n thangs esc'late, and esc'late they very well might, we must defend ourselves. And defend ourselves we will. But, y'are to never discharge your weapon 'til it gets to that point. Your team leader will have the discretion on that, an' no one else. Th' last thang we need is a messy killin' scene that'll draw th' authorities back to us. We don't want nobody in trouble with the law, and we certainly don't want nobody dead. 'Specially any fellow red-blooded Texans. Unnerstand me?"

"Yes, Sir," the group responded.

"Nah, the second rule of engagement pertains to the law, and I'm talkin' 'bout both the po-lice and the CBP," Voorhees said, as the image on the screen changed to project the logo of U.S. Customs and Border Patrol. "We don't wanna 'tract no unnecessary attention. Even though what we's doin' is technically outside the law, we ultimately want 'em to be glad we's out there. So that means we ain't gonna cause no messes if we c'n avoid it. We wanna force 'em to surrender, take 'em in to the author'ties, and be on our merry way. Quick and quiet. Don't give that little lady now runnin' CBP or our very own Sheriff Brown any reason to question what we's doin' and how we's doin' it.

"An' unless we can't avoid it," Voorhees went on, "we's gonna just leave the bandits tied up at their door, make a call, and then fade inta the night. Like ding-dong-ditch, if'n it makes y'all unnerstand better.

"Speakin' of our fine sheriff," Voorhees said, "I just spoke with his boy this mornin', even invited him t' join us this evenin'. Otis Brown, Son – you here?"

Otis sat frozen, thunderstruck by Voorhees' directly calling him out. He hadn't been prepared for this. The other men were starting to look around, their eyes searching among the crowd. It was only a matter of time before someone spotted him.

"Here," Otis finally said, raising a hand.

"Otis Brown," Voorhees said, clearly pleased. "Please stand up, Son, so ever'body c'n see you."

Otis reluctantly stood up, putting his hands in his pockets.

"As many o'y'all know," Voorhees began, extending both giant paws out in Otis's direction, "Otis is one o' the many TIFF members who're military. But he ain't *just* military; he's a hero among men. And he is a *survivor*. Saved many lives an' killed plenty o'the enemy while on tour. Was a P.O.W. in a Taliban prison camp for six long weeks an' survived that. Got hisself both a Purple

Heart an' even th' Silver Star. Then he comes back, decides he's gonna help protect our border. Then he gets ambushed in an attack that kills sixty-some people, an' survives *that*. Even managed t'save somebody's life in the process, I hear.

"This's a true hero," Voorhees continued. "This's a man who knows how t' fight, t' lead, and t' stay alive, an' I'm honored to have 'im join our ranks. Ever'body stand up an' give 'im a hand."

And with that the entire room of men got to their feet and applauded Otis.

Otis felt a hot rush of embarrassment course through his body; his cheeks flushed a deep red. The last place on earth he ever wanted to be was in the spotlight, and Voorhees had just turned the entire sun itself directly onto him.

And worse, Voorhees had put him in a tough spot with the hundred-plus men in the room, including several that knew him, who now thought he had joined the TIFF.

Had this been Voorhees' intention all along? To back him into a corner, make all the men around him believe he had joined, without giving him a chance to explain himself?

Either way, now the word would be out that Sheriff Brown's boy was in with the militia; there was no turning back from that. At the very least, he would need to speak with Allerton and McTeague to make sure none of it got back to Silas – for everyone's protection. At least he had that leverage on those two, given they were cops.

But two of Silas's troopers didn't make as big a story as his own boy, who also happened to be a CBP officer and a war veteran. If he were to join, it would state a clear lack of faith in local law enforcement – by the sheriff's own boy, no less.

No; he would need to tell Voorhees he was out. But he couldn't do it in front of all these men. He would pull him aside after the meeting.

His mind came back into the moment. Realizing he was still standing while many others had sat down, he returned to his seat.

"Nah, we got team assignments for alla you in the room," Voorhees returned to the topic at hand, motioning to another man near the front, who got up and began handing out a stack of papers. "Twenny teams total, and each one o' you is on a team. Like I said, some teams're big, some small, but ever' team's important to our mission.

"When we're done here," Voorhees continued, "we need alla you who're noted as team leader or team spotter t'come on up and collect your comm'n'cator and bi-no'clars, an' get a debrief o' what's go'happen t'morrah night, which you will share with your teams. The rest o' ya can be on your merry way for the evenin'. Ever'one unnerstand loud n' clear?"

"Yes, Sir!" responded many in the group.

Tomorrow night.

Otis sat back in his chair, biding his time. He would confront Voorhees when the meeting was done.

17

The blindfold had gone on the moment the black Humvee turned off the main highway onto a dirt road.

"Why – why are you blindfolding me?" he blurted out in a trembling voice.

"Hombre, you are going to need a little more spine if you are going to work for the Jackal," the voice from the front passenger seat said. "Especially a coyote. What will you do if you are caught by the gringos?"

When Enrique said nothing, the voice said, "Whatever you do, you'd better not give anything up. If you do, you might as well stay with the Americans. You don't want to come back here."

"Do you know what the Jackal does to coyotes that give up information?" the low, raspy voice next to him finally chimed in.

The front passenger chuckled darkly. "Why do you think he is looking for another coyote in the first place?

"You've seen the bodies with no heads, hands, or feet on the TV," the front passenger added on. "Those are not just coyotes. Those are coyotes and their *families*. He kills the coyote's family right in front of him, makes the coyote watch before he kills the coyote himself."

Enrique felt a warm, watery feeling running down his inner thigh. He began trembling uncontrollably.

Suddenly the men burst out laughing. "It worked – the hombre wet himself!" the front passenger exclaimed.

"Wh-what?" Enrique said. "I-I don't — "

"Part of your initiation," the front passenger said, "but you'll probably need a new pair of trousers."

"So … it wasn't true?" Enrique said, still trembling.

"About what the Jackal does to snitch coyotes?" the front passenger said, his laughter fading. "No, that's all true. He will kill you, family or no. No question."

Moments later, the Humvee came to a halt, and the blindfold was removed. Enrique looked around to see that they were now inside a compound of some sort: stone walls at least twenty feet high with barbed wire strung along the top surrounded him. He suddenly wanted to run, but that was not an option now. He was inside his uncle's world, and there was no turning back.

The compound was made up of at least four buildings that Enrique could see, each of white stone with a terra cotta-shingled roof. The three in the foreground stood one story high; the fourth, which loomed behind them, rose up four stories, allowing a view outside the high walls. His eyes moved back to the walls; there were lookout towers at each corner.

"Welcome to *Santa Maria*, boy," the man who had been driving said. Enrique recognized him; it was Hernandez, the henchman who was at the hospital with his uncle, once again wearing the spiked black wristbands.

Hernandez gestured toward the nearest building. "This way."

Enrique followed, walking through the wide, two-inch-thick metal door into a large open space. It appeared to be a giant meeting room or mess hall of some sort, with twenty or so long tables spread evenly about the massive stone floor. Several chandeliers clung tightly to a high ceiling. French-style doors stretched along the back wall, opening up to what looked like an expansive garden.

"Wait here," Hernandez said, then left the room.

Enrique took a seat at the nearest table. He glanced around the room once again, taking in its sheer size.

He'd never really wondered how much money and power his uncle wielded until this moment. The man had been mostly out of their lives since Enrique was a small boy, when his mother had told him that his uncle had moved to the wrong side of the law. Even though Javier had lived only across their neighborhood at the time, Enrique was forbidden from speaking to him from that moment on. Then, after Enrique's father died in a car crash when he was twelve, his mother moved him and his infant sister Juanita out of the neighborhood they'd been living in Enrique's whole life, to the small apartment they were living in now. Since then, his uncle had moved out of the old neighborhood into larger and larger homes, until ultimately building this massive compound Enrique had finally set foot in today.

Now it was clear to Enrique why his mother had moved them further away from his uncle's clutches: the lure of the money, the nice things, the luxury and comforts, would have tempted the young boy that Enrique had been more than his mother could control, especially without the influence of a father in his life.

He was glad she could not see him now.

Even though he was doing all of this for her, she would have never allowed him to do it. She would have rather died, he was certain.

But what choice did he have? He would rather have her alive.

And it was too late to turn back now.

"Enrique, my son," a voice called out from behind him.

Enrique turned to see his uncle Javier walking in his direction with a bottle of wine in his hand, the ends of the black long-coat he always wore trailing him subtly just below his knees. He went behind the wet-bar to retrieve two glasses from a shelf, then turned and gestured for Enrique to join him.

"I had every confidence that I would see you here someday," his uncle began as Enrique sat down. "This moment makes me very proud, gives me great pleasure."

Enrique was silent for a moment, then finally said, "Why?"

"Because you are *family*," Javier smiled, starting to open the bottle. "And this should be a family business. You know that I was never blessed with a son, never blessed with any children. So you were always like a son to me. When your father died and my dear sister took you away, it was a very dark day for me.

"I have built all of this," he said, spreading his arms out and gesturing to their surroundings. "But I have had no one to share it with. All of that changes today. And our timing could not have been better. Soon, we will be doing much greater things. But now, we must get you ready for your new role."

"A coyote," Enrique said quietly.

"Yes, yes," his uncle nodded. "Your, shall we say, entry-level job. It will give you a good perspective to learn the business from the ground up."

Enrique pondered it for a moment. "What — what makes you think I can do this job?" he finally managed to say.

"You are a smart, cunning young man," his uncle began. "You always have been. You have good instincts, and you are a quick learner. Several of my lieutenants urged me to start you out as a mule, but that is beneath you. Mules are easy to sacrifice, easy to replace. To me, the coyote is the most valued member of any organization. So you will work your way up from there."

"What about —" Enrique began.

"Your mother?" Javier read his thoughts. "She will have the very best care available. I am flying in a specialist from Mexico City to care for her."

"And Juanita? I can't just leave her alone."

"All runs are overnight," Javier explained. "Starting at midnight. You can see your sister off to bed and be there when she wakes in the morning."

Enrique didn't like the idea of leaving his sister alone in their apartment overnight; theirs was not the safest neighborhood. He would have to add an extra deadbolt on their door at the very least. And hope she never looked for him overnight.

But, he reminded himself yet again, his mother was now going to be all right. She was going to be taken care of. And that alone was reason enough for this.

"Thank you, Uncle Javier," Enrique said.

Javier smiled broadly. "Of course, boy. You are family."

At that moment a voice called from behind Enrique. "Jefe. We have them."

"Who?" Javier said, looking past Enrique.

"Alvarez and Lopez," said the henchman who, like many of the others, was dressed in black and powerfully built, with tattoos up and down his muscular arms.

Enrique watched his uncle's face harden.

"Take them to the clubhouse," Javier said.

In that split second, Enrique appeared to vanish in his uncle's mind: Javier walked by him, brushing him to one side as if he weren't even there.

When Javier was out of view, Enrique looked around him, unsure of what to do.

Who were Alvarez and Lopez?

Letting curiosity overrule his better judgment, he decided to follow them.

18

Once team assignment sheets had been passed out to the room, many of the men began getting up from their chairs.

Voorhees was standing at the side of the head table surrounded by several men. Otis decided to let the crowd thin out before he headed in Voorhees's direction.

However, before he had a chance to do that, Kyle Farnston quickly approached him, stepping over rows of chairs to reach where Otis stood.

"Ha-haaaaa," he exclaimed, throwing a wide-armed handshake out to Otis. "Ah knew you'd come to your senses, I *knew* it. We's excited to have ya join, brother. Havin' you on board's gonna make a real *diff'rence*."

Before Otis could respond, a second man approached him from the left. He turned to see that it was Ty Wallace, his usual wild-eyed expression jacked up even further with excitement, the uneven smile spreading and retracting with each twitchy blink of his eyes.

"Otis Brown," he said with a cracking voice. "We's *finally* hit the big time. And I get to be on your team n' less! We's a gonna kick some serious ass together, man."

"My team?" Otis cocked his head, turning from Wallace to Farnston. "What's he talkin' about, Kyle?"

Kyle frowned. "Aint'cha seen the assignment sheets yet, Otis? You's a team lead! Y'got four o' us on your squad. Ty n' m'self, plus a coupla youngsters who could certn'ly use a leader like y'self."

Farnston produced a sheet of paper, and Otis scanned it.

"How the hell'm I — " Otis said, shaking the sheet of paper in his hand. "I ain't even – 'scuse me, I need to talk to Voorhees."

Otis stepped through Farnston and Wallace, heading in Voorhees's direction at the front of the room. Voorhees, who'd looked up to spot Otis coming toward him, shook hands with a few of the TIFF members surrounding him, then gently cut through the crowd to greet Otis.

"Otis Brown," Voorhees exclaimed, placing a giant paw on Otis's shoulder. "It's my honor t' welcome y'all to the ranks of the Texas Independent Freedom Fighters. We's a-gonna do some great thangs t'gether."

"I need t' speak with you in private," Otis demanded.

"Oh?" Voorhees said. "Well, o' course, o' course. Jes' gimme a few minutes t' handle some unfinished bid'ness here, and we'll grab a booth at the bar."

Otis nodded, then headed to the bar.

The bar was considerably more crowded and noisy now that the meeting was over. Otis looked for an open booth. He found one in the far left corner.

An older, rail-thin waitress with wispy, mostly pinned-up hair approached the booth. "What'll ya have," she said in a raspy voice, coughing once afterward.

"Just an ice water, please," Otis said, half-looking beyond the waitress, watching for Voorhees.

"Ya waitin' fer someone who's actually gonna buy somethin'," the waitress frowned at him, "or ya just gonna take up space in one o' my booths drinkin' water all night?"

"Uh," Otis said, clearly taken aback, "make it a beer then. Coors Light's fine."

"We only got Bud an' Miller," she said.

"Bud Light, then," he said.

She walked off. In her place Otis saw Voorhees's large frame lumbering over to the booth.

"S'what's a feller gotta do t' get a drink 'round here," Voorhees said, sitting down with a broad smile on his grizzled face.

"Order somethin' that costs money, for one," Otis said. "And ask nicely."

"Thank I c'n do that," Voorhees replied. "Gotta tell ya, the men's awful excited t' have y'all on board. We's a-gonna set this sumbitch right, you just watch."

"Yeah, that's what I wanted to talk to you about," Otis said.

At that moment, the waitress returned with Otis's beer. "What'll ya have, dear," she said, turning to Voorhees with a yellow-toothed smile.

"Sweetheart, I'll have me a scotch on the rocks, an' a shot o' Southern Comfort," Voorhees returned her familiar banter. "An' why don'tcha brang one back f' y'self while you're at it."

"Y'all know I would if'n I could," she said. "Be right back." And she walked off again.

Voorhees turned back to Otis. "S' what all's on y' mind, Son?" he said, leaning forward, a confident grin still across his face.

"Listen," Otis leaned forward as well, putting his elbows on the table and crossing his arms. "I appreciate the invite an' all to be a part o' your organization. I ain't quite sure how you got the idea that I was already in when I never said I was, but fact o' the matter is, I can't be a part of it. So I am respectfully declinin'."

Voorhees frowned and rubbed his bristly-haired chin. "Well, nah, I'm sorry to hear *that*," he said, clearly disappointed. "Havin' you on our team would certainly make a diff'rence, no question 'bout it."

The waitress came back with Voorhees' drinks. Otis took out his wallet, but Voorhees held out a large paw over Otis's arm. "I got it, son. Let's talk a bit."

The waitress set down the drinks and moved on to another booth.

"I'm the sheriff's son," Otis resumed the conversation. "If I was to join up with a bunch – no disrespect – a bunch o' outlaws, how would that look?"

Voorhees said nothing. He took up the shot of whiskey between his thumb and forefinger, then downed it before gently setting the shot glass back down on the table and sliding it toward the wall. He leaned back in the booth and then stared at Otis for a long moment, his furrowed brow making his deep inset eyes almost disappear. "Son," he finally said. "I c'n def'nitely git where you're comin' from. An' I respect it. So I ain't go' try to talk y' inta somethin' that don't sit well with who y'are."

He took a breath and leaned forward. "But if'n you'd just humor me for a few more minutes, I'd like t' share a story with ya."

"All right," Otis said, leaning back a bit and taking a swig of beer.

Voorhees took a drink of the scotch and set it back down, wiping his mouth. "Y'ever hear th' story o' ol' Pete Cooney?" he said.

"No," Otis replied.

"No, I figgered that wouldn't be a story your daddy'd tell ya," Voorhees said. "Happ'ned 'bout fifty or so years ago, back'n this place was a-boomin' all over. Railroad wuz runnin' through our towns ever' day. People wuz movin' t' the area in droves. Fac'tries couldn't keep up w' th' demand fer ever'thang that wuz bein' made 'round here."

"Musta been good times," Otis commented.

"Well, sure," Voorhees acknowledged. "But it wudn't without problems. Lotsa illegal activity, too. Wudn't no drug trade t' speak of back then, but plenty o' other thangs. Th' biggest o' which was the start o' traffickin' illegal workers up to th' fact'ries. Fact'ries needed a supply o' workers, and the folks from 'cross the border needed the jobs. Problem was, once there were enough workers, th' bid'nesses realized they could git the illegals on the cheap compared to locals. They started replacin' the locals with more illegals. So the fact'ries wuz boomin', but good, hard-workin' local people were findin' themselves outta work. Problem wuz, nobody could do nuthin' 'bout th' illegals. CBP wudn't then what it is now, and there wudn't no laws in place to handle this kinda thang, so there wudn't no way to deal with it. Legally, that is.

"So ol' Pete Cooney decided to take matters inta his own hands," Voorhees continued. "He, along with one o' his closest colleagues, grouped together a bunch o' men t' take care o' thangs. They kep' watch o' the illegals, saw where they came from, where they went back to. Followed 'em. And once they got to where they wuz livin', le's jus' say they convinced 'em to never come back 'cross th' border ag'in."

Otis stared at Voorhees. "What in hell'd they do to 'em?"

"Nobody got killed, if'n that's what yer thinkin'," Voorhees waved a hand in front of his glass of scotch. "But they did what they needed t' do to make sure the illegals knew they meant bid'ness. And best part was, word spread 'bout what wuz happenin' to illegals who wuz stealin' jobs from Texans, and that all but stopped all o' em from comin'. Soon after, people 'round here started goin' back to work."

"Sounds kinda wild west to me," Otis crossed his arms again.

"Call it what'cha will," Voorhees said. "Fact is, it worked."

Voorhees took up the glass of scotch and took a longer drink from it.

"There's another reason why your daddy never tol' you this story, son," Voorhees said as he set the glass down.

"And what's that?" Otis said, leaning forward again.

"Ya see, back then, ol' Pete Cooney wudn't no random outlaw. He wuz *Sheriff*."

Otis was about to take a drink of beer when he stopped. "Sheriff," he repeated.

"You heard me right," Voorhees said.

"Ain't no way could that o' happened," Otis said. "My grandpa was —"

"Deputy for twenny years, tha's right," Voorhees said. "An' he wuz Cooney's deputy fer th' first ten o' em."

"I didn't know who all my grandpa served under," Otis said, "but I do know that he'd a' never let anything like that go on."

"Heh," Voorhees grinned. "Yer grandpa not only let all o' it go on, he wuz Cooney's right hand man through all o' what they done. Some even say it was his idear from the start."

"I don't believe it," Otis said dismissively.

"Jes' ask yer daddy," Voorhees shrugged his massive shoulders. "Why would I lie 'bout that?"

"I don't know," Otis said.

"Point is, son, Cooney an' yer grandpa did what had ta be done," Voorhees countered. "Jes' like right now, we are doin' what's got to be done. Nah, listen. This's go' happen one way or 'nuther, whether you p'ticipate or not. Yer a good man, Otis, a great soldier, a gifted leader. Havin' you out there will prob'ly save some good Texan lives, if'n thangs get hairy. How could ya say no t' savin' some o' yer fellah soldiers' lives?"

Otis said nothing, just took a long swig of beer and then set down the bottle, turning it slowly with his fingertips on the table.

"An' sooner or later," Voorhees continued. "Your daddy's gonna be drawn inta this. Whether the TIFF takes on the cartels er not, it's go' happen. You saw what they's already done. You know it ain't go' stop there. Lucky fer you, you have a say in maybe puttin' a stop to it."

Otis continued to sit there, staring blankly at the bottle, letting everything Voorhees had just shared with him sink in. He wanted to go straight home and ask Silas if there was any truth to the story – and if his grandfather had really been part of it.

But somehow he knew that Voorhees was telling the truth.

And not just about the story ... but also about what would happen from here.

There was no wishing an end to what the drug cartels were doing. They'd already crossed lines with the checkpoint attack and the killing of one of Silas's officers. They were getting bolder with each move – there was no telling what they would do next.

And most important, Voorhees was right about Silas: at some point he would be fully engaged in this battle. Whether he'd be on the offensive or as a target; no one knew.

Regardless of how he felt about outlaws, or of his very own son considering becoming one of them, Silas was in danger — or would be very soon.

Otis could either sit idly by, waiting for something bad to happen, or he could do something about it.

He looked up from the bottle to the man sitting across from him.

Voorhees, who'd been patiently watching him while he was deep in thought, noticed he'd broken his stare. "S' what say you, Son? You wanna help some fella Texans solve this here problem?"

Otis took a long swig from the bottle, then he set it down.

"I'm in," he said finally.

19

Enrique stayed a safe distance behind his uncle, following him to a small, one-story building near the compound's back wall.

There was a small, high window on the wall nearest him. He stood on his tiptoes and looked inside.

His uncle stood over two men who were kneeling at the center of the floor. Both were bound at the wrists and ankles, with duct tape over their mouths. The one nearest Enrique appeared to have a broken nose, his face covered in bruises, cuts, and blood. Two henchmen stood near the left wall.

The room itself was small, maybe fifteen feet across each way, nothing more than an out-building, a shed — certainly not worthy of being called a clubhouse, he thought. The stone tile floor was a reddish color, with an even deeper-red rug at its center, upon which both of the bound men were kneeling. The walls were a typical stucco, torch-lights adorning them. The room had no other decorations except for a large, wooden foot locker in the shape of a treasure chest that rested under the window opposite Enrique.

His uncle turned to the two men. He grabbed the bloody chin of the one nearest Enrique and tore the duct tape off the man's mouth. "Now. Explain what happened to my shipment. If I'm satisfied, I may show you some mercy."

"Jefe, jefe — I — I don't … I didn't —" the first man stammered.

Oropeza put a finger over the man's mouth. "I'm going to guess," he said, tilting his head at his prisoner. "That you didn't mean to take a detour off your route and walk directly into a group of border patrol agents. You didn't mean to have one of our largest shipments fall into the hands of the Americans. And you didn't mean to give up vital information in the interrogation, forcing me to re-route shipments for a week. Hmmm?"

The man could only sit silently in terror, trembling as a drop of blood fell from his chin onto his knees.

"Despite this stupidity," Javier said, standing up once more, "you had been one of my best coyotes. Loyal to a fault. And I do believe you, that this was just a huge mistake. I suppose this should be worth something, no?"

The first man's eyes turned upward to look at Javier, a hopeful expression washing over his sweating, bloodied face.

The Jackal walked over to the large wooden chest at the far wall, behind his prisoners and out of their view. He knelt down and lifted the hinged lid all the way up so that it rested against the wall. His back to Enrique, he removed something from the chest that Enrique couldn't see.

"Yes, it is worth something," he said thoughtfully, turning so Enrique could see the heavy, long-spiked metal club he was holding.

"A quick and merciful death."

And with that, he swung the club like a baseball bat into the back of the man's head. Enrique could hear the dull sticking sound as one of the long spikes pierced both skull and brain, killing the man instantly. The other prisoner screamed as the Jackal pulled and wrenched the club from the dead man's skull, spilling blood and brains on the red carpet below. The man's body fell in a twisted heap into the carpet, wide-eyed and open-mouthed, next the other bound man, who continued to scream through the duct tape in abject terror.

Enrique's mouth dropped open in horror.

The Jackal began to circle the blood-stained carpet, gazing at the lone surviving prisoner intently.

One of the two gunmen by the door handed him a white towel, and he began to wipe down the club.

"Now," the Jackal began, "you don't get to be a man in my position without knowing things. I know the Americans have people working for me, just as I have people working for them.

"The one question was, exactly who was working for *whom*. I suspected a few of you, so I set each of you up with a huge shipment — and a lot of false information. Give you some incentive to give me up. And when you made it through one of our riskiest routes untouched, when the Americans magically showed up at the safe house, I knew."

He tore the duct tape off the terrified man's mouth.

"I want to hear you say it," he snarled. "You are working for the Americans."

"I – I," Lopez began stammering, panting heavily.

"SAY IT!" the Jackal shouted.

"I am ... I am working ... for the Americans," he finally said through tears.

"Yes, yes. Now, this begs the question," Javier said, touching the razor-sharp tip of a spike with his finger. "If we know the price of loyalty, what then is the price of *dis*loyalty?"

"No, no ... please," Lopez begged. "I have a family ... five children ..."

"For whom you have put food on your table at my expense," Javier snapped. "My only regret is that they are not here to see this. But I will have my men take care of them later. You will all be together again soon."

"No, no! Please –" Lopez cried.

Lopez began to scream louder as the Jackal raised the heavy club.

As the club swung downward, Enrique ducked from the window. He was unable to watch another second. His legs buckled underneath him, forcing him down to the earth in a heap. He was panting uncontrollably, soaked in a cold sweat.

The screams carried on for many long seconds, each scream more soul-wrenching than the last, until they finally stopped.

The clubhouse ... it all made sense to him in that instant.

How many times had his uncle killed in that tiny room?

He lurched forward and vomited all over the dirt walkway in front of him.

He got up on wobbly legs and wandered back toward the mess hall building, wishing he could run for his life.

20

Days later, Otis was just starting to work on the Jeep when he heard the sound of boots shuffling outside.

As the door opened, he dropped to the four-wheel cart on the floor and slid underneath the vehicle. His father's familiar grumble lightly echoed in the garage as the door closed.

"Mornin', Pa," he said.

"Otis," Silas replied.

"Gettin' bit of a late start today?" Otis said, reaching for a socket wrench.

"Late night last night," Silas said.

"Yeah?" Otis inquired.

"Yeah," Silas repeated. "Was halfway through a night's sleep when I got a call from Gus. Somebody brought in a group o' smugglers, just outta the blue. Station got an anonymous call 'round midnight, then Gus found 'em and their shipment chained up together in the back parkin' lot. Six of 'em, but not a sign o' who caught 'em."

"Huh," Otis said. "Ain't that somethin'."

"Yeah, ain't it," Silas said, a note of suspicion clear in his voice.

"Sounds like someone is savin' you some trouble, Pa."

"Uh huh," Silas said. Otis could see his father's old brown leather boots walking across the floor toward the fridge. "I hear you had a pretty late night y'self. Mama said she heard you come in 'round one o'clock, while I was gone."

"Yep," Otis said boredly.

"That's a couple nights now you been out late," Silas observed. "Two outta the last three, matter of fact."

"Coupla guys started a poker league," Otis said. "Gotta make some money somehow. Short-term disability check only goes so far."

"Hmmh," Silas said, the boots walking back toward the center of the concrete floor. "What guys?"

"Some ex-military guys," Otis answered. He could tell his father suspected something, and he knew he could never win this game against him. The less he said, the better off he was.

"Any of these guys happen t' be members of the Texas Independent Freedom Fighters militia?" Silas said.

Otis froze for a brief second, then regained his composure.

"Wouldn't know," he said. "They'd know better than to talk 'bout that 'round the Sheriff's son, Pa."

"Would they, now?" Silas said skeptically. "Because I been hearin' they're up to somethin' involving the smugglin', some kinda counter-offensive, which seems more'n coincidental, what with the group o' mules that wound up on my front step last night.

"On top o' that, I heard they been recruitin' current and ex-military. Maybe even some local law enforcement. You wouldn't know anything 'bout that, would you?"

"Law enforcement, as in police?" Otis asked, trying to deflect his father's line of questioning.

"I'm lookin' inta that, too," Silas said, undeterred. "But right now I'm talkin' about you an' *your* guys."

Otis thought through his situation for a second. He didn't want to lie to his father, but the truth of the matter was that he'd already started down that path with the whole poker story. The question was, how far was he prepared to take it?

But, consequences aside, he couldn't lose sight of why he'd joined up with the militia in the first place: to help his father; to protect him. By doing whatever was in his power to make sure the violence didn't spread into his town, into his own home.

So the answer was clear: he would do what needed to be done.

"I don't know anything about it, Pa," he closed his eyes as the lie escaped his lips.

"All right then," Silas finally said. "Your word is good enough fer me, Son."

His father's words stuck into Otis like a heavy blade, forcing him to close his eyes even more tightly.

"Sorry, Pa," Otis added, his statement ringing true in more ways than one.

"Just keep your eyes and ears open's all I ask," Silas said. "These folks may think they're helpin', but it's only gonna escalate things. Put even more people in danger. No one wants that."

Otis said nothing at first, then finally, "Of course, Pa."

The boots walked over to the door, then turned back to the Jeep one last time. "You have a good day, Son," he said as he opened the door.

"Be safe, Pa," Otis said quietly as Silas walked out of the garage, closing the door behind him.

21

Enrique's third day of coyote training was not going well.

It was just before noon, and the intense mid-day sun bore down on him with a blanket of heat. For the past two hours he'd been out in the desert, two of his uncle's top lieutenants drilling him on smuggling routes.

The drills were about moving with speed and quickly locating escape routes in cases of trouble. But the speed with which his uncle's men were forcing him to move, along with the rocky, unpredictable terrain, were causing him to fail miserably.

"Get up," Nava, his uncle's second lieutenant, ordered him. "We go again."

"He's proven to be not worth our time," Alejandro, his uncle's top lieutenant, said gruffly. "But we have to train him until el jefe sees him as we do."

He understood that their intention was not to help him along, but rather to convince his uncle that the man's weak nephew was not cut out for being a coyote.

At that moment, an ATV roared up along the high path above them. Enrique could see it was Hernandez.

"Enrique," he called out, waving Enrique forward. "Jefe wants you to meet him. Main building, front lobby. Hop on; let's go."

Moments later, Enrique found himself following his uncle through a long hallway and into an ornate dining room.

The room was long and narrow, with a twenty-or-so-foot long oak table that ran the length of the room. Candles were placed evenly every few feet atop a white runner that was laid along its center. Place settings of white china and pure silver rested upon white woven placemats, while eight wooden chairs were pushed in neatly along each side. An enormous chandelier hung above the center of the table from the high ceiling, and a finely polished marble floor reflected Enrique's gaze from underneath his dusty shoes. Large, oil-painted portraits of men Enrique recognized as historic Mexican pioneers and leaders hung high along each of the walls.

"Have a seat, my boy," Javier said as he took a seat himself at the head of the table. "Our meal will be out momentarily." He pulled out the chair next to him with one of his long, powerful arms.

Enrique took a seat at his uncle's side.

"Enrique, my son," Javier began, "what do you think we're doing here?"

Enrique was puzzled by the question. "What do you mean, sir?"

"What I do," Javier said. "My business; my life's work, which you are now a part of. What do you think it is?"

"I don't," Enrique began, unsure. "I mean … I …"

"It is fulfilling a *need*," his uncle explained.

"A need," Enrique repeated curiously.

"Not the pathetic, gluttonous needs of the Americans," Javier waved off the mere thought. "They are merely the means to our ends. I'm talking about the needs of our region, of our people. I am fulfilling *that* need. Do you understand?"

"I don't know," Enrique admitted.

"Our region needs food, money, jobs," Javier went on. "It needs *sustenance*, the engine of its own economy to keep moving. I am providing all of this through what we are doing."

Enrique tried to avoid looking skeptical. His uncle had many men under his employ, but it was nothing in the face of all the poverty that had spread across the region. More important, he wondered if his uncle had also considered all the death his drug empire had wrought upon so many lives, or if he had chosen to ignore that fact altogether.

"Every day, hundreds of our people leave our homeland for the false promise of what awaits them over the border," Javier gestured. "More opportunity, a better life, is what they are told. But they are unwanted there, and the moment they are caught, they are sent back. It even happened to you."

Enrique said nothing. He wondered where his uncle was going with this.

"But if we can build a better life for our people *here*," he leaned forward, "think about the effects it would have. The region, the country, would flourish."

"But, how would you do that?" Enrique asked.

"By simplifying," Javier answered plainly.

"Simplifying what?"

"How we do business," Javier explained. "Making it easier to increase production, distribution. Eliminating conflicts with other cartels. There would be less death and destruction, and more people working, earning a living, and buying local products. It would have a cascading effect on *everyone*."

Enrique remembered that his uncle had been an extremely successful businessman and economist, so he had no doubt that there was a fair amount of reasoning behind what the man was saying. He just didn't understand how it would all be done.

"But ... how would you do all this without catching the government's attention?"

"Hmmh," his uncle chuckled, leaning forward and resting his elbows on the table. "My boy, the government is actually *part* of my plan. People in my line of business, myself especially, have an ... understanding with them. Even though our business technically operates outside of Mexican law, there are many other factors at play. Unwritten rules that are followed. If one plays the game and stays within the rules, he will be allowed to continue on with his business.

"When you *do* see someone in our line of work taken down by the authorities, it is because he was *not* playing within the rules. Because, when it comes down to it, it is not about what is against the law ... it is about *control.*"

"Control?" Enrique repeated.

"Who controls the economy, the country, everything," Javier explained. "The government keeps us all under their thumb to maintain the appearance, the *illusion*, of control in the eyes of the people."

He put a hand on Enrique's shoulder. "My plan is to take that illusion and turn it more to *our* advantage."

"What will you do?"

"The plan itself is not important," his uncle leaned back in his chair. "It's what follows that will be the key."

Enrique waited for his uncle to elaborate, but Javier merely let his last statement hang in the air for many long seconds.

"One of the keys to life," Javier finally said, changing the subject, "is knowing what motivates people. Some men are motivated by money. Others by ambition. Still others by fear, and so forth.

"You, my boy," he gestured to Enrique with open hands, "are motivated by family. You want your dear mother, my dear sister, to be well. You want your young sister to be protected from our streets, and to want for nothing. Am I correct?"

"Of course," Enrique nodded.

"Then we are no different in what motivates us," Javier smiled. "You should know that family is of utmost importance to me.

"What *I* want," Javier explained, standing up and pacing over to the first portrait on the wall, "is for my work to live on beyond my days." He stood for a moment in silence, gazing at the portrait before him.

"I have thousands of people in my employ," he went on, "on both sides of the border. There are many who would want to step into my shoes. But this is a family business. So it is my wish that it will all someday become yours."

Enrique was stunned. He was not sure what shocked him more: that his uncle would someday bequeath his entire empire upon him ... or the very idea that Enrique could someday become a drug lord himself.

He realized that his mouth was hanging open, so he quickly closed it, trying his best to mask the dumbfounded expression on his face.

"So I need to know that you are committed, my boy," Javier sat back down and leaned forward, clearly ignoring Enrique's reaction, "now and from here forward, to this new life you have chosen."

Enrique was backed into a corner, and he knew it. He knew there was only one acceptable answer in his uncle's eyes.

But could he do it? He hadn't thought yet of the future; only of the present: bringing his mother back to health; being able to pay his bills. Nothing beyond that.

Now that he knew what his uncle's expectations were, the full gravity of it began to settle on him like an immovable weight.

"I will," he finally managed to say. There was no other answer.

"Good," Javier said, a smile spreading across his lips. "Now you can focus on your first run. Tomorrow night. My second-in-command, Alejandro, will join you. Follow his lead; you will learn from the best."

"All — all right," Enrique said, not quite sharing his uncle's confidence.

At that moment, two young women dressed in white cooking attire entered the room, ushering in a cart with several steaming-hot dishes on top.

"Ah, lunch is served," Javier observed.

The two women placed the dishes on the table and removed the steel covers, bowed to Javier, and quickly left the room.

Enrique hungrily surveyed the spread laid out before him. Five large serving dishes steamed on the table, piled high with Mexican delights. Nearest to him were the Spanish rice and refried beans, behind which were dishes stacked with enchiladas, tamales, and grilled chiles and peppers. He had never seen so much food on one table.

"Come now, my boy, eat up," Javier said, taking up a pair of tongs and digging at the mound of enchiladas. "There is plenty for both of us."

Enrique gorged himself as if he hadn't eaten in days. He felt guilty enjoying this delicious meal while Juanita was forced to eat the meager scraps he'd prepared for her lunch at school. But his first payday would be coming, and with that he could fill their pantry and more.

Despite the promise of a better life that had been put before him, Enrique wondered what his uncle's plans were, and who would be put in harm's way as a result.

22

The fading light of sunset had receded from the sky as Rage and the other squad members filed in for their final briefing.

In the briefing room stood three giant screens: the face on the first screen, Rage immediately recognized as Dunlap; the second was none other than Edward Armstrong, the Deputy Defense Secretary himself. The third screen showed a zoomed satellite image of the Juarez region. In front of the screens stood the two NSA agents who had been briefing them every day thus far, Michael Cade and Clarence Miller.

"Let's get started," Miller began. "Now I don't need to introduce either Deputy Defense Secretary Armstrong or General Dunlap to any of you. So let's get down to the business at hand. General Dunlap, Sir?"

"Agent Miller," Dunlap acknowledged him before turning his attention to Rage and the SEALs. "Men, I don't need to reiterate the importance of this mission to you: it is a message to the world that the United States will not stand for terrorism within our borders. Our target is an extremely dangerous man and cannot be underestimated. Deputy Secretary?"

"Thank you, General," Armstrong said, then addressed the men. "As you know, our target is not only dangerous, he is also exceptionally intelligent, cunning, and resourceful. The billions he has made in the illegal drug trade give him a huge advantage: an army of loyal foot soldiers, a vast compound, and you can count on an impressive cache of weaponry to defend that compound.

Not to mention this is on his home turf, which has been strategically built upon a very treacherous landscape.

"But you are our very best, and we've prepared you for success," Armstrong continued. "You capture the target, dead or alive, and bring him back to face justice."

"And most important, we want you all to come back home alive," Dunlap added. "As the Deputy Secretary said, you are America's bravest and best. Godspeed, men."

Both the first and second screens went dark.

"As you already know," Miller said, arising from his seat by the podium, "our deployment is set for 2300 tomorrow night from Biggs Airfield in El Paso, which is where you will do your final prep. We will be departing from here at 2300 tonight."

"Transport will be two MH-60 Black Hawk helos," Cade began. "Collins, Johnston and Mirer will be in the first helo; Capt. Stevenson, the Specialist, and our two CIA agents in the second."

"As has been the plan thus far," Miller started again, "L.Z. will be one hundred meters outside the compound's northeast corner, near the main structure. Helos will return to higher altitudes and will await your all-clear signal. You will blow the wall, entering the compound from the northeast. Kill or capture the target, along with the top lieutenants we've identified for you, and fend off any inbound threats for the eight-minute window that our CIA Agents need to do their work. Once the all-clear has been given, the helos will retrieve you at the same L.Z. as the drop. Understood?"

"Yes, Sir," the SEALs replied.

"All right, then," Cade said. "Final round of drills begins at 1900. See you back here for departure at 2300."

23

Back in the Pentagon, General Jack Dunlap remained in his seat, deep in thought.

He heard the War Room's security lock disengage, followed by footsteps tapping loudly on the polished tile floor. He didn't turn around to acknowledge them; he knew who they belonged to.

"Took you so long, Edward?" he said. "Stop for coffee?"

"Another phone call," Armstrong answered, taking a seat to Dunlap's left.

"From?"

"Collins, who else," he said flatly. "But this time he had the President piped in, who just spoke with Mexican President Vincennes an hour ago."

"And?"

"Everything's a go," Armstrong said. "Vincennes has informed his inner circle as well. They foresee no issues."

"How many in the inner circle, again?"

"Five," Armstrong answered. "Vincennes himself, Vice President Alverno, his Defense Minister, Secretary of State, and Chief of Staff."

"Too many," Dunlap murmured.

"I wouldn't be concerned, Jack," Armstrong observed. "It's considerably smaller than our inner circle."

"But we're not the ones allowing another country to execute a military insertion within our borders," Dunlap argued.

"No, we're not," Armstrong said. "But you of all people understand why we have to do it this way. This isn't Pakistan or some other country across the globe. This is our neighbor, one of our closest allies."

"On a ruling-party level, yes," Dunlap acknowledged. "I don't disagree with that. But it still puts the mission at risk. Especially on a shortened deployment timeline. Our men could've used the normal amount of preparation, not to mention intel, which we're still gathering by the second."

"Jack, what are you most concerned with here?" Armstrong questioned.

"A lot of things, Edward," Dunlap scowled at his longtime colleague. "I'm concerned about sending our men into a dangerous situation not fully prepared. I'm concerned about any surprises the enemy has in store for us, that we've failed to identify for our men. And most of all, I'm concerned about the integrity of everyone who's been given knowledge of this supposedly top-secret mission."

"So," Armstrong surmised, "you're concerned that someone in Vincennes's inner circle will give up the details of the mission to the target."

"Yes," Dunlap said more loudly than he'd intended, capturing the attention of the agents and intel officers in the War Room.

Armstrong remained silent for a moment. "You know this as well as anyone, Jack," he finally said. "If the target has anyone even close to Vincennes's inner circle, this is only the beginning of our problems."

24

As Friday afternoon rolled slowly into evening, Otis began to clean up the garage and prepare for the night ahead.

Friday suppers at the Brown household were normally whatever Otis wanted; it had always been his night to decide what was on the menu ever since he was twelve years old and wise enough not to choose macaroni and cheese every time. His mother was a good cook, the best Otis knew, so Silas had once told him it would be a crime to waste her talents in the kitchen on something you could pour out of a box.

But tonight's supper would not be at the Brown household; instead, it would be at Wendy's Diner right in town, eight o'clock sharp. He'd told his mama that he was finally going over to go see Alyson, the girl who worked behind the counter there. Annie had always thought there was chemistry there, and she had been telling Otis to go to talk to her ever since he'd gotten back from active duty months ago.

In part, he was speaking the truth: Alyson would be there, but also waiting for him would be Kyle Farnston and Ty Wallace, along with Bobby Swank and Jeb Ferrell: the four members of Otis's border-watch team.

While Otis knew both Farnston and Wallace well enough, Swank and Ferrell were just two green eighteen-year-old kids whose fathers had strong-armed them into joining the TIFF.

Otis shook his head at that thought. He now knew that part of his job would be to make sure those two young men stayed alive if any violence broke out.

Their Friday night assignment would be to cover the infamous smuggling route known as *Garganta del Diablo*, or Devil's Chasm, the most dangerous route across the entire Texas-Mexican border. It was extremely difficult to navigate, and it was filled with rattlesnakes, scorpions, and poisonous fauna, making it a last resort for anyone looking to cross the border into the U.S. The remains of countless illegals and smugglers had been found there over the years, only adding to its legend.

But given the TIFF's success in capturing smugglers along the main routes over the past three nights, Otis knew it wouldn't be long before the cartels were forced to use less-traveled ones like *Garganta del Diablo*.

Otis's team had not been involved in any of the TIFF's exchanges with smugglers or illegals as of yet, but he knew it was only a matter of time.

Their shift would begin at ten o'clock and run until two in the morning, at which time they would be relieved by another squad.

After finishing up in the garage, Otis went into the house to shower. As he walked through the kitchen, he saw his mother beginning to prepare supper.

"Ma," he said, "Pa home yet?"

"Not yet," she replied. "You know he's been gettin' home a bit late all week. Lots of extra activity down at the station and all."

"All right," Otis said, somewhat relieved. His mother was readily willing to believe he was actually going down to the diner to see Alyson, but he knew his father would likely have other suspicions. If he was able to get out of there before Silas got home, he would be all the better for it.

"Otis," Annie called to him as he was about to head down the hallway.

"Yeah, Ma?" Otis answered, stepping back to the kitchen so she could see him.

"Good luck tonight," she said, a hopeful smile coming to her face.

"Uh, thanks Ma," Otis said, suddenly feeling a pang of guilt he hoped didn't reflect in his voice. "You know, I'm just goin' over to see her, right? Get a bite to eat, nuthin' more?"

"Well, ya gotta start somewhere," Annie said, taking a pan from the cupboard and placing it on the stove. Otis could still see a tiny smile in her eyes.

"All right," was all Otis could say, before turning and lumbering down the hallway.

The hot shower washed away the day's dirt and grime but not a morsel of the guilt he'd caked onto himself over the past few days. First he'd lied to his pa about what he was doing, now he was lying to his mama about what he *wasn't* doing. It didn't matter that he was technically 'seeing' Alyson at the diner; his intentions were something other than what he'd told his mama, and that was lie enough.

He managed to shower and leave the house before Silas got home. He was on his way to the diner when his phone rang.

"H'lo?" he picked up.

"Sergeant Brown," the gruff voice returned. "Voorhees here."

"Hey," Otis greeted him back, a bit surprised. He knew Voorhees was an especially busy man during the hours leading up to shifts. He wondered why the man would be calling him directly.

"Got a nugget for yeh," Voorhees said. "Me n' mah other leaders are reachin' out to each squad tonight. Gotta spread th' word."

"An' what word is that?" Otis inquired.

"Got word from one o' our sources that th' cartels might start bringin' firearms with *all* o' their mule teams, not just some," Voorhees explained. "If not t'night, prob'ly soon."

"Where'd you hear this?" Otis asked.

"One o' your cohorts at CBP that I's friendly with," Voorhees said. "Said one o' their folks ov'heard one o' the detainees talkin' 'bout it while in custody last night."

"Hmmm," was all Otis could say, thinking grimly about what had happened to Officer Reynolds the other night. It sounded like that would no longer be a random occurrence. "S'pose it was only a matter o' time before things started escalatin'."

"Which is why we's all tellin' you 'bout it now," he said. "So you's prepared. Nah tell your men 'bout it, and keep us updated if'n y'see anything, a'right?"

"'Course," Otis answered.

Both men hung up.

Otis figured that some kind of change would happen at some point; he figured a drug lord could only lose so many shipments before taking some kind of action. But this was bold, brazen: the opponent was basically challenging the TIFF, and ultimately the U.S. authorities, to a giant game of chicken.

If this was true, whoever was running things on the other side of the border was either stupid, or a lot more cunning – and either way, more aggressive – than anyone would have expected.

At five minutes before eight, he rolled into town and parked right in front of Wendy's Diner. As he got out of the truck, he could see Alyson in the front window, wiping down the counter. He noticed when she caught a glimpse of him and subtly checked herself in the small mirror just below the clock behind the counter. He then happened to notice Ty Wallace leaning on the counter directly across from her. It was clear from his body language that he was trying to strike up conversation. And it was clear from hers that she was trying to avoid it.

Otis pushed open the glass front door, the familiar ring of the door chime sounding as he did so. "Ty," he acknowledged Wallace as he walked in. "Evenin', Alyson," he added with a tip of his Rangers cap.

"Hello, Otis," she said, smiling back at him. "Nice of you to bring your little meetin' here to the diner tonight." Otis thought he saw her expression shift subtly from pleasure to exasperation as her eyes moved briefly to Ty, but she smiled through it.

"Well, nah, like I say, we's here on official bid'ness, darlin'," Ty leaned in even further across the counter, a note of self-importance in his tone. "We gots three more comin' to talk about —"

"Heh, don't be ridic'lous, Ty," Otis stepped in next to Ty, waving him off calmly. "We're just a coupla ol' friends gettin' t'gether over supper, talkin' bout glory days. An' since you serve up such a mean patty melt —"

"Oh, I make 'em, too," Alyson said wryly. "Girl's gotta be able t'do multiple things in this town."

Unsure of what else to say, Otis let a grin spread across his face. "Well, like Ty said, we got a coupla more comin'. But in the meantime, d' you make the chocolate malts, too?"

"You betcha," Alyson said, setting down the wiping cloth and placing her palms on the clean countertop. "You want all the fixin's?"

"Fixin's?" Otis said, puzzled.

"Y'know," she said, a flirty smile coming to her face. "Whip cream and cherry on top?"

"Uh, sure," Otis said, taken aback by her playful demeanor. He felt his cheeks flush.

"Comin' right up," she said, turning back toward the cooler.

"Make 'at two of 'em," Ty cat-called at her. "Since y'all ain't got no whiskey."

"Nice touch, Ty," Otis said blandly.

"Thought so, too, eh?" Ty returned, clearly not catching Otis's sarcasm.

At that moment, Kyle came in, followed almost immediately by Swank and Ferrell. Swank had been with their squad for their previous two watches, but Ferrell had been mysteriously ill on both occasions. This was his first outing with the squad, and his discomfort was clear by his appearance: the boy was as white as a sheet, and he was sweating profusely. Either he was truly sick and his old man had finally forced him out of the house this evening, or he was nervous to the point of becoming a potential risk to the squad. Either way, it meant nothing but trouble as far as Otis was concerned.

"A'ight, we's all here," Kyle clapped his hands together. "Now what?"

"Let's grab the big booth in the back corner," Otis's eyes swept across the four men before him. "We got plenty to talk about tonight."

Moments later, Alyson brought out menus. "Malts comin' right up," she said.

"S'what's so special 'bout tonight?" Kyle asked as he opened his menu.

"First of all, voices down, alla you," Otis said in a low voice. "Only other time we met wasn't in a public place like this. T'night we don't have that luxury, what with Kyle's girlfriend bein' home an' all. Second, place's pretty quiet t'night, which means the few that're in here can hear everythin' bein' said. Understood?"

The four men nodded.

"Now," Otis continued, "here's what's happenin' tonight. We're gonna be coverin' what's bein' called the path of last resort. The Mexicans call it Devil's Chasm. Apparently it's the most dangerous smugglin' route of 'em all."

Each of the men seemed to understand what that meant, and each showed a different reaction. Everyone but Ferrell looked disappointed.

"But don't think for a second that we won't see action 'cause of this," Otis raised a finger. "We been squeezin' 'em on nearly every other route all this week. It's only a matter o' time before they start turnin' to the ones they think we won't be at."

"Well, hell, Otis," Kyle finally spoke up. "Even if'n they do send runners through there, no guarantee all o'em make it out alive."

"Dayum straight," Wallace echoed. "Looks like 'nuther night, no action for us. Shee-it."

"One other thing," Otis waved off their protests. "Startin' t'night, I want'chall to be extra vigilant. Voorhees called me not twenty minutes ago, sayin' the cartels are startin' to bring a little extra firepower with 'em. Now I don't know if their intention'll be to intimidate or actually act, but I want'chall t' be ready either way. Understand?"

Wallace leaned forward. "And what if'n they act?"

"Then we'll act in kind," Otis said in a slow, deliberate tone.

At that moment, Alyson showed back up with the malts and set them in front of Otis and Wallace. "What c'n I get y'all?" she asked sweetly.

Each of the men ordered a meal and drink.

Wallace watched Alyson walk back to the counter, then made a grunt of approval before turning back to Otis. "An' who fires first?"

"*We* don't," Otis said warningly. "Only if provoked, or if we got no other choice."

'Well, hell, Otis," Wallace said. "When the hell we gonna know, when one of us got a bullet in our chest?"

"I'll give the signal," Otis said, staring Wallace down. "You don't like it, your attendance ain't mandatory."

"Hell, I knew *that*," Wallace challenged. "Not like ol' Ferrell here, right?"

Ferrell shrunk back in his seat as Wallace turned and sneered at him.

"Leave it, Ty," Kyle chimed in.

"Enough o' this," Otis said, anger rising in his low voice. "Let's finish with the business at hand, and then we can part company 'til the meetin' point at ten."

Several moments later, after Otis had wrapped the debrief while the men finished their supper, he noticed that something had gotten Kyle's attention by the front door. He turned to look for himself.

A man wearing a black hooded sweatshirt had come in and was leaning forward on the counter by the cash register. He was talking to Alyson, who stood completely still, a frightened look on her face. He was holding something in his right hand, obscured from view by the register. When the man moved, Otis could see the left sleeve of his sweatshirt dangle weightlessly. The man was missing his left arm.

"Is that ... Sam Brockman?" Kyle said.

"I believe it is," Otis said, recognizing the man's physique. A local man, Brockman had lost his arm while on a tour in Afghanistan six months ago. Shortly after being diagnosed with PTSD, both his parents had died in a terrible car crash, and his disability checks couldn't keep up with the medical bills and other expenses. Since falling on hard times, the man had become a recluse: no one had seen him around town in weeks, until now.

Taking a breath, Otis got up from his seat.

"Otis, hell you doin'?" Kyle protested.

Otis didn't respond as he began walking toward the front of the diner. Alyson had removed the drawer from the register and had begun pulling out the cash and placing it in the brown paper bag the hooded man had brought in with him. As she glanced in Otis's direction, her eyes grew even wider and she began shaking her head slightly, warning Otis to stay back.

But Otis kept approaching; he already knew the man had a gun in his hand.

"You don't wanna do that, Sam," he called out to the man.

The hooded man jolted as his name was called aloud, a clear confirmation to Otis that he was in fact Sam Brockman.

Brockman turned toward Otis, pointing the gun at him.

"I know you don't wanna do that, neither," Otis said calmly, placing his hands slightly in the air. "Just gimme the gun, and let's talk about this."

"I don't wanna talk, Otis, I wanna eat!" Brockman screamed, pulling down the hood with the gun still in his lone hand. "I jes wanna eat!"

"I know, Sam, I know," Otis said in a sober voice. "Let me help ya. Hand over the gun, and we can figure things out."

"No, no," Brockman shook his head vigorously. "Y'all had yer chance. I tried to get me a job, no takers fer a one-armed man. Alyson here tried settin' me up with a girl, but no one wants to date a one-armed man."

"And yer thankin' her by pointin' a gun at her?" Otis said.

Brockman jerked his head back to Alyson. "No hard feelin's, nuthin' personal," he said apologetically to her. "I ain't got no money. I jes gotta eat."

"Sam, you're part o' this community," Otis said, still keeping his distance to keep Brockman calm. "That means we're here for ya — us — your neighbors. Maybe we can't help ya in every way, but we can sure try. Why don't you let Alyson here make ya a cup o' coffee an' somethin' to eat, and we can have a seat and talk about it."

Brockman's eyes darted to Otis, then back to Alyson. The crazed, scared look in his eyes had subsided a little. "You don't unnerstand, Otis," he said, his voice trembling. "I ain't got no money, no food in the cupboard ... I ain't got no family, no friends, no life. What'm I doin'? What'm I s'posed to do?"

"We can talk about it," Otis said. "Just gimme the gun. Let's take it down a notch, all right? You're a good man, we all know that. Let's just sit down and talk."

Brockman hesitated, just standing there, the gun still raised but no longer pointed at anything.

"Come on, Sam," Otis said.

Without a word, Brockman stepped forward, gently laying the gun down on the counter. "What've I done," he mumbled, burying his face in his arm.

"You've done nuthin' tonight," Otis said, putting an arm around him, walking him over to the booth behind where they stood, and letting him sit down. "No harm, no foul. Ain't that right, Alyson."

Alyson hesitated for a moment, the frightened look faded, but still present in her eyes. "Yes," she nodded, catching Otis's meaningful glance toward her. "Yes, right, Otis."

"Hell you mean, done nuthin', Otis?" Wallace stood from the booth and started walking toward them. "He done pulled a gun on Alyson here!"

Ignoring Wallace and keeping his eyes on Brockman, Otis half-turned back toward Farnsworth. "Kyle, get him the hell outta here, *now*," he growled.

Without hesitation, Kyle got up, motioning for Swank to join him, and they grabbed the protesting Wallace by the arms and forced him out the front door without a word.

"We'll eat somethin' here and talk things out," Otis put a hand on Sam's shoulder. "Then I'll drive ya home, and we can talk more on the way."

"All right, Otis," Sam said, dejection still heavy in his voice.

"Just gotta handle a couple things first, all right?"

"Sure," Sam replied. "O' course."

Otis picked up Sam's gun from off the counter and walked over toward Ferrell, who was now alone in the booth, his eyes wide with a combination of wonder and fear. He handed the gun to Ferrell. "Figured you could use one o' these, right?"

"Uh," was all Ferrell could say.

"Guessin' you don't own one, 's'what I mean," Otis added.

"Uh," Ferrell said again, before finally admitting, "no. Guess ah don't."

"You're gonna need some ammo for it, is all," Otis told him. "Don't worry, though, I got some o' that caliber."

"Huh?" Ferrell managed. "What d' you —"

"It ain't loaded," Otis whispered with a sly wink.

"Oh," Ferrell said. "How'd you —"

"I just knew," Otis said. "Now why don't you go out there and tell the men I'll meet y'all at the rendezvous point at quarter to ten, and we'll head to our position from there. I'll bring some ammo for ya. All right?"

"Yessir," Ferrell said and got up to head for the door.

Otis headed back to the booth where Brockman sat. Alyson brought two cups of coffee. "On the house," she said. "So's whatever you want, Sam."

"Thank you," Sam said. "Just somethin' with meat 's'all, please. I ain't picky."

"I got just the thing," Alyson said. "Comin' right up."

Otis glanced up at Alyson as she walked back to the kitchen. He smiled then turned his attention back to Sam.

After devouring two of Alyson's famous patty melts, Sam looked at Otis gratefully. It was clear that he was having trouble finding words.

"Why don't you head on out to my truck parked outside," Otis said to him. "I jes gotta settle up with Alyson."

"Thought she said it was on the —"

"Just go," Otis implored. "Be right behind ya."

As Sam walked out the front door, Otis got up and lumbered to the register, pulling out his wallet. Alyson met him on the other side of the counter, a curious look in her eyes.

"Get all them hundreds back in the drawer?" he said.

"Kept two for m'self," she joked back, then saw his wallet in his hand. "Told you this was on the house, Otis."

"Can't let'cha do that, young lady," Otis said. "Plus, still gotta pay for the men's supper, unless someone else stepped up an' did it."

"That I'll give ya," she nodded. "An' no – no one did."

"Figgered," he said. "I'll get 'em later."

"Well, you were busy, too, at the end," she said, an awkward smile coming to her face. "Thank you."

"Y' don't need t' thank me," Otis shook his head.

"Yes, I do," she argued, then glanced back toward the booth where Otis and the other TIFF members had sat. "I heard what you said to the boy in the booth ... how'd you know the gun wasn't loaded?"

"It's not Sam's way," he said. "I know him. He'd sooner shoot himself than hurt anyone else. Even desperate as he was. Plus, it was too light to be loaded. Could feel the weight."

"I hope he can get help," she said.

"I got some ideas," Otis confided. "But right now I gotta go. I'll see ya around."

"Bye, Otis," she said.

He turned for the door and was just about to push it open when he stopped.

"Alyson," he said, half-turning back toward her.

"Yeah, Otis," she replied.

"I, uh," he began awkwardly. "I know this isn't really the time to ask somethin' like this, but ..."

She waited for a second, then: "Ask me what, Otis?"

"Well, uh," he struggled. "Would you uh, like to go have dinner, or somethin', sometime?"

"I'd like that, Otis," she said, a smile coming to her face.

"Uh, someplace other than here, I mean," he said, then stopped himself. "I mean ... that came out wrong ..."

"I know what you meant, Otis," she replied with almost a giggle. "And like I said, my answer is yes."

"Well, a'right then," he said, not sure what else to say. "I'll uh, I'll call ya."

Otis walked out of the diner, trying to conceal the smile that had inexplicably come across his face. The familiar sound of the door chimes jingled as the door shut softly behind him.

25

At the compound's far north end, Enrique waited for Alejandro.
It was just past ten o'clock P.M. Enrique had gone home for a few hours that afternoon to help Juanita with her homework. Then he left at around eight o'clock, telling her he had to go to work, once again dodging her suspicious questions as he ran out the door.

Now as he waited, one of his uncle's ATVs sped toward him and came to a halt, almost running him over.

"Get in, boy," Alejandro's voice called out behind the blinding lights in Enrique's face. "Almost time to go."

Enrique obeyed, hopping into the cart's passenger-side seat. As he did so, he noticed two enormous armored trucks headed toward them. Alejandro kept the ATV where it was, allowing the two trucks to pass before them. He saw Alejandro's gaze follow the trucks as they went by. Once they had passed, he began moving forward again.

"Where are we going?" Enrique asked.

"The Garage," he answered. "Where all the product is kept."

Seconds later, Alejandro had parked the ATV near the Humvee in which Enrique had first been taken to the compound days before. Enrique could see Hernandez and the other man who'd accompanied him on that first trip, loading items into the back of the vehicle.

As he got closer, he saw what they were loading: guns. Big ones.

"That's a lot of guns," Enrique commented.

"You afraid of the gun, eh, boy," Alejandro said judgingly. "Don't be. The gun is our lifeblood. In time you will learn this. If you live that long."

"Why so many?"

"El jefe has lost some shipments recently," Alejandro explained. "Vigilante activity along the border. This is our answer to it."

"Will I – have to carry one?"

"Of course you will," Alejandro answered. "Starting tonight, all groups will be joined by an enforcer. Both the enforcer and the coyote will carry."

Moments later, the SUV sped through the front gate and into the open night beyond. They turned off the main road onto a bumpy trail. A mile or so out, they came upon a large hill surrounded by brush, cacti, and trees. They drew closer, revealing a narrow clearing ahead. As they entered the thicket, long branches stretched out above them, shielding the clearing from any view from above.

They moved slowly through the clearing, tree branches lightly scraping the vehicle's roof and sides. Ahead, Enrique could see that the path ended at a rock wall.

The driver produced a walkie-talkie and spoke into it: "Garage. Vehicle Six approaching."

Suddenly, the rock wall ahead of them began to move; a large section about the size of a garage door separated from the rest, moving several feet to one side, and revealed a massive opening to the inside.

"What in the world ...?" was all Enrique could say.

As they stepped out of the truck, Enrique got his first glimpse inside the huge room: it appeared to be some kind of warehouse, with rows of metal shelves stacked high with packages. The packages were wrapped tightly in duct tape and were of all shapes and sizes. In the foreground were men dressed in military-style fatigues, all holding rifles. As Enrique walked through the opening, he could see more men and even some women in the back, standing at long tables, wrapping items tightly in cellophane and duct tape.

How had his uncle built a warehouse into the side of a foothill? Even after all he had seen thus far, Enrique wondered to what extent all of his uncle's resources stretched.

Alejandro began speaking in a low voice with two of the armed men. Enrique walked past them toward the rows of shelves. Everything was sorted by product: marijuana, cocaine, heroin, methamphetamine, even some things Enrique didn't recognize. There were at least a hundred packages in all, maybe two hundred.

"Boy," Alejandro called to him. "Make yourself useful; help them load up."

Enrique turned to see two pickup trucks back their way in. Three men approached with wheelbarrows, while others began removing packages from the rows of shelves, tossing them to the men with the wheelbarrows.

"How much are we taking?" Enrique asked.

"All of it," Alejandro answered. "The place will be full again tomorrow night. Now get moving. We are wasting time."

Several moments later, Enrique and the others had loaded both pickups.

"All right, let's go," Alejandro told the driver as he began walking toward the SUV. "Boy, follow me. And suck it in, we've got a few more coming with us."

As Enrique opened the back door, he understood Alejandro's meaning: already in the back seat were two men, both with guns resting at their feet, nozzles pointed toward the ceiling. The one nearest to him, a man about his age with tattoos on his forehead and up and down both his arms, gave him a menacing look.

Enrique squeezed in, closing the door behind him and reluctantly pressing himself next to the tattooed man, who pushed back against him with his considerably larger shoulders, forcing the breath from Enrique's lungs.

"Where is tonight's drop point?" the gunman furthest from Enrique asked.

"Vasquez stash house for us," the driver replied. "Magana stash house for the others. Jefe wants us to split the drop points due to all the gringos' activity lately."

Ten minutes later, they arrived at their destination: a fenced in, rundown, one-story house. Enrique could see three large dogs roaming the front yard as they turned into the driveway, each of the dogs halting in its tracks to watch the SUV go by, though not one dog barked.

"They're trained not to bark, but to simply attack if they sense a threat," Alejandro said. "Boy here is the only one who hasn't been here before, so we'll see how they take to him."

"Heh," the driver laughed. "Boy may not be a threat, but they can smell fear, too. I'd worry about that if I were him."

"Si," Alejandro snickered. "So no soiling your trousers, or they might come right up and bite you where they smell it."

The SUV cabin roared with laughter.

Seconds later, the SUV came to a halt before a two-car garage. Enrique could see one of the trucks they had just loaded parked to the side, and next to it sat another SUV. Men began unloading the truck's payload into wheelbarrows. Others opened the rear lift-gate of the second SUV and had started to unload its contents as well: more guns.

The doors opened and the men got out, the tattoo-faced man next to Enrique shoving him out the door as it opened. "Around the side," Alejandro motioned to the group, and all the men followed him to a wide opening on the side of the garage.

As he stepped inside, Enrique could see it was much more than just a garage: the enormous room stretched to take up what must have been half of the house as well, the walls having been knocked down to create a larger space.

He immediately understood why: there must have been fifty, maybe sixty men inside of the cavernous space, most of them with what looked like large burlap rucksacks in their hands, lined up in groups of four and five.

Then the main garage door opened behind them. Wheelbarrows rolled in, stacked high with packages, followed by four men, each carrying armloads of rifles. The wheelbarrows stopped at the center of the garage and were quickly unloaded in stacks before each group of men. Alejandro walked to each line, several sheets of paper in his hands. The man at the front of each line was given a sheet. The coyote. Once each coyote had a sheet in hand, he began handing the packages before him back to the men who stood behind them. The mules.

Then came the guns. The four men who'd brought them in by the armload began moving from one line to the next, handing one to each coyote.

As the mules stuffed packages into their rucksacks, the coyotes examined the sheets of paper that had been given to them. Enrique turned to see that the garage door was closing once again.

"Each of you knows the drill," Alejandro called out to the group, looking around as he did so. "You are to examine what is on your manifest. Your map, your shipment. Memorize it all, and then I will collect your sheet from each of you. Not one manifest is to be taken from this safe house. If you are caught, nothing must fall into the gringos' hands. If it does, you know the consequences.

"All groups will be accompanied by an enforcer beginning tonight," he continued. As he spoke, several of the armed men who had been standing around the garage began walking toward where Alejandro stood. One by one, he pointed each man toward a group, and moments later, each and every one of the groups had two gunmen at the front: a coyote and an enforcer.

"Pack your shipments and leave," Alejandro announced to the assembly; then he walked over to Enrique. "We go with them." He pointed to a four-some of mules. Standing at the front of the line was the tattooed man he'd ridden with in the SUV, holding three rifles.

"Lobo here will be our enforcer," Alejandro said as they neared the group.

The tattooed man handed what looked like a sniper rifle to Alejandro, then tossed a rifle straight at Enrique's head. He bobbled and caught it before it hit the floor.

One by one, the coyotes walked over to Alejandro, handing him their manifests. Then each group filed out of the garage one by one, until it was only Enrique, Alejandro, Lobo, and the four mules. Alejandro pulled a sheet from his pocket and scanned it.

"Where we going, Jefe," Lobo said.

"It's our lucky night," Alejandro replied. "We're going the path of last resort."

"Not *Garganta del Diablo*," Lobo replied, skeptical.

"Why wouldn't it be?" Alejandro answered, handing the sheet to Enrique.

"Maybe el jefe wants the boy dead, after all," Lobo threw a menacing gaze toward Enrique, "but he shouldn't have to drag us down with him."

Glancing nervously from Lobo to Alejandro, Enrique took the sheet and read it. He glanced toward the mules and noticed their clear discomfort upon hearing this news. He didn't know what this route was or what it meant for them, but judging by their and Lobo's reactions, it was not going to be pleasant.

"Take a good look and give me that back, boy," Alejandro told him. "Remember the route, the map, and the destination."

Enrique took another look at the sheet, this time more closely. At the top of the sheet it read 'Garganta del Diablo.' The route appeared to head to the north and east. It also appeared to zig-zag quite a bit. Total distance was four kilometers; their destination was a drop point just across the Rio Grande, where a vehicle would be waiting to take the shipment.

"How are we getting across the river?" Enrique asked.

"We swim," Lobo said mockingly. "And if you slow us down, I shoot you."

"We take a raft," Alejandro said. "But if you don't keep up in the valley, maybe we *will* make you swim."

"Or shoot you," Lobo repeated. Enrique noticed the two cloves of garlic in his hand just as he tossed one to Alejandro.

"What's that for?" he asked.

"To put in your shoes, to keep the snakes away," Alejandro said. "The valley is full of them."

Enrique didn't ask why they didn't have a clove for him; clearly a snake-bite would be an ideal way for them to unload him in the desert valley.

"Now, hand it over, boy," Alejandro said, motioning to the sheet still in Enrique's hand. "You are wasting everyone's time."

Without a word, Enrique gave the sheet back to Alejandro.

Alejandro took the sheet and set it atop the stack already in his hand. He withdrew a lighter from his pocket. He lit the stack afire, walked over to the row of steel barrels by the garage's back wall, and dropped the burning pages into one of the barrels.

"Now," he said to them all, "let's get moving."

26

It was 10:47 P.M. at Biggs Airfield just north of El Paso, Texas; Rage and his team were t-minus thirteen minutes until deployment.

The SEALs were equipped with body armor, night-vision goggles, an M-16 rifle along with a .45-caliber sidearm, comms, and short-range explosives. Even the two CIA operatives were sporting body armor and sidearms. Rage was equipped with the only things he ever brought on a mission: his Gift, his instincts, and a team whose primary purpose was to cover his back.

As the two MH-60 Black Hawks began starting up outside, Agents Cade and Miller called the team in for one final briefing.

In the small room, the screen in front of them lit up with an image of the target's compound, taken from directly above.

"This image was beamed to us just ten minutes ago," Cade said. "Again, like most nights, the grounds have cleared out by now. Good intel places the target and his top lieutenants within the compound every night at this time, along with approximately seven to eight armed guards."

"But again," Miller came in, "we don't know exactly what he has in that facility: weaponry, hidden attack points, booby traps."

"So the key here is caution," Cade said. "We do not know what awaits you around every hidden corner, or inside the buildings.

"One last time," Cade continued, and the image on the screen changed to show photos of three men. "Your primary target is Javier Oropeza, a.k.a. the Jackal. His top two lieutenants, Arturo Nava and Alejandro Garcia, are secondary. Orders are to kill or capture. But don't expect any to go down without a fight. So do what's necessary.

"As we've briefed you on previously," Cade went on, "the Jackal has been known to employ several body doubles, similar in height, weight, and appearance. The lack of any recent photos of him may make properly identifying him by plain sight even more difficult. However, our sources within the Mexican government confirm that he sustained gunshot wounds in the upper left leg and lower right torso during a firefight with Juarez Police eight years ago. You will be able to identify him by the scars from those wounds."

Meaning shoot first, ask questions later, Rage understood.

"Atten-tion!" Stevenson barked, standing up and turning toward the men. The SEALs rose, followed by Rage. "One last cross-check of your equipment, and then proceed to your assigned transport. We depart at 2300. Four minutes."

Less than a minute later, Rage had boarded the MH-60 and was fastening his five-point harness for the journey south. Donaldson was doing the same in the seat next to his; Zooker had already buckled himself into the jump-seat across from Donaldson.

At that moment, Stevenson boarded the craft and began buckling himself in as well. "Compound is four clicks past the border. We'll be in the air about nineteen minutes before hitting the L.Z., due south and west," he shouted over the din of the spinning rotors. "Upon hitting the L.Z., proceed and keep it tight to the wall. Collins and Mirer will implant the charges, and the Specialist and I will lead through the opening. CIA, you will have your window: eight minutes and we're in the wind."

Donaldson and Zooker nodded in acknowledgement.

"Clear for liftoff," Stevenson said to the pilot through his earpiece.

Rage felt the Black Hawk begin to pull heavily upward. He watched Biggs Airfield drop further below them before disappearing from view as the MH-60's picked up speed, cutting their way through the warm night air toward their destination.

27

Otis checked his watch; just after eleven o'clock P.M. His team had been at their coverage point for a little over an hour.

The group sat atop a steep hillside about ten yards off the northern riverbank of the Rio Grande, concealed by trees. Swank and Ferrell sat atop two large rocks off to the side, while Farnston and Wallace rested against a couple of trees. Otis stood behind a tree toward the center of the clearing where they sat, peering through his binoculars at the Rio Grande's southern bank.

"Aww, c'mon, man," Wallace moaned impatiently. "Where th'hell are they, man? This's bullshit. We's been stuck with a dead end. Ag'in!"

"Keep it down, Ty," Otis said calmly. "It's still early. And anyone on th' other side hears you, they'll be turnin' around."

"C'mon, Otis," Ty said, dropping his voice to a harsh whisper. "Cain't y' use some o' your influence t' get us a better route? Voorhees'll listen to ya."

"Shut up, Ty," Kyle chimed in. "Y' know all this stuff's a crapshoot. Voorhees don't know who's a'gonna be comin' through, when or where."

Otis looked back at Swank and Ferrell. Both young men remained seated on the rocks, quietly observing the others' conversation.

Otis turned his gaze back toward the border and pulled up the binoculars. The full moon was their only source of light, which didn't translate to good visibility through a zoom lens. He wished he still had his night-vision goggles from tour. His best bet was to pick up movement through the brush along the southern bank. If any activity was spotted, Otis's men would have little time to plan.

He scanned the southern bank for a few long moments; nothing. As he'd told Wallace moments ago, it was still early, but even he was starting to get impatient.

"Y'hear that?" Swank whispered from behind them.

As Swank said the words, Otis heard it, too: a low. humming sound, coming from the north behind them.

The two helicopters passed over them from only a few hundred feet up, the air churn swaying the tops of the trees above them. Otis looked on as they swept across the night sky, then quickly disappeared from view.

"Hell wuz that?" Ty exclaimed, holding his camouflage hat to the top of his head.

"Black Hawks," Otis said. "And stealth ones, by the sound of 'em."

"What're they doin' all the way out here, at this hour?" Kyle asked.

"Trainin' exercise?" Ferrell piped in.

"Not a bad guess, but no," Otis said. "They crossed the border, an' at high speed. They're goin' in for somethin'. What, I don't know."

Within seconds, the low hum had vanished into the night, leaving the group in silence once again.

"Should we call it in?" Swank asked.

"No. Gotta keep radio silence unless we need help," Otis answered. "Plus, we don't even know what it was."

Not another minute passed before they heard another sound in the distance, again behind them to the north. Turning around, Otis saw a faint glow over the hillside followed by headlights breaking over the ridge, about two hundred yards away.

"Hell's this, now?" Ty murmured.

"Keep low an' stay still," Otis said in a low voice. "Don't move 'til I say."

The men remained motionless as the vehicle slowly approached. As it neared, Otis could see that it was a truck – a Dodge Ram from the looks of it, a slightly faded red. It finally came to a stop about twenty-five yards from them. The driver switched off the lights, but no one emerged from the truck.

"What d'we do?" Ty whispered.

"We wait," Otis said, "an' we watch both sides, north and south. That's a pickup vehicle."

"What's that mean?" Swank said.

"Means we're gonna have company," Kyle answered.

"'Bout damn time," Ty whispered.

"Not 'nuther word," Otis whispered harshly. He turned around and took up the binoculars once again, scanning the south riverbank. Still no activity.

"All right, gather up," Otis said, motioning the men to move in closer. "We got a pickup vehicle to the north, and I'll betcha a group o' mules headin' our way from the south. Neither knows we're here, and I wanna keep it that way 'til it's too late for both of 'em. S' here's what we're gonna do. Kyle. You, Swank, and Ferrell're gonna stay here, keepin' watch o' the river. Call for backup the minute you see anyone appear on the other side. Ty, you an' me's gonna head up to that truck. We'll take care o' that driver so he can't warn the incomin' party."

"What're we gonna do to 'im?" Ty asked, an almost hopeful tone in his voice.

"Nuthin' bad," Otis shook his head. "Just shut 'im up for a bit. Just follow my lead, and don't do anythin' I don't tell ya to. Now come on."

"What do we do if I start to see activity on the river?" Kyle said as Otis tossed him the binoculars.

"Just let me know when we get back," Otis said. "Even if they show up now, it'll take 'em ten minutes to load up an' cross the river. We'll be back in five."

Without another word, Otis and Ty ducked down into the desert fauna for cover, then they silently began making their way toward the pickup vehicle.

28

A full moon presided over *Garganta del Diablo*; the occasional sound of rattlesnakes was the only thing to break up the hum of desert insects that filled the valley.

The group walked in a single-file line, Alejandro in front, followed by Enrique, then the four mules, with Lobo bringing up the rear. Alejandro had his long rifle slung over his back, a flashlight in hand to help navigate the difficult terrain ahead of them.

Enrique, who had figured he was in as good shape as any of the others, was exhausted; the rocky, uneven route had forced them to go up and down large hills, then through this valley that even in the middle of the night somehow still managed to contain the sweltering heat of day.

The route itself had certainly earned its namesake. The ground constantly changed beneath their feet: rocks large and small didn't just litter the path; they *were* the path, and with every step came the risk of twisting an ankle or falling down one of the steep ridges.

Then there were the plants and creatures that populated the valley. Aside from the rattlesnakes – which, to Enrique, it seemed they encountered every twenty seconds – large insects were everywhere. Buzzing in Enrique's face, biting him along the arms and back of his neck ("You need to spray next time, boy," Alejandro had told him after the fact), they had forced him to spend every moment of the journey swatting at one part of his body or another. He could even hear the mules chuckling quietly to themselves from behind him.

Aside from his rifle, Enrique was also tasked with carrying the group's supply of water. With the mules each carrying fifty-pound burlap packs on their backs, he was left to carry the two one-gallon jugs for the entire trip. He carried both jugs in one hand as often as he could, to free up the other one to swat at bugs; but all too often his hands ached, and he had to carry one in each.

They came upon a thick line of trees. Alejandro stopped, then turned around to address the group: "This is it," he told them in a whisper. "Over this ridge is the river; there are two rafts hidden in the trees. Lobo – you take the first two mules in the first raft; boy, take the second two in the other. Pickup vehicle will be waiting on the other side, beyond the hill. Be quick."

He switched off the flashlight. "No talking once we're in the trees," he ordered.

At that moment, Enrique could hear a noise – a low hum, off in the distance. He saw that Alejandro and the others had noticed it, too: all of them began to look around in different directions, trying to pinpoint the source of the incoming noise. Then, without warning, the two helicopters were upon them, soaring directly overhead, just above the treeline. Enrique ducked instinctively, as did a few of the mules, the force of wind from the massive blades blowing down upon them. And then just as quickly as the helicopters had appeared, they were gone.

"What ... *was* that?" Enrique thought aloud, as the hum faded to the south.

For a long moment, Alejandro stared in the direction where the helicopters had disappeared. "Nothing we should be concerned with," he finally said. "We have a job to do. Let's get moving."

They entered the thicket of trees growing along the riverbank, Enrique's eyes doing their best to adjust to the deeper darkness, now without the light of the moon or Alejandro's flashlight to guide them. He took each step carefully, still almost tripping twice, before Alejandro whispered, "Halt."

There were the two rafts, both leaning against two trees near the clearing just before the riverbank. "I will wait here," Alejandro told them. "Go straight across, pickup vehicle, and back. Go."

Following Lobo's lead, Enrique set down the water jugs, grabbed hold of one of the rafts, and quietly joined the mules going down to the riverbank, towards the waiting Rio Grande.

29

The two MH-60's flew at high speed toward the Rio Grande, sweeping the low sky just above the treeline.

Rage stared out the open side door, watching the moonlit desert landscape move swiftly below. In his headset, he heard the chatter between the pilots and Stevenson, mostly tactical details, when something caught his attention:

"Bodies ahead, on both sides of the river," the co-pilot's voice issued.

"How many?" Stevenson replied. "Movement?"

"Five, six on each side," the co-pilot responded. "Movement south of the river, looks like."

"Smugglers," Stevenson said. "Alert CBP once you've dropped us."

"Ten-four," returned the co-pilot.

Moments later, Rage felt the helo begin to slow. They were approaching the landing zone. The chatter between Stevenson and the pilots picked up again. Rage could see a steep slope that beveled the edge of a small canyon; beyond it stood the target's compound, surrounded by a high wall.

Seconds later, they were in vertical descent. He saw the other MH-60 descending at the same rate as they were, fifty meters to their right. Stevenson continued to issue commands to the pilots of both helicopters. Rage felt the soft landing of the MH-60 touching down and readied himself for deployment.

There was a bright orange flash of light to their right, followed by a deafening roar that immediately took away Rage's hearing, filling his head with a terrible ringing sound. The helicopter rocked to the left, tipping onto its spinning blades, which sliced into the desert rock and sand, sending shrapnel everywhere. He saw Stevenson shouting into his headset, but he could not hear the words. There was no time to think; they needed to get out of there. As the helicopter rocked back upright, Rage tore off his five-point harness, freeing himself from his seat, and then he grabbed at Stevenson's harness. Stevenson pushed back hard at him, motioning forcefully for him to sit down, continuing to shout orders angrily into the headset as if there was a chance the wounded Black Hawk was still of any use to them. He saw the other MH-60 burning brightly against the night sky from the opposite-side door, and he knew they had seconds at the very most.

The helicopter rocked once again, this time much harder, as another RPG made a direct hit, sending Rage flying from the craft, his head missing the twisted and frayed metal blades by mere inches. A second and third RPG followed, consuming the MH-60 completely in a fireball that rose high into the air. Rage felt his consciousness slipping from him as he was blown further away from the chopper, propelled violently into the air by the sheer force of the explosion. He finally made a hard, rolling landing against the desert floor, momentum forcing his body to continue rolling down the steep slope, until he dropped into the depths of the canyon that yawned wide below.

30

The Ram was parked at the edge of the rocky path that passed for a road, its headlights switched off.

Otis knew it wouldn't be an easy task to subdue the driver before he could warn the incoming mules, given that the man could easily blow his horn or flash his lights before they got inside the vehicle to him. The area surrounding them was so quiet, even a simple shout for help might do it. So the element of surprise was vital.

Suddenly, they caught a break: the door opened, and the driver stepped out. From where he and Ty sat crouched in the desert foliage, Otis could hear the flick of a match being struck, followed by the tiny orange glow of the end of a cigarette.

This was their chance.

He motioned to Ty to stay close behind him and began moving to the right, toward the rear of the truck.

Within seconds, they had snuck up on the driver, Otis taking him down with a quick knock on the back of the head with his elbow. The driver immediately fell to the ground. Otis tied his wrists and ankles with some rope he'd found in the back of the truck, and he and Ty hoisted him into the truck bed, setting him down gently. Otis took the keys from inside the cab and threw them into the high brush.

"He'll be out for a little bit," Otis said. "Long enough for us to figger out what's comin' from the other side."

"Heh," Ty whispered. "Y'shoulda let me hit 'im. I'd've had a little more fun with it."

"That's exactly why I didn't," Otis returned.

They walked back to their position on the riverbank in silence. As they approached, Otis noticed that Kyle had taken his spot behind the large tree, binoculars in hand.

He moved quickly up to Kyle's side. As he did so, he could see movement on the river: two large rafts had begun to cross.

"You call for backup?" he whispered to Kyle.

"The moment I saw 'em," Kyle answered. "Connors' group's headed our way, E.T.A. fifteen minutes."

"We ain't got fifteen minutes," Otis said, then glanced back at the rest of the group. Ty looked ready, a might too ready for Otis's taste, while Swank and Ferrell looked plain scared. The only way he could protect the two boys would be to limit their roles in what would happen next.

"Hand me those, willya," he whispered to Kyle, gesturing for the binoculars. Kyle did so, and Otis got a look for himself. Packed into each raft were three men, along with two large burlap sacks. Two of the men paddled while one kept watch ahead. Otis assumed that one of the two men keeping watch was the coyote. He would make sure to figure out which one. If the man knew anything about the attack on his border crossing or the murder of Paul Reynolds, Otis would make him talk before turning him in.

Otis turned back to his men. "We follow the plan," he said. "Stay at your positions, follow my lead. We stay hidden 'til I announce ourselves. Kyle and I'll be out front. Ty, you're backup; stay right behind us. Swank, Ferrell, stay to the sides but keep your arms pointed firmly at the opponent. Do not waver, but do not shoot. We clear?"

The group nodded.

The two rafts were only moments away from reaching the riverbank.

"Positions," Otis whispered to his men. "Be ready."

As the rafts reached shore, Otis could see that the two men who had been keeping watch were armed with semiautomatic rifles. Voorhees's intel had been right.

Otis and his team looked on from their positions in silence while the six men stepped out of the rafts. The two armed men scanned their surroundings while the mules pulled the rafts up onto the riverbank, then loaded the burlap packs onto their backs. Otis observed the two armed men closely. Though he couldn't see their faces, he could easily tell that the larger of the two was the leader: he was more confident in holding his fire-arm and more direct in whispering commands to the mules. The smaller of the two, by contrast, looked like their opponent's version of Ferrell; his body language was hesitant, unsure, as if he didn't want to be there and was ready to run away at any moment. Judging by what he saw, Otis bet that this was his first run. A rookie.

The smugglers began climbing the small ridge toward the clearing where Otis and his team waited. Otis backed away from the tree and held up a hand as a signal to his men. The darkness remained on their side as his team stood in the shadows of the trees surrounding them, out of the moonlight.

A head appeared at the edge of the bank, then a body came into view as the first man climbed up onto the clearing. Then a second, third, fourth, and fifth. As the fifth man reached the clearing and the sixth man's head appeared in view, Otis shone his flashlight upon them.

"Alto. Stop," he announced. "Drop your weapons. Hands in the air, where we can see them."

The group of men froze in the bright light. Otis could see that the leader was in front, followed by the four mules, with the rookie bringing up the rear.

Holding his sidearm in his left hand and the flashlight in his right, Otis scanned the group. The four mules stood motionless, a similar look of anxiety and fear upon each of their faces. The rookie stood just off the edge of the clearing, hands in the air with one arm shielding his eyes from the bright light, but he placed his rifle on the ground immediately. Only the leader stood defi-antly out front. His hands were raised as well, but he held on to his rifle. Otis shone the light on his face to see the man was smiling.

"I said, drop your weapon," Otis ordered him.

A grin still spread across his face, the leader slowly lowered his rifle, set-ting it on the ground before Otis's feet.

"Don't do nuthin' stupid," Otis said, moving toward the leader and picking up the rifle. He tossed it over to Farnston. "Now. You're the leader, I'm guessin'."

"No habla Ingles," the man said in a deliberate tone, his expression unwavering.

"That's how it's gonna be, then," Otis said darkly, then he turned his atten-tion to the rookie, who still stood just off the clearing. "You. Step on up here."

The young man did so, climbing up to stand at the edge of the clearing, hands still raised. Otis walked toward him.

As Otis's gaze met his, he immediately recognized him.

It was the boy he'd saved the morning of the bomb attack.

As Otis's eyes widened in surprise, he could tell that the rookie recognized him as well.

"What the hell ..." was all Otis could manage to say. The boy's fearful gaze seemed to turn a hue of regret.

"You and I ... we have ... some things to talk about," Otis said, a wave of thoughts hitting him all at once. He thought back to that morning. His instincts had been wrong: the rookie had in fact been a part of the attack. He had to have been; there was no other explanation. But had he been merely a distraction, or had he been the trigger man?

So many dead ... his friends and colleagues, family men and women, good people ... and this kid had played a part in it.

Otis's face hardened at the thought of all the blood on his hands.

"Kyle, radio in," Otis called back to Farnston. "Have 'em bring the van to our checkpoint."

But before Farnston could make the call, a low boom could be heard far off in the distance.

Otis glanced past the young man before him, toward the south horizon. The rookie half-turned toward the source of the sound as well.

"The hell," Otis could hear Farnston say.

"Stay focused," Otis ordered his men. "Kyle, make the call."

As Farnston put the handset to his mouth again, a second boom echoed in the distance, followed immediately by a third. Then a fourth.

The air seemed to hang around them as if waiting for something else to happen. Everyone from both sides stood motionless.

"Kyle," Otis finally said, keeping his eyes on the rookie. "We got a job to do. Now do it."

A shot rang out. Otis saw Farnston's head snap violently backward, then he dropped to the ground in a heap.

Sniper!

"Everyone *scatter!*" Otis screamed, diving toward the ground. "Get to cover!"

Chaos ensued. Men from both sides scrambled in all directions. Another shot was fired, missing Otis by mere inches. Then automatic gunfire erupted immediately all around them.

He rolled toward a large rock where he saw Swank and Ferrell had taken cover. He grabbed Swank by the collar. "You boys get the hell outta here, *now*" he shouted above the din. "Head for the checkpoint. Understand me?"

Both Swank and Ferrell nodded.

"Stay the hell low," Otis added. "Don't stop for nuthin'. Now go."

As Swank and Ferrell disappeared, Otis poked his head just above the boulder, rifle pointed toward where their opponents had stood. He saw the flashpoint come from the trees on the other side of the river just as Ty jerked backward and crumpled to the ground. He could see bodies on the ground, along with three or four burlap sacks. Two of the dead were his own men, but there were at least four or five strewn about. Both Kyle and Ty were gone; there was nothing he could do for either of them. He didn't have time to assess the carnage, though; there was still an active shooter out there, not to mention the man who'd been directly involved in the bomb attack.

As that thought crossed his mind, he could hear the sounds of splashing water. One or more of the smugglers was trying to get back across the river.

Otis leapt over the boulder and somersaulted to Kyle's body, grabbing the semiautomatic. No time to check for rounds. He fired into the woods across the river, toward the sniper's position, giving himself some covering fire. As he reached the edge of the clearing, he saw that there was only one crosser: the rookie.

In his panic, the rookie had run right past the rafts and was going to swim for it.

This was his chance to get him.

Firing more short bursts into the trees across the Rio Grande, Otis made a run for the river. The rookie had a pretty good lead on him, there was no question about that; but Otis was a fast swimmer: he had no doubt he would regain ground while crossing the river. One of the rafts might have been a better option, were there not a sniper hidden somewhere in the woods. In the water – partially obscured from view, blending with the current – he would at least have a fighting chance; in a raft, he'd be nothing more than target practice.

Tossing the semiautomatic and his walkie-talkie aside, he reached the river's edge and dove in, hitting the water at full speed. This stretch of the Rio Grande was only forty yards across, but even with Otis's fast strokes, it felt like an eternity, knowing that at any second the sniper's bullets could come slicing through the water around him.

He stayed underwater as long as he could between each breath, forcing as much air as he could into his lungs each time he surfaced. He had to assume that the sniper had a night-vision scope; but the closer he got to shore, the less of an angle the sniper had on him from the woods.

When Otis reached the shore, he felt relief as he saw no one awaiting him, but still he took no chances, clambering out of the water as quickly as he could, heading for cover in the thick brush a few yards from the riverbank.

He realized that he'd given up the advantage of a firearm the moment he dove into the river. He still had the combat blade sheathed in his boot, but he was now powerless if there were to be any exchange of fire.

And he was now in enemy territory, with no method of communication.

The dangers were many: there was at least one active shooter, very likely more; the terrain was unfamiliar, and visibility was poor.

But he knew the darkness could be used to his advantage as well: many of the missions he'd run in Afghanistan were night raids; he'd learned to leverage the dark as his ally. He was also an excellent tracker, thanks to his father taking him hunting as a teen. As long as the trail stayed warm and he kept moving, he had a chance to catch his target.

In the strip of moonlit terrain before him, he could see where the rookie had come upon shore: the weeds were freshly trampled, and he'd cut a path that led directly through the brush and into the woods beyond.

Otis took a rough measure between the prints to gauge the man's pace: he was running. It was clear that the rookie was in a panic, which meant that he would be taking the straightest path to wherever he was going, not taking care to cover his tracks, and he would need to stop and rest soon, at which point Otis could gain the most ground on him. Most important, he may not yet have realized that he was being followed, which meant that Otis would have the element of surprise on his side.

As he neared the far edge of the woods and saw the long stretch of desert terrain beyond, he stopped and listened for any signs of movement around him. The sniper was still out there, somewhere; he needed to be mindful of that fact with every step he took.

Several seconds passed. Nothing.

The sniper could have abandoned his position and moved to another, or he may have left the woods entirely to rendezvous with the rookie.

Otis scanned the ground and found the rookie's tracks once again. Where the ground cover ended, he could see the wet footprints in the dried dirt and sand, extending into the desert landscape beyond.

Otis stepped out of the woods and began running, staying near cover where he could, zig-zagging his route to throw off any sniper fire, moving quickly in pursuit of his target.

31

Enrique had been running for what felt like hours; his heart raced, his lungs burned, and his feet and ankles felt as if they would tear from his legs with every step.

He had tripped over rocks and patches of low-lying brush, but it was sheer exhaustion that finally brought him to his knees, crashing to the dusty, hard desert floor.

They had barely reached the riverbank on the American side when he heard the gunmen, ordering them in English to surrender. He had known right then that they were not American authorities; all of the police and Border Patrol agents he had ever encountered addressed him in Spanish.

Everything that happened next was a blur: the big officer who had saved his life, the explosions in the distance, the gunfire, the mules shot dead, Lobo disappearing into the trees. Then he was running back toward the river, sprinting right past the rafts and diving into the water. He swam as fast as he could; when he reached the shore he tore through the woods, bouncing off trees that he couldn't avoid in the sheer darkness. He stayed on his feet as best he could, until he hit the clearing several yards later, where he ran even faster, until finally he collapsed where he lay now, staring up at the night sky.

He thought about how his uncle would react. He had *failed*. On his first run.

Would his uncle punish him? Or worse, punish his mother or Juanita?

He had seen Lobo escape into the trees. But where was he now?

And what about Alejandro? He realized that it was he who had shot the Americans from across the river.

His breathing had finally begun to slow. He willed himself to sit upright. He would need to get moving soon. Though he didn't know where he would go, there were still plenty of dangers out here in the desert. And even with a clear night sky, it was still very difficult to see the uneven terrain of Garganta del Diablo ahead of him.

And he had no water to drink.

He decided the stash house was his only option. He could find the way.

He glanced around one more time to be sure of his bearings and then began walking in the direction of the stash house.

32

"What the hell just happened, Jack?" shouted Armstrong after the video feed went dark.

The large array of screens in the Pentagon's War Room had suddenly gone blank, black and white static filling every one of them. Dunlap, Armstrong, and the twenty-nine other Intelligence Officials and staff were left in a stunned silence.

"They're down," Dunlap replied, his voice a mixture of tension and shock. "We have to assume both helos are down. We need to send in Second Squad for an insert-and-rescue immediately. Best case, we work to see if we can get any of that feed back up to see what's going on down there."

"We're working on it, Sir," the engineer next to him replied. "Looks as if the signal was interrupted at its source —"

"Which means?" Armstrong asked impatiently.

"That the units themselves have been incapacitated, Sir."

"Jesus," Dunlap said. "Keep working on it. And keep me updated."

"What in the hell could have happened, Jack?" Armstrong sat back in his chair, running both hands through his thinned white hair.

"There was a cam unit mounted to each soldier's helmet, with the exception of CIA and Specialist," Dunlap thought it through aloud. "If all units were in fact taken out, something big had to have hit both helos, and we can only assume the worst."

"Damn it," Amstrong said. "How could they have taken down two of our MH-60's?"

Dunlap ignored his old colleague and got on the comm. "Get me General Norris," he said.

Seconds later, the line blinked, and Dunlap picked up. "General," he said into the handset. "Send a drone to map point oh-three-two-three. I want heat signatures, infrared video, still shots, two full sweeps. We need to know status of helicopters and every single body on the ground. Then we need to prep Second Squad for an insert-and-rescue."

"How could this have happened?" Armstrong said. "The intel on the target was sound. The teams were prepared for every scenario."

"Except for the one where they knew we were coming," Dunlap retorted.

"Jack," Armstrong said, leaning forward in his chair, "what would you have had us do: not tell the Mexican government of our new timetable? I told you before; this isn't Pakistan or some other second-tier ally. They needed to be properly prepared."

"And look at the result," Dunlap replied, then waved his hand dismissively. "No question, the target had a mole; we should have prepared for *that*.

"It doesn't matter at the moment," Dunlap cut himself off. "What matters now is finding out what's going on down there and getting those men out of there alive. I just pray to God that we're not too late."

Armstrong received a call on his secure line. "Armstrong," he answered. "Yes, we'll be there. Ten minutes."

Armstrong hung up; his face had turned white.

"What is it, Edward?" Dunlap asked.

"The President is calling an emergency all-hands meeting in the Situation Room," Armstrong answered. "An attempt was just made on President Vincennes's life."

33

The pale desert moon loomed high in the night sky as Otis tracked his target.

He had no idea how far he'd gone. At least two miles, maybe three. He was beyond winded, and his feet and legs burned from running along the rough terrain.

Now that clarity of mind had begun to sink in, he realized that this was probably the stupidest thing he could have done. After seeing two of his fellow servicemen being gunned down, he'd run blindly after the coyote, across the river and into Mexico, without any concern for his own safety, or the safety of Swank and Ferrell, whom he'd left behind without knowing what other dangers might still be awaiting them.

And he had no food or water on him, and no gun – just his hunting knife.

Panting, he stopped for a moment and scanned his surroundings. This was a dangerous landscape, he knew: rough terrain, with many predators throughout.

But there was no turning back now. He had come too far.

And he still had the element of surprise on his side. Stupid or not, no one would expect a gringo to follow someone this far into enemy territory. He would need to make the most of this sole advantage.

He resumed his pursuit, again checking the tracks in front of him, as well as looking behind him to landmark where he'd been. He was thankful for the tracks that he and his target had made: they would be his guide back home.

Moments later, Otis cleared a ridge and could see the faint glow of lights in the distance. A house. He could see a small amount of dust being kicked up far down the hill. Someone was running in the direction of the house.

Otis began moving down the rocky hillside in pursuit.

When he was within about a hundred yards of the house, he could see the barbed-wire fence surrounding the property. Beyond the fence stretched a long driveway that led to the main one-story building. A single truck was parked in the driveway, another red Dodge Ram, jacked up high on enormous tires.

Good, Otis thought; the lack of vehicles meant there probably wouldn't be very many men inside the house.

Getting past the fence wouldn't be a challenge: it was only about waist-high.

He had seen the coyote jump the fence but then had lost sight of him.

As he drew closer to the fence, Otis noticed three dogs, all rottweilers, circling the truck. None of the dogs barked at the truck, but rather, they were quietly, persistently circling it, every few seconds going up onto their hind legs and pressing their front paws against the outside of the truck bed, sniffing eagerly.

Something was inside the truck bed. Some kind of small animal, Otis figured.

Otis had heard that some cartels had dogs trained to attack directly rather than bark at any possible trespassers, but he had never before seen it in person.

He watched from a distance, hidden from view by a patch of thick brush. There was very little wind tonight, but for what air flow there was, Otis was thankful that he was downwind from the dogs. He just hoped that the wind wouldn't shift on him.

He thought about how he would approach the house. Although the dogs were currently focused on whatever was inside the truck bed, he knew that their attention would shift the moment they noticed him.

Then, something happened that Otis didn't expect: a head popped up in the truck bed before ducking back down. A man was in there.

A small, lean frame rose from the bed, wobbling to his feet. It was, without a doubt, the coyote. He was shaking something in his hand: a long, thin object. As the coyote took a step toward the edge of the truck bed, one of the dogs jumped high into the air – Otis could hear the snapping of its powerful jaws even from that distance – and the man jolted in surprise, falling backward and crashing down into the bed.

Otis shook his head. Why was the coyote hiding at his own stash house?

Then the coyote got back to his feet and began shaking the object again, this time a safe distance from the edge. Otis got a better look and saw that it was a crowbar. Was he actually crazy enough to try to fight off the three dogs?

But instead of trying to fight the dogs, the coyote did something else entirely: he threw the crowbar as far as he could.

The boy began motioning wildly with his arms in the direction of the bar. Otis realized that the coyote was trying to urge the dogs to chase after the crowbar. Even in that moment, Otis almost had to suppress a laugh. Rottweilers were guard dogs, not retrievers. The coyote was proving himself dumber by the second. Hell, getting him back across the border was probably the only way to keep him *alive*. He wasn't sure how he'd even gotten *this* far without getting himself killed.

The dogs had begun circling the truck once again when Otis heard a subtle noise behind him. Pebbles moving.

He drew his knife and turned around just quickly enough to see the butt end of the rifle before it slammed into the side of his head.

34

H is eyes opened.

At first, he could not see; everything was blackness. Then, what light his eyes
did allow in came only as a blur. Bright spots moved about his field of vision;
he did not know whether they were real or part of his imagination.

Shapes began to form, then colors. The shapes, he did not recognize. The
colors were different shades of dark: black, deep gray, brown, a deep blue.
Then black again. Then nothing.

He could feel his ears. At first he heard a low hum, then it became louder.
It grew into a violent crescendo, running roughshod through his ears, his head,
his body. Deafening.

Then, nothing again.

He could smell something burning – something burned. Meat of some
sort. And there was the taste of blood on his tongue – a lot of blood.

The hard, uneven surface beneath him pressed into his back, his arms,
his legs. He could feel several hard, jagged, pointed things sticking into him;
whatever they were, they had punctured his skin in many places. As his nerve
receptors began to pick up sensation again, the pain became unbearable. He
wanted to scream but could not force enough air from his lungs; the only sound
that issued from his wide open mouth was a faint wheeze.

He tried to move but could not. He willed himself harder. Still nothing.

Moments passed. The pain that resonated throughout his body did not
subside, but he felt strength returning to him. He could feel his blood flow

increase; his muscles begin to twitch. When he opened his eyes again, what was at first a darkened blur slowly came into focus as a deep blue night sky, a white moon staring down intently at him.

The throbbing pain, the jagged points stabbing into his back, and the oddly putrid smell of charred meat still dominated his senses, but he slowly began to feel in control of his own body again. His eyes moved to the left, the right. He twitched the muscles in his arms and legs. Slowly, he lifted his head and looked about him.

He was in some kind of canyon or gorge, judging by the high walls of rock that surrounded him. He was lying on his back at a slight angle, his head farther down than his feet, which explained the head rush he was feeling as the flow of blood in his veins continued to increase. The rocky surface of the canyon floor around him was uneven, which explained the sharp protrusions that had pierced the skin all along his backside. He had no idea how much blood he'd lost or if he had any broken bones.

He tried to move again, slowly, and was able to pull his arms up. Small rocks and pebbles cascaded from his arms; he was covered in sand. Then he lifted his legs. He could feel the wetness of the blood on the back of his arms and legs from being cut and scratched in so many places. He turned his right arm over in the moonlight and saw through his shredded sleeve that there was a deep cut that ran almost the length of his forearm. But he was thankful that somehow, there seemed to be no broken bones.

Then he saw the shrapnel.

It was metal, about a quarter-inch thick, lodged in his right shoulder, just beyond the collarbone. It was protruding out about three inches. He had no idea how deep it went into his flesh. He was certain that it was limiting any blood flow to his right arm, but he was equally certain that if he removed it, there was a good chance he would bleed out.

He needed to find help.

He would first need to lift the rest of his body off of the rocky floor of the canyon.

Taking a breath, he placed his fists on either side of his head, then he bent his legs fully, tucking his feet as close as possible to his bottom. He was going to lift himself into an arch, to pull his back directly off the ground. As he moved into position, every single inch of his body screamed out in agony; the movement of each muscle seemed to ripple and amplify the pain into the next muscle, and the next. He tried again to scream, and this time what expelled from his lungs was a terrible, primal, howling roar that bounced off of the canyon walls for long seconds before fading into the distance.

He took a deep breath again, readying himself. His entire body was trembling. Finally, he began to push off with both hands and feet — the beaten, torn-up muscles and limbs throughout his body straining — and hoisted himself from the rocky surface. He screamed again, this time louder, longer, even more soul-wrenching than the first. He felt the jagged points of rock begin to pull from his flesh, some lodged in much deeper than others, maybe even an inch deep in some places, a few of them catching on his torn flesh as he pulled. But he kept arching, kept willing himself off the ground, until finally he had freed himself.

As he rolled over onto his side, catching himself before going face-first into the rock, the pain from twisting his flesh hit a new peak, and he became sick all over the rocky canyon floor.

Panting heavily, he wiped his mouth and sat up. He scanned the barren landscape around him.

Where was he?

How did he get here?

His tried to retrace his steps, how he had nearly gotten himself killed — broken, beat, and scarred, left for dead in this deep ravine.

To his surprise, he found himself with no recollection of anything that had led up to this moment.

His mind worked harder, trying to look further back, straining to recall, to retrace any moment that might provide a clue as to how he had gotten here.

He took a breath and closed his eyes, trying to relax, to clear his mind.

He sat in silence for long moments, his eyes closed, doing all that he could to shut out the throbbing pain in his head, his entire body. He let the emptiness of the desert settle upon him like a soft rain, allowing the thoughts, the memories to come to him at their own pace.

There was nothing.

It was as if his mind was empty, wiped clean.

He did not know where he was, how he had gotten here, or how to get home.

He did not know where home was.

He did not even know *who* he was.

Then he realized: he must have something on him: a wallet, ID card, something that would at least tell him his name, and maybe that would trigger something.

Slowly, agonizingly, he stood up and began patting himself down. His hands moved along what remained of his torn-up clothing, searching for pockets.

He found six pockets – all of them torn up, all of them empty.

He looked around once again: high rock walls loomed to his left, his right, and behind him. He knew that he was in no condition to climb, so he began walking in the direction he was facing, in search of a way out of the ravine.

He looked over his torn clothing in the moonlight. His right sleeve was shredded to the point of being almost gone. His pants were torn in several places, including a long tear that ran along most of his right leg. He took a second look at the deep cut that ran along his right forearm; the blood had seemed to dry somehow, and the cut didn't look as deep as when he'd first noticed it. It didn't matter; he knew he needed medical attention.

Curiosity then turned his attention to the clothes themselves. They looked like fatigues of some sort, like the kind the military would wear. But they were all black, with no markings on them whatsoever. His heavy, black boots were as non-descript as the fatigues themselves.

Why in the world was he dressed like that?

His thoughts then turned to his location. He wondered exactly where he was. He knew that he was in a canyon, in a desert somewhere.

As he walked, he felt his strength continue to return to him. Every step seemed to get easier. He began to feel as if he could climb out of the gorge, maybe get a look around at where he was.

He walked for what felt like several minutes and then made his way over to the side of the canyon to his right, to a point where the slope was reasonable, the canyon wall at its lowest. Placing his hands on the rocks before him, he began to climb.

The task was far easier than he'd imagined. Whoever he was, he was in incredible physical condition. In a matter of minutes, he had scaled the wall, and now he stood at the edge of the gorge, looking out at a desert landscape laden with rock and desert fauna in the foreground, with foothills and small mountains in the distance.

There was no sign of any human presence in his line of sight, but he could see a faint glow of light that appeared to be coming from around one of the foothills.

He dusted himself off and began walking, heading toward the source of the light.

35

Jack Dunlap had only been inside the White House Situation Room once before, and the tension from that previous visit paled in comparison to what he was witnessing now.

Lined along the main long table were the Vice President, White House Chief of Staff Jezowit, Secretary of Defense Collins, Secretary of State Braun, Director of Homeland Security Deegan, FBI Director Jones, CIA Director Lunkenheimer, and the Joint Chiefs. Several other top officials and advisors stood against the far wall. The President himself was pacing along the back wall, farthest from the large projector screen many were staring at, arms crossed, as he glanced between the gathering of his staff and the images on the screen.

On the screen itself was a live report from the Mexican National News service, showing the chaos that had ensued in Mexico City since the attempt on President Vincennes' life less than one hour earlier.

A polarizing figure for his firm stance on the war on drugs in his country, Vincennes had millions of ardent supporters as well as detractors, and it seemed as if all of them on both sides had emptied into the streets of Mexico City.

Riots swarmed. Fires raged. Cars were overturned. Entire police squadrons were overrun. Gunfire echoed everywhere.

Vincennes had been taken to an undisclosed location for emergency medical care; the extent of his injuries was unclear. Also unclear was whether or not he would survive. The only detail available was that his motorcade had been attacked while in transit to his residence from a state dinner.

It was also unclear who was responsible for the attack.

What was more, given this development, all top-level communication between the U.S. and Mexican governments had temporarily broken down. State agencies were still in communication, but anyone in Vincennes' inner circle who had knowledge of the current operation in the Juarez region was currently unreachable. If the U.S. was to go in for a rescue mission, it would be outside the knowledge and therefore the permission of the Mexican government, which would violate several existing accords between the two countries.

This was the core of the debate amongst the President's senior advisors.

"We have very little choice here," Defense Secretary Collins argued. "We have men down, and we don't know if there are survivors. We need to go in."

"At the risk of our relationship with Mexico?" Secretary Braun countered. "Doing so would violate several long-standing agreements. I strongly advise against it."

Dunlap knew that this discussion was well above his rank. He glanced at Armstrong, who also watched silently as the debate escalated before them.

At that moment, Collins turned to Armstrong. "Deputy Secretary," he addressed him, "will you please provide the group with a status of the drone reconnaissance your team ordered of the landing zone?"

"The Predator completed its fourth and final sweep of the L.Z. not ten minutes ago," Armstrong addressed the group. "Images confirm both MH-60's down. As of now, there are no signs of survivors within the L.Z. itself; however, infrared revealed a possible survivor in the ravine just to the north."

"So," the President chimed in, "one possible survivor."

"Yes, Sir," Armstrong confirmed.

"But we're not sure he's ours," the President pressed.

"We cannot confirm that at this time, no, Sir."

The President turned to the Secretary of State. "How long until we reestablish contact with Vincennes?" he asked.

"We don't know," Braun responded. "It depends on the extent of his injuries and how quickly they can set up a comm. center wherever he is."

The President pulled at his chin, deep in thought. "There is no question that, whether there is one survivor or many, we need to get in there quickly. But to Secretary Braun's point, we cannot do so at the expense of our agreements with our neighbor and ally. And per our eyes in the sky, we don't yet know if we even have any survivors.

"Secretary Braun," he said, making his decision. "Continue trying to establish contact with Vincennes. Secretary Collins, you do the same for our men down there. Do not stop, do not rest, until it's done. We will hold off our rescue mission until either we have the opportunity to communicate our intent, or we have confirmation that at least one of our men is alive down there."

Dunlap could see that Collins clearly wanted to argue, but he knew that the President's decision was final.

Moments later, the two men were walking toward the car that waited to take them back to the Pentagon when Armstrong broke the silence.

"We haven't had a moment to discuss the recon footage," Armstrong said.

"I know that," Dunlap replied. "You're wondering the same thing I am: if the heat signature that the drone found belongs to one of ours."

"I am," Armstrong confirmed.

"That wasn't detected 'til the final fly-over," Dunlap said. "And we had to order the bird back so we could report in. I'll order another sweep, give us a closer look."

"If there's anything to see by then," Armstrong thought aloud.

"Obviously my concern as well," Dunlap agreed.

"What are the chances it is one of ours?" Armstrong wondered.

"No idea, but pretty unlikely," Dunlap said. "It was thirty meters from the L.Z. First, the subject would have to have somehow gotten out of the helo before the blast. Then, if he escaped, he would have been thrown several meters into a gorge that's who-knows-how deep. If the concussion from the blast didn't kill him, the fall certainly would have."

"Unless," Armstrong began.

"You're thinking it could be the Specialist," Dunlap said.

"The only one who could have survived all that," Armstrong said.

"Clearly," Dunlap concurred. "But that kind of punishment is likely beyond even *his* limits."

"But if it is him ..." Armstrong began.

"Then it changes everything," Dunlap said.

36

"*Vaminos!*" the voice boomed suddenly from outside the truck bed.

Huddled down, Enrique looked up to see the silhouette of a tall man walking in his direction, carrying something large over his left shoulder.

His eyes moved back to the yard to see that the dogs had scattered and were now pacing around the yard once again, as if they'd completely forgotten about him.

As the figure moved closer, Enrique saw that it was Alejandro. The object over his shoulder appeared to be a large body.

"Stupid boy," Alejandro snapped at him. "I should let the dogs in after you right now, but I don't want to have to clean up the mess. That is my truck, after all."

Alejandro slid the body down from his shoulder, sending it crashing onto the ground. "Help me carry this bloody mess into the house."

Enrique climbed out of the truck bed and picked up the man's legs to begin carrying him. He saw that it was one of the gringos from the river, the man who had saved his life at the border crossing. His face was bloodied, with a huge welt on his forehead, as if he'd been struck by something very hard.

"He's – he's alive, right?" Enrique said.

"And lucky to be," Alejandro said. "Just as you are."

"How – how did he get down here?"

"How do you think?" Alejandro sneered. "He followed *you*. You led him right here."

"But how? I was — I was careful —"

"Not careful enough," Alejandro said. "He was tracking you, staying far enough behind so your dull senses couldn't pick him up. Lucky for you, I was tracking *him.*"

"What are we going to do with him?" Enrique asked.

"We're going to keep him here," Alejandro said. "Jefe wants one of the outlaws."

"For what?"

"For interrogation. And to send a message back to the Americans."

Enrique had seen his uncle's way of sending messages before, and he knew it would mean a horrible death for this man. He found himself suddenly feeling sick.

They carried the unconscious man into the house. A small kitchen lay before them, then a doorway which led to a larger room. The kitchen was filthy, with trash and debris all over the counter, and it smelled as if something had died there. Overall, the place was cramped and terribly dim, with only one small lamp lit in the kitchen and another that he could see flickering, barely on, in the room beyond.

A few steps later, they set the gringo down against the far wall of the main room, near a metal post that had a short chain and pair of handcuffs attached to it.

Alejandro pulled the man's wrists up against the post and cuffed them tightly.

"What happens next?" Enrique finally said, breaking the long silence.

"We wait," Alejandro said, "for the other groups to return from their runs. Once everyone has returned, we will take this one back to *Santa Maria.*"

"How long?"

"It will be a while," Alejandro said, taking a seat in a worn folding chair. "No more questions, boy."

Enrique had no idea how much time passed before Alejandro's phone rang.

He picked up the phone. "What did we say about radio silence, muchacho?" he spat angrily into the handset. "Jefe is going to —"

Then he went silent, listening intently to whatever was being said on the other end of the line. His ire-filled expression transformed into one of disbelief, then back to anger. "All right," he finally said in a low voice. "Get everyone you have. I'm leaving now."

He hung up and turned to Enrique. "Change of plans," he said. "You stay here with the gringo until I return. Don't talk to him. Wait for the others to arrive."

"What's happening?" Enrique asked.

"Distress call from the Garage," Alejandro said darkly. "It's under attack."

37

From deep inside *Santa Maria*, Javier Escondido Oropeza sat watching a news report of the carnage in Mexico City.

He had been informed of the Americans' coming attack on *Santa Maria* hours before, and he had been ready for them. Now their war machines lay in smoking ruins outside his walls, their soldiers dead.

Following that effort was his attempt on Vincennes's life. Though not successful, it would be only a matter of time before one of his men on the inside would finish the job. Once that was done, he had the resources to ensure that one of his insiders would become the next president — one more in line with his long-term goals.

But his message to Vincennes had been clear: allowing the Americans to attack one of Mexico's most important citizens would not come without repercussions.

Before, the Jackal had run his operations mostly unimpeded by the authorities. The President would spew out rhetoric against the cartels to the masses, while the Jackal would provide his administration with information leading to arrests of officials in other, competitive cartels throughout Mexico. These high profile arrests suggested that Vincennes was in fact winning the war on drugs.

But with this move by Vincennes, the time for such agreements had now passed.

And in a similarly promising development, Alejandro had captured one of the American outlaws who had been intercepting his shipments in recent days. He would learn all that the man had to share, and then he would send the man's body back home in pieces, to send the outlaws a message as well.

But what happened moments ago was the one thing he had not expected. A distress call from the Garage revealed that it was under attack — by whom, he had yet to learn. He had ordered all his top enforcers not currently on runs to that location, to neutralize the threat and figure out who was behind the attack.

He had no idea who was bold — no, stupid — enough to invade one of his main distribution hubs, but whoever it was, it would not take long to squash them.

Over the past few years, he had systematically crushed his primary competitors in the region, and many of their former employees now worked for him. He knew of a few budding drug gangs who had made inroads with small-time dealers, but there was nothing he perceived as ever becoming a threat.

His satellite phone rang. Alejandro. He picked up.

"Update," he said.

"En route," Alejandro replied on the other end. "Had to secure the prisoner."

"Once you've handled the situation at the Garage, bring the gringo in," the Jackal ordered him. "I want an audience with him tonight. Report back when you've secured the Garage."

He hung up and turned his attention back to the news reports.

38

Several moments earlier, the midnight moon shone over the desert landscape as the man in black walked toward the beacon of light ahead.

With each step he took, he felt his body continuing to grow stronger. His limbs, muscles, and bones all seemed to become more fluid, more solid, with every passing moment.

It was a strange sensation; he felt as if he could launch into a sprint, leap high into the air, even punch a hole through a wall. This energy began to excite him; he wondered if this was how a bird felt when it first began to take flight.

Instinctively, he glanced down at his injured arm. He looked back up for a split second before he stopped and looked at the arm again.

It appeared as if it was completely healed. The blood was still there, dried and caked onto his skin, but there was no sign of any wound.

He ran his finger along where the deep gash had been. Aside from the blood that he clearly saw, it was as if the injury had never happened.

Had he imagined the injury? Was the blood on his arm from something else?

He felt dizzy from confusion; he shook his head to regain his focus.

Regardless of what he had just seen with his arm, he still needed medical attention for his other injuries — including the shrapnel lodged deeply in his shoulder, which he knew he was *not* imagining — right away.

The light was still far away. He was becoming impatient. He began walking again, picking up his pace, noticing that the painful limp he'd had when he first climbed out of the gorge had gone away completely. He began to run.

He had no idea how fast he was running, but the sheer wind against his face told him he should probably slow down before he lost his footing or tripped over the uneven, obstacle-laden ground beneath him. Though somehow, even in the darkness, he seemed to be able not only to see, but also to avoid the many rocks, bumps, dips, and desert plants he encountered.

Before he knew it, he was upon the source of the light. There was a thicket of trees that led up to it, but it looked as if the light was coming directly from a hillside – there didn't appear to be any kind of building in the area.

He entered the thicket and could see the source of the light ahead. It *was* coming from the hillside itself: someone had actually bored an enormous hole into the side of the hill and made a home out of it.

He didn't know what to make of all of it, but he kept walking forward until he was standing in the massive entrance.

Immediately, he realized that it was not a home but some kind of warehouse, with several rows of empty metal shelves. There were a few wheelbarrows off to his right. Directly beyond the shelves, he could see some men and women standing at long tables, wrapping packages large and small in duct tape and cellophane.

Then he saw the men with the guns.

As he stood there, one of them noticed him, and began shouting at the other gunmen in a language he could not understand. They pointed their weapons at him and, without warning, opened fire.

As the bullets flew, his body seemed to act of its own accord, ducking and dodging the incoming fire. One of the bullets grazed his left elbow, slicing just under his skin; the second hit him square in the right shoulder, shredding the wound around the shrapnel.

Before he knew what was happening, he was outside, beyond the front door, climbing the steep hillside at a breakneck pace. Despite the excruciating pain in his right shoulder, he was able to scale the rocky wall with ease. Once he'd reached the top, he looked over his wounds. The bullet he had taken in the shoulder had twisted the shrapnel in such a way that it tore into his flesh with his every movement. Without a thought, he ripped the shard from the open wound in one swift motion. He screamed loudly, the pain exploding throughout his body, almost causing him to pass out.

He was panting, heart racing – not from the terrible pain in his shoulder, but from something else he couldn't pinpoint.

No time to ponder it. He could hear the voices coming up the hillside. He looked around desperately for some kind of weapon. There was nothing more than a few small rocks, not even the size of a tennis ball. And he couldn't run; he had no idea if there was another way down the hill.

He saw the first man's head appear just at the ridge. He had no options; he was out in the open and would be an easy target. He was out of time.

It was in that moment that instinct took over.

He rushed the edge of the hill and straight-kicked the first gunman in the head, sending him flying backward into the second man, who was climbing directly behind him. Both of them tumbled down the hillside, crashing into a heap several meters below. Two additional gunmen were flanking the leaders up the hill and immediately opened fire on him. He leapt over the line of fire and somehow landed immediately between them on the steep ridge. He tore the rifle from the grip of the gunman nearest to him, smashing him in the face with the butt end. Before the first gunman began to fall, he grabbed the man by the head and twisted hard, hearing the neck snap easily under the force of his strength. He then threw the limp, lifeless body full-force at the second gunman, who couldn't react in time to dodge it. He watched as the two bodies cascaded down the steep hill, landing close to where the first two gunmen had crashed to earth.

Seeing no one else in pursuit, he leapt down to the bottom of the hillside and stood over the bodies of his four would-be attackers, all bloody and broken, two of them face down, the other two facing up toward him, gazing emptily into the night sky. Getting his first good look at them in the moonlight, he saw that they were dressed in fatigues, similar to what he was wearing, but all had some kind of emblem at the shoulder that he did not recognize. He looked closer and saw that it was a black bird of some kind, wings spread wide, with two machine guns crossed just underneath.

As he stared at the bodies, the realization washed over him like an enormous wave.

He had just killed four men.

And how he had killed them ... so quickly, so *easily* ...

Effortlessly ...

It had almost seemed ... natural to him.

Who was he?

What was he?

He stood up and became aware that he was breathing heavily again, his heart racing, blood coursing through his veins with some form of energy he couldn't understand. And then he realized: this was not fear for his life; this was something else entirely. It was some kind of innate compulsion, racing through him like a terrible juggernaut, threatening to take over his entire consciousness.

It almost felt like ... *exhilaration.*

He shook his head again, trying to clear the confusion from his mind.

He looked down at his fists and saw that he was clenching and releasing them every second, his fingers pressing hard into his palms with every clench, like a steam engine ready to boil over.

Suddenly a clatter of noises came from behind where he stood: footsteps, shouting. He turned just in time to see a bright light trained on him; behind it, four more gunmen had stopped at the mouth of the garage, all pointing rifles at him. They seemed to pause for a split second, clearly taking in the sight of their four dead comrades whom he was now standing over. Then, as abruptly as the others had done moments before, they opened fire on him.

He once again let instinct take over, dodging the incoming shots with an ease he could not understand, then leaping forward at his attackers. But, unlike moments before, he was clearly more comfortable, more in command of the abilities that had allowed him to somehow dodge arrays of bullets, scale massive rock walls with ease, and kill with such terrible strength and skill.

In a matter of seconds, all four gunmen were lying dead at his feet. He felt an odd, momentarily release come over him, which he suddenly realized he'd also felt moments before, just after taking down the first four attackers.

Was this something he had done in his life before?

Had he been a murderer? A criminal?

And why did killing feel so effortless ... perhaps even fulfilling ... to him?

A strange mix of remorse and confusion washed over him. He lurched forward to vomit, but all that issued from his mouth was hot, putrid breath.

Then he remembered ... there were more inside. They would be coming for him.

His eyes grew darker; he felt that insatiable urge build within him once again.

Without another thought, he rushed the doorway of the warehouse, a terrible roar announcing his arrival, anticipating more of them to be inside, ready to attack, to kill.

But as he rounded the corner and scanned the room, he saw no men with guns.

Instead, all he saw were the partially hidden bodies of four people, two of them men and two of them women, trying their best to conceal themselves behind the steel table they'd been laboring over when he'd first entered the room moments before. He could hear someone whimpering, another crying, and a third whispering something in a pleading tone, in the same unfamiliar language he had heard the gunmen using.

He strode toward the table, the urge overpowering his every thought, a ravenous appetite for violence coursing through him. He would enjoy this.

He reached the table. Without warning, he tore it from where it had been bolted to the floor. He threw it far behind him, sending it smashing into a large steel shelving unit, toppling the entire unit to the floor with a resounding crash.

As he looked upon the four terrified souls huddled to the floor, embracing one another in desperate fear for their lives, another wave of confusion washed over him, halting him in his tracks. He wanted to lash out at them —

But he found himself rooted to the spot where he stood.

He shook his head angrily and forced himself forward, grabbing the man closest to him — a young man, maybe in his teens — and pulling him up so they were face-to-face.

The urge was overpowering. He realized he was snarling, tiny bits of spittle flying from the sides of his mouth with every panting breath he took. He saw the man shaking — not only from fear, but from the unsteadiness of his own grasp.

He would not — could not — do this.

With a roar of defeat he let the terrified man drop to the floor. He began smashing his fists together like some kind of wild ape, his feet stomping the floor, searching desperately for someone, something to lash out at.

But there was no one.

He fell to the stone floor and began pounding his fists into it as hard as he could, until the floor itself had cracked and his fists were red with his own blood. He rose up and screamed a terrible, primal scream that echoed loudly in the vast room.

Then, without turning back, he launched into a sprint, vanishing into the night beyond.

39

The big red pickup jumped ridges and traversed rough terrain as it made its way toward the Garage.

As Alejandro drew near, he saw the lights of two other vehicles approaching from other directions as well.

Since the attack, he had not heard one update from the Garage on who the attackers were, how many there were, or if they had been dealt with.

He arrived and took up his AR-15. The others had parked their vehicles as well and approached him, also with rifles in hand. He counted ten men.

"Split into three groups," he told them. "Nava. Take three around to the right. Hernandez, three to the left. You two — come with me. Shoot to kill, no hesitation. One group makes contact, radio in — the others head to that position."

As they made their way into the room, they saw the carnage that had ensued: bullet holes in the walls, shell casings on the floor. Two rows of shelves had been knocked down, on top of which lay the twisted remains of a metal table. At the back of the room, he saw four figures huddled together against the wall. The packagers. They had always worked behind the large table at the back of the warehouse. That table now lay in a mangled heap over twenty feet from where it had been bolted to the floor. Alejandro saw that the bolts themselves were still in the floor, bent and twisted, as if the table had been ripped from them in one swift, abrupt motion.

The packagers kept their faces hidden, as if they couldn't bring their eyes to face whatever had happened in the room.

Alejandro kept his guard up as he approached them, the AR-15 ready to fire.

His mobile unit sounded. It was Nava.

"Contact?" he spoke into the mobile unit in a low voice.

"Bodies," Nava replied. "Outside. Eight of them."

"Who?"

"All ours. Dead."

"Any sign of the enemy?"

"No," Nava said. "Nothing. And no blood. It looks like their ... necks were broken."

Alejandro swore under his breath. "Keep looking, and stay alert. If they're still here, they're extremely dangerous. Again, shoot on sight. Out."

Alejandro put away the mobile unit and took a step forward. As he did so, he noticed that the stone floor beneath his feet was cracked. As he looked closer, he saw that it was pocked with tiny divets and broken pieces of stone, as if someone had smashed something repeatedly onto the floor – something hard enough to break the stone surface.

He approached the packagers. There were two women, both around twenty, a teenage boy, and an old man, who was huddled over some rosary beads, whispering intently to himself with eyes closed.

"What happened here?" he demanded.

The two women hesitated, but both glanced up in Alejandro's direction. The old man kept his head down and eyes closed, continuing to whisper into the rosary beads.

"One of you. Talk," he ordered them.

"A – a man ..." one of the women began.

"Who?" he implored. "What were they after?"

"Nothing ..." the woman continued feebly. "He took nothing ... he came in ... they started shooting at him ... he disappeared ... and then he came ... he came back ..."

"What did they say?" Alejandro urged her on, ignoring the old man.

"He said nothing," she said, the terror in her voice rang with every word. "He came in ... he was going to ... to kill us ... and then he ... he *stopped*."

"Where are they now?"

"I ... I don't know ..." the woman said.

"How many?"

"One ..." the woman answered. "There was only one of them ..."

"*ONE?*" he said incredulously, grabbing her by the wrist. His anger was growing; his patience wearing thin. "*Who?* What did he look like?"

"A gringo," she winced as he squeezed her wrist. "Wearing black ... covered in blood ... and the eyes ... the eyes of the devil."

The old man said something into the rosary beads, more audible than whatever he'd been saying before, but still barely above a whisper.

Alejandro noticed this and glanced in the old man's direction. "What did you say?" he leaned down into the man's face. "Look at me when I talk to you."

"Diablo," the old man repeated into his rosary beads, keeping his eyes closed, his gaze away from Alejandro's menacing visage. "Diablo ... Diablo ..."

Alejandro stood back up and smiled malevolently. "Diablo, eh?" he sneered.

Then, without warning, he took the AR-15 and smashed the old man in the side of the head. The man fell to the floor. The two women screamed. Alejandro hit him again. Harder. A third time, until the old man's blood began to pool on the stone floor.

Alejandro towered over the man's body. "The only devil you need to fear is *me*."

The screaming had drawn the attention of the other groups, who ran into the room with rifles pointed. "What happened?" Nava said. "Where is the enemy?"

"Gone," Alejandro said, turning away from the packagers.

"What do we do now?" Hernandez asked.

"We set up a perimeter here in case he returns," Alejandro said. "Four of you will stay. Others will do the same at the safe houses, in case something bigger is going on. The rest of us will hunt him down. I will let the Jackal know what happened here."

"'*He*', you said?" Nava questioned. "What happened outside? That cannot be one man."

"I don't know," Alejandro said darkly. "But whether there is one of them or twenty, we are going to end this tonight."

40

The dark room slowly came into focus as Otis opened his eyes.

The side of his head was throbbing. He reached up to touch it and realized he couldn't: both of his hands were handcuffed. His eyes followed the cuffs to the chain that wrapped behind him, then to the metal post he was leaning against.

Where in the hell was he?

His mind retraced his steps back to the firefight at the border, to chasing the coyote … to the safe house. Then nothing. He must have been knocked cold and taken inside.

He looked around the low-lit room: a run-down couch and a few folding chairs were the only furniture; there was a doorway at the far end to his left and a lone window to the left of the doorway. The faux tile floor beneath him was worn and filthy, and it had begun to separate and curl up along many of the seams. He also saw the faded remnants of some blood stains that had been hastily wiped from the floor. He turned to see similar traces on the wall behind the post.

He wasn't just a prisoner here; he was going to be tortured, killed – likely both.

The room was empty; none of his captors was present. He needed a plan before whoever was holding him returned.

As that thought crossed his mind, he heard movement just beyond the doorway. He looked up to see a young man, shorter than he was and slight of build, enter the room. As the man passed into the low light, Otis saw that it was the coyote he'd chased across the border, the same one from the attack at South Fitchburg.

When the coyote noticed that Otis had come to, he stopped in his tracks, startled, then turned back toward the doorway for a moment, hesitant.

Otis knew two things in that instant: he knew there was no one else in the house; that for some reason, the coyote had been left there alone with him. He also knew that the coyote represented his best chance to get out of this: he could tell, just by observation, that the kid had no stomach for the business he'd gotten himself involved in and didn't have it in him to kill anyone. Maybe he could somehow use this to his advantage.

He decided to ask the question that had been burning in his mind since seeing the coyote at the river.

"What do you think you're doin'?" he said simply.

The coyote almost jumped where he stood, clearly not expecting his captive to talk. "Wh-what?"

"What are you doin' here," Otis said, "with these people. Doin' this. I don't know you from Adam. But it doesn't take much to see that you're ... not like anyone else in your line of work."

"What's that supposed to mean?" the coyote said.

"It means," Otis leaned forward a bit, pulling taut the chains that tied him to the post, making the coyote take a step back, "that you don't look like a killer. Don't think you got it in ya. That you're in over your head with the people who're around ya, and you don't know how to dig yourself out."

"You don't know what you're talking —" the coyote began.

"So the question in my mind is," Otis interrupted him, "what'd make someone like you, get involved in somethin' like this."

"That's none of your business," the coyote said.

"Somethin' personal, then," Otis said. "Wasn't your choice. A debt owed, someone's got somethin' on ya, somethin' like that. Am I right?"

"No, it's —" the coyote began, then: "Listen. The others are just outside that door. Don't make me go get them. You'll be sorry."

Otis shook his head. "No, I don't believe they are," he retorted. "Matter of fact, I think it's just you an' me in this house. And I also think you're dreadin' when the others come back, fer a lot o' reasons."

"You don't know anything," was all the coyote could say.

"I know that when they come back, they're gonna kill *me*," Otis said matter-of-factly. "And you know it, too. And worse, you're gonna have to watch.

Or maybe — maybe they'll even make you do it. An' I don't think you wanna watch it, much less be involved."

The coyote said nothing.

Otis allowed a moment to let his statement sink in, then broke the silence: "You ever kill a man before?"

The coyote hesitated, then finally said, "Yes."

"You sure about that?" Otis questioned. "Killers don't hesitate, an' you just did."

The coyote did not respond.

"The thing about killin' a man," Otis said. "It's one of the few things you can never take back. Can't undo. Don't matter why or how you did it. Once it's done, it's done. No turnin' back. You ever had that feelin'?"

"Don't — don't ask me any more questions," the coyote said tersely.

"Then I'll just say one more thing," Otis said. "Whatever's gonna happen next, when those men walk through that door, you don't wanna be a part of it. You might even wanna stop it. I can tell it on you. An' right now, you're the only one who *can* stop it.

"That point of no return," Otis continued, "we're not there yet. I can't promise that I can help you get out o' whatever mess you've gotten yourself into, but I can promise you this: if you let me go, my blood won't be on your hands.

"An' you never know," Otis added. "When they're done with me, they might kill you, too. After all, you're the one I followed here. Don't take a genius to figure that out, so I'll bet it won't be long before the others do, too."

The coyote said nothing, clearly contemplating Otis' last statement. Then he turned to leave, stopping at the doorway. "There's — there's nothing I can do," he finally said, and disappeared from view.

In the next room, Enrique sat down in a worn folding chair, his head spinning around the comments that the border patrol agent had just made. Would they really make him murder the man in cold blood? Would they then kill him for leading the man back to their safe house?

And this was not just any man; this was the man who had saved his life.

And if they killed him — what would happen to his mother and Juanita? They could not survive without him.

But if he let the gringo free, what would his uncle to do him then? And to his family? He would kill them all, without question.

If he made the decision his conscience was leading him to, he would have to get to his family before his uncle did. Take them far away, out of his uncle's reach.

But where was that, exactly? His uncle was one of the most powerful men in all of Mexico. There was nowhere in the entire country that his family would be safe.

So that was the answer: he would do nothing. He *could* do nothing.

But perhaps he could get his family to safety before his uncle reached them. There was always a chance. If he did nothing tonight, there was no chance the man who had saved his life could avoid a terrible death.

And right now, he was the only one who could stop that from happening.

He had no idea how long before the others would return. But he knew that once they did, he would have to go along with whatever they had in store for the gringo. He would not be able to do anything to save the man.

His window of time was shrinking.

He glanced at the wall and saw a small keychain hanging on a hook.

Otis kept his head down in the grim silence, waiting for the sound of foot-steps to return. The house had been deathly quiet for several moments now; whatever the coyote was doing in the other room, he was doing it very quietly.

He'd begun this foolhardy chase into Mexico with the sole purpose of bringing the coyote back with him: he'd been certain that the coyote was in-volved in the border attack, and Otis would get him back into the states for the authorities to interrogate him.

But now that he'd spoken to the man, seen him face to face and looked into his eyes, he knew the coyote was nothing more than a pawn in the whole thing; he could tell that circumstances had somehow not only put him at the border checkpoint that morning but had also sucked him into whatever life he was now forced to lead.

A few moments later, the footsteps returned. Slow. Hesitant. Otis raised his head to see the coyote's silhouette in the doorway. He stood still for a moment, saying nothing, then: "What will you do if I let you go?"

"I'll run," Otis said. "Just like you should."

The coyote did not move. "They know — they know where my family is."

"Then you should get them away from here," Otis said deliberately. "Far away."

The coyote took a few steps forward. Otis could see the key ring in his hands.

"There is no safe place for us to go," the coyote admitted, taking another step forward. "They are everywhere in Mexico. They will find us."

"Mexico's a helluva big country," Otis replied. "I'll bet there're places that'll allow you to get out of this life. You're taking a good first step right now."

"My sister is only a child. My mother is in the hospital," the coyote said, his voice cracking slightly. He took a few more steps forward. "I don't know what we will do."

Otis didn't understand why the coyote was telling him all this. "There are always options," he finally said, keeping a close eye on how far the coyote was from him.

"Will you help us?" the coyote finally said.

This took Otis by surprise. "How can *I* help you?" he asked.

"You can get us into America," the coyote said hopefully, stepping toward Otis a bit more. "Help us get across the border. We will be safe there."

"An' how do you expect me to do that," Otis replied flatly.

"You work on the border," the coyote said, stopping dead in his tracks. "You can get us across."

"I'm afraid I can't do that," Otis said plainly.

The coyote hesitated, then: "If you don't help me ... I won't let you go."

It was already clear to Otis that the coyote was trying to use setting him free as leverage for help in getting his family into the U.S., but Otis knew he could never agree to that. If he agreed, he would be lying. And to him, lying was no different than begging for his life. He had survived months in a Taliban prison camp without once begging for his life; he wasn't about to start now. Even in this desperate situation.

And it didn't matter now, anyway. The coyote had come close enough.

Enrique could not understand the gringo's motivations: Enrique was the only one in the world who could set him free. All he wanted in return was safe passage for his family to the United States. But the man was refusing.

Enrique now knew the gringo was right: once Alejandro and the others returned, they were both as good as dead. They had to get out of there.

But the man was giving him no choice: if he didn't agree to Enrique's demands, he would be left chained to the post — left to die. He must have understood this.

Enrique had just begun turning to leave the room when suddenly, his legs were cut out from underneath him: a powerful leg had whipped out and tripped him up, forcing him to fall hard on his back, directly within the gringo's reach. The man wasted no time, wrapping both legs around Enrique's arms, then pulling Enrique into a headlock in one blinding motion. Before Enrique understood what had hit him, he was gasping for air in the man's tightening grasp.

"Hand me the keys," the gringo said. "I don't wanna hurt you. Hand me the keys and I'll let you go. Don't, and I'll break your neck. Understand?"

Enrique could not breathe; the man's long, powerful arms, even though bound by handcuff and chain, had found their way around his neck and were squeezing him with such terrible strength that he thought he would pass out at any moment. He tried to pull his hands up to counter the vise-like grip on his neck, but they had been immobilized, also caught up in the gringo's tremendous grip. He kicked and flailed his legs about wildly, trying to wrench himself free, but it was no use. The man was too strong, and he seemed to know exactly what he was doing. It was clear to Enrique that the gringo could and would easily break his neck if he didn't comply.

Somehow, inexplicably, Enrique realized he had kept his grip on the keys. He instinctively made to move his arm to hand them to the gringo but was reminded he could not. "Okay, okay," he said. "They are in my right hand."

"Drop 'em on the floor," the American said. "Where I can reach 'em."

Enrique did so, and as the man reached down to get them, he loosened his grip on Enrique's neck and arms. Realizing that this was his only chance, Enrique pulled an arm free and jabbed a fist upward at the man. It was a lucky shot, connecting with the gringo's chin, clearly taking him by surprise while he was focused on collecting the keys. His grip loosened further, enough so that Enrique could wriggle free. In a panic, he clambered to his feet and ran from the room.

As Enrique rounded the corner, heading toward the back of the house, the back door flew open in front of him, forcing him to stop cold in his tracks. A lone figure appeared in the doorway, and Enrique immediately recognized the hateful, tattooed visage of Lobo, a look of genuine surprise on his face.

In the other room, Otis's chin smarted from the jab he'd taken, but he didn't have the luxury of allowing himself time to recover. He didn't know whether the coyote was running blindly away or going for a gun, but he had to assume the latter.

As he sat up, he heard a door fly open in another room. His initial thought was that the coyote had high-tailed it and run, but then he heard the voices: the others had returned. There was no time; he needed to make his escape now.

He located the key ring and gathered it up in his hands, quickly trying each key he thought would fit the cuffs. On the third try, he hit pay dirt, and the cuffs dropped from his hands as he stood up.

From the other room came shouting, followed by the sound of a pleading voice, all in Spanish tongue. Then came a crashing sound, followed by a second, much louder than the first. Otis surveyed the room for an escape route: the lone window was too small for him to climb through, and there was only the one doorway, which led directly toward the source of the noise. If he was going to escape, he would have to go through whatever was going on in the next room.

Enrique was caught off guard by the sheer sight of Lobo, whom he'd forgotten about as soon the shooting had begun back at the riverbank. From that moment, he'd had no idea whether the enforcer had survived or not. Now that he knew, a terrible fear surged through him, freezing the blood in his veins.

Lobo's clothes were spotted with blood; a thick coating of it oozed down his left arm, where Enrique saw that a bloody tourniquet had been tied tightly around his bicep. His eyes were wide, manic; he looked as if he was ready to tear something to pieces, and Enrique was the only one in his view.

Enrique took a step back. Lobo lunged forward at him, grabbing him by the throat.

"You," he snarled into Enrique's face. "Coward. You abandoned the group!"

"No," Enrique gasped, choking from Lobo's firm grip. "I-I –"

"Shut up," Lobo roared, throwing Enrique hard to the floor. "You are only a coyote because of your bloodline. But your uncle is not here to protect you now!"

Lobo swung a leg hard into Enrique's stomach, lifting him off the floor with the force of the kick. Crying out in pain, Enrique turned over just in time to see the wooden chair being swung down upon him, and he rolled out of the way just as the chair shattered on the floor. He kept rolling as a second projectile smashed onto the floor, this time a small table. He tried to crawl away, tried to get his arms and legs underneath him, but the moment he stopped rolling, Lobo kicked him hard again, this time connecting with the back of his head. The room spun on him; spots flashed in Enrique's vision as he saw Lobo withdraw the hunting knife from his thigh holster, tossing it from one hand to another.

He screamed out in terror, closing his eyes as Lobo swung the hunting knife down on him. But just as he felt the blade touch his skin, he felt something just as quickly pull it away, then came the sound of a loud crack from above him.

He opened his eyes to see that the gringo had entered the room, and was now locked in a struggle with Lobo.

Seconds earlier, Otis positioned himself to get a look at what was happening in the room next to his. What met his eyes came as both a shock and a relief: while he'd feared that many had returned to the safe house, he was relieved to see only two men in the room: the coyote and a newcomer, dressed in sleeveless black fatigues and covered in tattoos. But shock quickly set in when it became clear that the second man was trying to kill the coyote.

Otis turned back to the shadows, trying to think. He didn't understand what was happening or why, but he knew two things: first, the tattooed man clearly represented the larger threat to Otis's escape. Second, if Otis didn't do something, the coyote would be dead in a matter of seconds.

The newcomer had pushed the coyote to the doorway just a few feet from where Otis crouched. Otis considered his options – then he saw the hunting blade. As the man swung it down on the coyote, Otis instinctively kicked at the man's arm, knocking the knife out of his hands and sending it across the room. He then immediately followed up with a straight jab to the man's face, connecting directly with his nose, sending the sharp, cracking sound of breaking bone and cartilage throughout the room. The man staggered backward, and Otis wasted no time, following with an uppercut to the man's chin, then a straight kick to his chest, sending him crashing into the far wall.

Otis checked to make sure that the tattooed man appeared to be out cold, then he reached down and pulled the coyote up by the hand. "I'm gettin' outta here," he said. "I suggest you do, too."

The coyote seemed to want to say something, but he simply heeded Otis' advice, heading directly for the back door, Otis following close behind. As he reached the door, the coyote turned back toward Otis, then exclaimed, "Look out!"

Otis turned in time to see the tattooed man advancing on him, hunting knife in hand. There was no time to react; the man had raised the blade when from behind Otis came a long, narrow object that swung out toward the assailant, throwing off his attack.

It was all Otis needed. He quickly dodged the blade and then grabbed the attacker firmly by the knife-wielding wrist, overpowering the tattooed man's own strength and turning the blade directly into his chest, where it sank cleanly into its new target. The tattooed man's eyes grew wide, then empty, as his life rapidly drained from him. Otis held the wrist tightly, supporting the man's full dead weight for another long second before letting him drop to the floor.

Otis turned to see the coyote, eyes wide in shock. He was holding out a broomstick, the long, narrow object that had been put between Otis and the hunting knife seconds ago. It was the one thing, along with the coyote's quick thinking, that had saved Otis from certain death.

There was no time to reflect on what had just happened. They needed to leave before any others arrived.

"Come on," Otis said. "There's gotta be a truck or somethin' you can take to get outta here."

Otis pushed through the back door, the coyote following him, into the back yard. Otis spotted an all-terrain vehicle parked about twenty feet beyond the edge of the house.

Then he saw the lights in the distance. A vehicle was approaching.

Then he remembered the dogs. As quickly as they came to mind, he saw two of them approaching from the perimeter fence. He had no idea where the third was.

"Shit," Otis waved over to the coyote. "C'mon. We got trouble headed our way, and lots of it."

Otis ran over to the ATV, the coyote quickly catching up with him. He hoped that the keys had been left in it, because they were now too far from the house to avoid the dogs.

He hopped on and praised his luck: the keys were in the ignition. He started it up as the coyote climbed in behind him. The dogs were almost upon them, and the headlights drew closer in the distance.

"Hold on tight," Otis yelled back to the coyote. "Gonna be a bumpy ride."

He cranked on the throttle just as the first dog reached them, the bike lurching forward with a jolt. He heard the coyote cry out, wrapping his arms around Otis's midsection; the dog must have gotten a hold of his pant leg.

"Just hang on tight as you can," Otis yelled out over the rumbling motor. "We'll shake 'im."

Otis cranked the throttle one more time and took a hard left turn toward the fence. Out of the corner of his eye, he saw the dog roll away into a cloud of dust. He straightened the bike out, heading for the driveway, the only opening he'd seen.

"Aren't you going to turn the lights on?" the coyote called out from behind him.

"Can't risk bein' seen," Otis said. "We just gotta get clear o' here for now. The terrain's pretty rough, so just hang on best you can. Gonna be some big bumps."

They cleared the fence and Otis took another sharp turn, away from the driveway to avoid being seen by the oncoming headlights. Within seconds, they were at least out of the headlights' line of sight. But not in the clear just yet.

Otis became quickly aware that he'd completely lost his orientation after getting knocked cold. With the moon obscured by clouds, and having no access to a compass, he had no way of telling which way was north or south. And in his haste to track the coyote, he'd failed to landmark anything to give him any sense of direction.

He would have to figure out a way home later. His immediate need was to get away from that stash house and avoid being detected.

The terrain was beyond bumpy; even with Otis's skill at driving all-terrain vehicles, he almost knocked them both off the bike several times.

Long moments later, they finally reached an even surface. A road. It was unpaved but flat enough that Otis could finally pick up some speed. He looked back and saw that the headlights had reached the stash house. They had gotten out of there not a moment too soon.

The coyote holding tight behind him, Otis switched on the ATV's headlights, heading away from the stash house as fast as the bike could carry them.

41

The dim lights of Vasquez stash house glowed an orange hue against the night sky as Alejandro neared the fence.

The hunt for whoever had been behind the attack on the Garage weighed most on his mind, but he had his orders: get the gringo and nephew back to *Santa Maria*.

Hernandez had joined him for this trip, mostly as added muscle to help control the gringo, since he knew that the Jackal's worthless nephew wouldn't be of any help.

He noticed the dogs running around frantically, circling the edge of the driveway. He got out of the truck and heard them growling and whimpering, which they only did when something was terribly wrong.

He reached into the truck and removed the AR-15 from the back seat. He motioned for Hernandez to take the house's right flank, while he took the left.

When he came around the rear of the house, he noticed that the back door lay wide open.

He raised the AR-15 and approached the door. He saw Hernandez come into view from the other side of the house. He motioned for him to stay close to the wall.

He rounded into the back room of the house. The room looked like there had been a struggle, with pieces of smashed wooden furniture littering the floor.

Then he glanced directly down and saw the blood. His eyes followed the trail of deep red to his right and saw the body on the floor. It was Lobo: a knife had been driven straight into his chest.

He looked closer in the dim light and saw a small amount of blood still trickling from the wound. Lobo had been killed not moments ago.

Without hesitation, Alejandro swept the AR-15 into the room where the gringo was being kept.

The man was gone.

He must have somehow broken free and killed Lobo during his escape.

But what about the nephew? Alejandro assumed he had to have been killed also, his body somewhere within the house.

They quickly swept the remainder of the house. No sign of the boy.

Had the gringo taken him hostage?

He went to the post. He saw the handcuffs on the floor and kneeled down to examine them, when his knee hit something hard and sharp.

It was the key ring to the stash house, including the key to the cuffs on the post.

The gringo had been set free.

There was no one else in the house but the nephew until Lobo had arrived. No intruder could have gotten past the dogs.

The Jackal would never believe him, but he had to assume that the nephew was somehow involved. He saw no other logical explanation.

He would need to inform the Jackal immediately.

42

Dunlap was examining digital images of the Juarez region when exhaustion finally began to set in.

It was well past midnight. He heard Armstrong's footsteps coming up behind him, returning from his closed-door meeting with Collins's Defense Council.

"Updates?" he heard Armstrong ask as the footsteps stopped to his left.

"Still nothing concrete," Dunlap replied. "We've done several more sweeps with multiple drones. Teams are still poring through the images they took — we have hundreds now — looking for any signs of activity from the wreckage, movement in the surrounding area. Nothing real so far. What about contact with the Mexican government?"

"Still nothing," Armstrong replied. "The President has had Secretary Braun doing everything but going down there himself and knocking on doors. But after the assassination attempt, his contacts either don't know anything or aren't talking."

"And no change to the President's position," Dunlap guessed.

"And we shouldn't expect one, either," Armstrong said. "At least until some form of meaningful contact has been made, or we have confirmation of survivors."

"As expected," Dunlap nodded grimly. "So — we keep looking from the air."

"What else do you know about our possible survivor?" Armstrong asked.

"Heat signature disappeared shortly after it was discovered," Dunlap said. "Because it was in a deep ravine, we can't send one in for a closer look or we'll lose the remote signal. One of ours or no, we have to assume whoever it was has terminated."

At that moment, one of the lead analysts, a bespectacled, buzz-cut kid named Stewart, briskly approached Dunlap with a tablet in hand.

"Sir," he said, "I think you'll want to have a look at this."

Both men leaned in as Stewart pulled up text and images on the screen.

"We've been monitoring activity on land lines and cell towers in the Juarez region," he began, "and we came upon some chatter that we've traced back to numbers registered to known members of Oropeza's organization — including one that we believe belongs to Oropeza himself.

"I have the transcripts here, just back from the translators," Stewart went on as he removed a flash drive from the tablet and stuck it into a slot on the map table.

The text appeared in large block letters on the map table's enormous screen, detailing a string of conversations between Oropeza and one of his top lieutenants.

"You can see that much of the chatter seems to center around someone they refer to as 'the gringo,' as well as an attack on what we suspect is one of their facilities — it translates loosely to 'garage,'" Stewart explained. "They also refer to a nephew — we believe they're talking about Oropeza's nephew, the same one from the border attack two weeks ago. We're still trying to piece together details on much of it — but now that we're locked onto their signals, we can monitor them real-time, and even zero in on their locations."

"So are you suggesting that this 'gringo,' as they call him," Armstrong began, "is who attacked their facility?"

"No, we don't believe so," Stewart answered. "From the transcripts, the aforementioned sounds as if he's being held captive in one of Oropeza's stash houses or bunkers. And timestamps on the conversations suggest that the attack they mentioned happened not only while this individual was in captivity, but also several miles away from wherever he's being held."

"So we're talking about *two* wild cards, here," Dunlap surmised.

"Yes," Stewart agreed.

"But operating separately?" Armstrong questioned.

"We don't know enough to assume anything at this point," Stewart said. "But we'll continue to monitor all activity from these mobile units, and we'll try to pick up other units as they get in contact with the ones we're already tracking."

"Keep up the good work," Dunlap told Stewart.

As Stewart walked away, Armstrong turned to Dunlap.

"I know what you're thinking, Edward," Dunlap interjected before Armstrong could speak a word. "The truth is just as the analyst said: we don't know anything yet. And we're certainly not going to jump to conclusions."

"But you're suspecting the same thing I am, aren't you?" Armstrong cut in.

"*Hoping*, is more like," Dunlap countered.

"But who else could it be?" Armstrong argued. "Tell me of another American, Caucasian, whoever that would be down there in that region that we *wouldn't* know about. Anyone Homeland or CIA ever sent down there has been of Hispanic background in order to blend in. There *is* no one."

"Edward, it could be anyone," Dunlap said. "The attacker could have been just a rival drug gang. The American, just some poor soul who wound up at the wrong place at the wrong time. We have no idea – and not enough intel to draw from. Yet."

"Of course," Armstrong said. "But play along with me. If it *is* him – if the Specialist somehow survived and is in the field down there –"

"Then the only thing on our minds should be to get him out of there, stat," Dunlap said firmly.

"But if we can find a way to communicate with him," Armstrong suggested, "there's still a chance we can salvage some of the mission."

Dunlap's expression became angry. "I'm going to pretend I didn't hear any of that," he said.

"Jack, listen to me," Armstrong began, "Secretary Collins and I understand where you're coming from. But the fact of the matter is, we've already expended a great deal of blood and treasure on this mission. If we have one – maybe two – of our men still down there –"

"I can't believe what I'm hearing," Dunlap said. "Are you saying you've discussed this possibility with Collins?"

"He and the President green-lit this mission," Armstrong said. "That means that we need to keep them in the loop on every development we come across. Collins feels – and I agree – that if we have an opportunity to take down the target while the mission is still in play, we should seize it."

"The mission *is* no longer in play, Edward," Dunlap countered. "We have men down. No communication. Hell, we don't even know if the Mexican President is still alive. This is nothing short of foolhardy."

"But if any of our men are alive and able," Armstrong said calmly, "they've trained for the mission, they've trained for contingencies. Even for something like this. You know this better than anyone, Jack. And let's not forget that we have Second Squad prepared for the insert-and-rescue. But you know that they're also prepared to complete the mission itself – you authorized this yourself."

"And the reality is," Armstrong continued, "that there is an imminent threat *now*. It's the reason we accelerated the insertion timeline to tonight. Another insertion would take weeks to prepare for. A new strategy would have to be drawn up. Soldiers trained. Who knows what the target has planned for tomorrow, as the intel suggests, or even after tomorrow? By the time we get another opportunity, more innocent American lives could be taken. If we have boots on the ground, we have to act *now*."

"But the fact remains," Dunlap maintained, "that we have no idea who – if anyone – is alive down there. Everyone but the Specialist is carrying comms equipment. Why haven't we heard from anyone?"

"It could be for a number of reasons," Armstrong said. "The equipment was damaged when the helos were attacked, the most likely. And as far as survivors, I'm talking about being prepared to act *if* it turns out we have any down there. Until we get the intel, we won't know, but we need to be ready to act if there are."

Dunlap exhaled hard. "What you're talking about here ... sending more men in when we've already been taken off-guard once, and we have no clue what other surprises may be waiting for us down there ... you might as well put them all in a firing line right now."

"But we know the risks of doing nothing," Armstrong said. "The enemy has already attacked us once. He knew about our retaliation and was even prepared for it. And, most important, another threat is imminent. Things have escalated, Jack. If the opportunity is still there, we need to seize it."

"You're betting on a very faint possibility," Dunlap said. "And if any of my men are still alive ... the thought of putting them in any further danger ..." his voice trailed off.

"I know these are your men, Jack," Armstrong said. "But it's *our* mission. And ultimately, it's neither your call nor mine. The President and Collins are discussing it right now, and I expect Collins to convince the President to give the 'go' order if it becomes available to us."

"Well, then, I suppose it's already decided," Dunlap said flatly.

"Right now, the priority is determining who may have survived, and re-establishing contact not only with them, but with the Mexican government,"

Armstrong said. "If we get to that point, you need to be ready to execute the plan for re-insertion."

"If it gets to that point, then it's no longer a covert insert-and-extract," Dunlap said darkly. "So we'd better be ready for all-out war."

43

It was a few minutes before one o'clock in the morning when Javier Oropeza's satellite phone rang once again. It was Alejandro.

"Jefe," Alejandro began. His voice was tense. "The boy and the gringo. They are not at Vasquez. They are gone."

"How is that possible?" the Jackal snarled.

"The shackles were unlocked," Alejandro said. "The keys on the floor. Someone let the gringo go. And Lobo is dead."

"Lobo is dead? How?" Javier said.

"Stabbed in the chest, his own knife," Alejandro explained. "He –"

"Where is Enrique?" the Jackal said.

"Gone," Alejandro replied. "No one is here. We've searched everywhere."

"The gringo must have taken him," Javier surmised. "Find them. And I want the gringo alive."

"Jefe," Alejandro's voice came across the line, sounding hesitant, "there was no one else here, and the shackles were unlocked. Someone let the gringo free."

"Are you suggesting," Oropeza challenged, "that Enrique was somehow involved?"

"No ... I don't know ... I'm only trying to understand –"

"You don't need to understand anything," the Jackal barked. "All you need to do is follow orders. Now find them. Alive. And bring them to *Santa Maria*."

"Of course, Jefe," Alejandro replied.

"Have you any updates on the men who attacked the Garage?" Oropeza added.

"Nothing yet," Alejandro said. "I have eight field commanders out looking, but none of them has even seen a sign. And witnesses at the Garage said there was only one of them, so he will be even harder to find."

"If what you say you saw at the Garage is true," Oropeza said, "that cannot be the work of only one man. There are more. Keep the men looking. Find them. And when you do, bring them to *Santa Maria* as well."

"Yes, Jefe," Alejandro said.

Javier hung up the phone and sat back in his chair, deep in thought.

He did not like Alejandro's assertion about his nephew and the gringo's escape. Enrique was not many things, but if he was anything, he was obedient. He was loyal. And his loyalty was always to family. He would never do anything that he knew would go against his uncle's wishes.

But if what Alejandro said was true — that the house was otherwise empty, that no one else *could* have released the gringo — it cast a shadow of doubt in his mind. And a shadow of doubt had always been more than enough to convince him to take precautions.

He knew exactly where to begin.

44

The man in black walked across the barren desert landscape, his mind spinning with each step he took.

He had no idea which direction he was headed or how long he'd been going.

The face of each man he'd killed remained fresh in his mind, as if somehow he'd taken a mental snapshot of their expressions in the instant he'd ended their lives. Now, the terrified visages of all eight rotated in the forefront of his mind as if on some macabre turntable, the red hue of blood filling out the background.

He was not concerned by how easy it had been for him to physically kill each of them. No; it was how natural the acts felt that alarmed him. His strength and speed, which seemed to increase tenfold when engaged in conflict, were exhilarating; but what he found even more exhilarating were the violent acts themselves he'd committed – it was an urge that built upon itself with each neck he snapped, each bone he shattered. As he recalled each with vivid imagery in his mind, he had to suppress a smile. How could someone take such joy in doing such terrible things?

It should have been a curse, but in the dark corners of his mind, it almost felt like some kind of blessing, some kind of … gift.

He tried not to dwell on the conflict that raged in his mind over his doing such things and to focus more on understanding who he was and what he was doing here. Finding answers to those questions would surely give him guidance on everything else.

He saw yet another set of lights in the distance. A house. Perhaps they would tell him where he was and where he could find medical attention. Medical attention he was no longer sure he even needed.

He began walking toward the house when he heard something approaching from behind. It was an engine, still far off in the distance, but gaining volume quickly. He could see the headlights break over the high ridge about fifty meters behind him, one of them brighter than the other, bouncing with every bump and dip the vehicle encountered. With nothing else to be seen across this barren landscape, he had to assume that the vehicle was headed in the direction of the house.

The vehicle drew closer. With the bright headlights shining on him, he couldn't make out who was inside, but he could tell it was a large pickup truck.

The truck slowed to a crawl as it approached, then stopped completely.

Unsure of what to do, he stood before the shining lights for a long second, then decided to raise his arms high in the air to indicate he was no threat.

BANG. The first bullet missed his leg by inches as the flashpoint appeared atop the cabin; the second grazed his left shoulder.

Losing his footing on the rocky ground, he stumbled backward, falling on his back. He quickly regained his footing and launched himself into the air, leaping out of harm's way as more bullets sliced into the spot where he'd stood.

Arturo Nava's orders had been to lead his squad to stash house E, where he would relieve the squad of enforcers currently staked out there, and send them out on patrol. All patrols had one directive: to find the gringos that had torn up the Garage and bring them back to *Santa Maria* alive, so that the Jackal could make an example of them.

They only had a description of one of them: a small gringo in torn black clothing.

With Gutierrez in the cab with him and Gomez and Rodriguez riding in the truck bed, he'd combed this stretch of desert for the past twenty minutes or so, his men looking for any sign of the perpetrators.

The moon had been bright earlier, but clouds had settled in, and now the far-reaching dark did not allow him to see much beyond the high beams of his headlights.

They had just cleared a ridge near stash house E when something caught Gutierrez's attention.

"I see something up ahead," Gutierrez said. "Movement. Off to the right."

Then, Nava noticed it, too — a lone man, standing about thirty meters ahead of them, watching them as they approached.

Nava slowed the truck as they came closer. The man wore what looked like black military fatigues, torn and tattered in several places. He was covered in blood. But even with the blood, it was clear that the man was a gringo.

He had no idea if there were any others or if the man was alone, but they had him; he was not going to escape.

"Gomez," he called through the cab's open back window, "two shots. Knees. On my signal."

At about ten meters' distance, Nava stopped the truck completely. As he did so, the man did something completely unexpected: he put his hands up high in the air, as if surrendering.

"Now," he ordered.

As Gomez fired, the man stumbled backward and fell.

Then, inexplicably, he disappeared.

"Find him," Nava ordered his men. "And fan out. There are others who have to be nearby. Shoot to wound unless given no choice."

But before anyone could make a move, the truck rocked with the weight of something hitting it. Nava turned his head to see movement in the truck bed, then he felt blood hit the side of his face as he heard Rodriguez's gut-wrenching scream. Then Gomez cried out, before a smashing sound against the truck bed cut his screams to silence.

Gutierrez had turned toward the back window and began firing his AK-47 blindly into the truck bed, when Nava saw a hand reach through the open passenger window and grab Gutierrez by the neck. He heard Gutierrez's cry cut short, saw his wide eyes roll up into his head as the hand quickly closed around his throat, crushing it. Then, in one swift motion, the hand yanked Gutierrez's limp body out through the open window, disappearing into a sea of black outside.

Nava did not hesitate; he floored the gas pedal, causing the truck to lurch forward, bouncing up and down along the rocky landscape, directly toward stash house E. He had no idea what had just hit his men, but getting to the house was his only chance.

As the truck rocked with every mound and trench it encountered, he fumbled for his mobile phone, hit speed dial to Alejandro's number, and issued the distress call: "Nava, approaching stash house E. Being ambushed. All my men are gone. Send help – now!!"

He could hear Alejandro's voice come through the other end, but there was too much static to make out what he was saying.

Then the phone flew from his hand as the truck hit a deep trench, causing the entire vehicle to almost topple over. Then he realized: he hadn't hit anything – the truck was *being* hit by something, rammed from the side, rocking it up onto two wheels.

He stood on the gas pedal, ignoring the terrain, trying to gather as much speed as possible in hopes of outrunning his pursuer. But as he neared the stash house, the truck was again rammed from the side, once again going up onto two wheels. However, this time the vehicle did not regain its balance. It rolled onto its side and then flipped over completely, sending Nava spilling inside the cab, his face smashing into the ceiling as the truck came to a rocking halt.

Nava lay on the truck's ceiling, fighting to stay conscious. He wiped blood from his forehead. He saw his right hand dangling but could not feel it; what he *could* feel was the intense pain shooting out from his twisted ankle. He tried to move, but the pain overpowered him. It was as if he was pinned down.

He turned his head to peer out the windshield. Even though his vision had blurred, and white spots danced before his eyes, he could see the rear of the stash house only about ten meters ahead. The crash had killed the engine, but the headlights remained on, bathing the scene before him in an eerie white light. He had reached the back yard, mere inches from crashing the barbed wire fence that circled the perimeter.

He noticed the three dogs approach the fence, then saw the back door fly open. Four of the Jackal's enforcers emerged, all carrying assault rifles. Nava recognized two of the men as Lopez and Maldonado. Maldonado immediately noticed the truck and gestured to Lopez and another of the men to approach it.

That was when Nava saw the gringo perched on the roof of the house.

He tried to call out, but only a faint wheeze issued from his lips. He cleared his throat, gathered as much air as his battered lungs would allow, and tried again. "Behind you!" he tried to shout, but it was not loud enough. The two men approaching could hear his voice, but clearly they could not make out his words.

He heard his mobile phone ring. He turned to the source of the sound to see that it had also landed on the ceiling, only inches from his head. He reached for it desperately; grabbing hold of it, he peered at the cracked screen and saw that it was Alejandro.

"Nava. You called," came Alejandro's voice. "Do you have him?"

"At stash house E, target is here," Nava panted. "He took out my men, turned over my truck. You have to send more men, now."

"He turned –" Alejandro began, then cut himself short. "Stand your ground. I will have two more squads there in minutes. Shoot to kill if given no choice – do not let him escape."

The line went dead as Alejandro hung up.

Nava peered back up at the roof and saw the gringo still perched there, waiting, like some kind of wraith. Somehow, the dogs had not yet picked up on his scent. He glanced back toward the ground and saw that Lopez and the second man, whom he now recognized as Encarcion, were almost to the truck, rifles pointed at the cab.

"Identify yourself," Lopez called out as he bent to one knee to look into the cab, just on the other side of the fence.

"Nava," he replied. "No time; he's on the roof."

"Nava," Lopez repeated. "What happened to you? *Who* is on the roof?"

"The gringo," Nava shot back. "No time – kill him now!"

As Lopez turned to stand up, Nava could see a set of black boots land next to him, then heard a harsh snapping noise before Lopez immediately dropped to the ground. Gunfire erupted all around as he saw the wraith move with an almost inhuman speed, first to Encarcion's position, who was quickly dropped as well, then to Maldonado and the fourth enforcer. All Nava could do was look on as the wraith quickly and brutally ended their lives.

The dogs had been chasing the wraith ever since he'd dropped from the roof; once he had finished with Maldonado, they were upon him. But instead of killing them, he picked them up with lightning quickness, one by one, and threw them over the barbed-wire fence. The dogs squealed in terror as they flew through the air, but Nava heard each one land, crying as they ran away into the desert.

Then the wraith turned back toward the truck and began walking in Nava's direction.

Nava searched the cab desperately for his rifle. He felt around in the dark with his one good hand, but wherever it was, it was not within arm's reach.

He looked back out of the cab, scanning the yard for the wraith.

But the man had disappeared.

He reached for his cell phone, scooped it off the ceiling, and dialed Alejandro.

As the line was answered, Nava heard a raspy voice outside the open window say, "Hello."

The phone was knocked from his grip as the truck was once again rocked hard, rolling onto its side, sending Nava crashing against the passenger-side door. Then hundreds of shards of glass exploded into the cab as the windshield was smashed in. He cried out as a powerful hand grabbed him firmly by the collar, pulling him out of the cab and face to face with his attacker.

Nava felt frozen in terror as he gazed directly into the dark, demented eyes of the wraith; they were the blackest eyes he had ever seen. It was as if he were staring into the eyes of the Devil himself.

The man was considerably smaller than Nava: at least six inches shorter, with trimmed black hair. He had a thick, muscular frame which still gave no indication of the inexplicable acts of strength Nava had witnessed in the past several moments. The wraith appeared to be half-man, half-beast: he was panting uncontrollably, tiny bits of spittle flying from his mouth, nose curled up like a rabid wolf growling at its prey.

Then the man in black spoke: his harsh, raspy voice issued words that Nava could not understand. English.

He could not utter a response for a brief moment; then the wraith shook him, barking more unfamiliar words into his face. "No – no comprende," was all he could say, his heart pounding, not knowing what the man would do next.

Then Nava heard the sounds: a vehicle was approaching. Two vehicles. His last thought was a sliver of hope as the devil in black turned his attention briefly in their direction; Nava swore he saw the man's scowl fade to reveal the slightest grin as his face was bathed in the oncoming headlights.

Then the devil turned back toward him. The man placed a bloody hand over his face, and the world around him immediately went to black.

45

"Stand your ground," Alejandro barked into his phone moments earlier. "I will have two more squads there in minutes. Shoot to kill if given no choice – do not let him escape."

Alejandro hung up and dialed a second number. "Vasquez," he spoke into the unit. "Take your unit along with Rivera's over to stash house E. The target is engaged with Nava's squad. Get there immediately and take him down."

"Yes, Sir," returned Vasquez's voice through the unit.

"We need to collect the gringo and the boy quickly," Alejandro said to Hernandez as he hung up. "Too many loose ends."

They continued to scour the landscape when Alejandro's phone rang. He glanced down to see that it was Nava again.

He picked up and was about to speak when he heard another voice on the line. It was definitely not Nava's. It was immediately followed by a loud banging noise, a crashing, then the sound of glass shattering. He then heard Nava's voice cry out, along with a shuffling sound, like something being dragged. Then nothing for a few seconds.

Then came the voice again: distant, as if a few feet away, but issued with enough force that Alejandro could make it out clearly.

"Do you know who I am? Tell me!" the voice was speaking English. It was raspy, deep, irate. Almost savage.

A banging sound, then the voice again: "Where am I? Why are you trying to kill me? Tell me or you die. Now!!"

Then Nava's voice came, much feebler, barely audible. Nothing for a few seconds, then a sharp crack. Another shuffling sound. Then nothing again.

Alejandro hung up. It was clear whose voice he had heard. The target had killed Nava and his squad, so now it was up to Vasquez and Rivera's units to eliminate him.

But there was something odd about what the target had said ... something that didn't make sense. He would have to inform the Jackal, once he'd recovered the boy and the gringo.

At that moment, Hernandez spoke up. "Movement ahead."

Alejandro switched on the high-beams and saw two figures running away from a small vehicle up ahead. It was an ATV. He couldn't make out who the men were, but he could see that one was significantly larger than the other — about the size difference between the nephew and the gringo.

Alejandro accelerated and then swung the truck around, cutting the targets off. He threw the truck into Park, grabbed the AR-15, and got out.

In the high-beams, it was immediately clear that they'd found who they were looking for. Both men raised their arms above their heads as Alejandro stood before them, the AR-15 pointed at them.

46

"What in hell do you think you're doing, boy?" Alejandro quickly advanced on Enrique.

Moments earlier, Enrique and Otis were motoring across the desert on an ATV they'd stolen from the stash house, when the bike began to cough and sputter, until the motor completely died, and they coasted to a halt. The gringo tried to restart it once, twice, a third time – to no avail. It had run out of gas.

Then, the lights appeared on the horizon. They tried to run, but there was no place to run to. The vehicle had seen them and quickly caught up to them.

Alejandro lunged forward, pulling him up by the collar so they were face to face. "Do you think your uncle can protect you from *this*?" he snarled. "Once I tell him what I've seen here, what do you think he'll do?"

Enrique tried to mutter something, but couldn't.

"I was at the stash house," Alejandro went on. "I saw Lobo dead. The keys by the post. It wasn't hard to figure out what happened. And it won't take much to convince the Jackal that *you* were involved."

"There's no need to harm the boy," the gringo suddenly chimed in, using broken Spanish. "He was standing guard. I broke free, killed your man, and took this one hostage with me."

Enrique's gaze moved from Otis back to Alejandro, who looked surprised by the gringo's interruption. Alejandro said nothing; he simply pulled a large pistol from a holster in his belt, strode around the large American so that he was directly behind him, and pointed the gun at the back of his head.

The American remained still, keeping his hands high in the air, not saying a word. His expression was stoic, almost calm, in a way that Enrique did not understand. Either he had faced many situations like this one before, or he had no idea of the gravity of their predicament.

"There's no point in lying," Alejandro said to the American. "Neither of you will walk away from this alive."

Then, without another word, he smashed the butt end of the pistol into the back of Otis's head, sending him falling forward, unconscious.

Alejandro directed his gaze back at Enrique. "You're lucky the Jackal wants you both alive," he said.

"Get in the truck," he prodded Enrique with the nose of the pistol. "Front seat. Hernandez, load the gringo into the back and keep your sidearm on him."

Once they were all in the truck, Alejandro retrieved his mobile phone from the dash. "I'm calling your uncle, then we're going back to *Santa Maria*," he said. "When we arrive, I wouldn't expect a warm welcome."

47

Dunlap was drawing up insertion scenarios on the map table when he heard Stewart's voice come from behind him.

"Sir," the young analyst said urgently, "we have something."

Having heard Stewart's tone, Armstrong sidled up to where Dunlap was standing.

"What've you got?" Dunlap said, turning from the table.

"We'd been continuing to monitor chatter among Oropeza's field commanders," Stewart began. "And we picked up an anomaly. It might be one of ours."

"Who?" Armstrong pressed.

"We're running voice-recognition right now," Stewart said. "The audio isn't perfect, and the dialogue isn't making much sense. But the voice is speaking English."

Stewart plugged a USB drive from his tablet into the map table. Menus popped up on the massive surface, and Stewart opened a file with a few swipes and taps of his fingertip. "Listen," he said.

The map table's sound system came to life. Both Dunlap and Armstrong leaned in to make out the audio, but the volume was ample enough to hear.

The first thing they heard was a deep, raspy voice that sounded as if it weren't speaking into the phone but was maybe a few feet away from it. As if speaking to whoever was holding the phone.

The voice simply said, "Hello." English.

Dunlap knew the voice. But he continued to listen intently.

The next sound they heard was a loud banging noise — once, twice — followed by the unmistakable din of glass shattering. Then came another voice, this one different from the first, crying out — the words unrecognizable. Then some more banging, shuffling. Then nothing.

Then the voice again: farther away now: "Do you know who I am? Tell me!"

Then more banging sounds, followed by another missive: "Where am I? Why are you trying to kill me? Tell me or you die. Now!!"

Then the other voice came, quieter, pleading. Stewart pulled the volume bar to the right so they could hear the words.

"No — no comprende," was all the voice said.

Then a sharp crack, followed by more noises, then silence.

"That's all we have," Stewart said, pulling the volume bar to the left again. "We're running it against each of the men and should have the results momentarily."

Dunlap had heard enough to know who the voice belonged to. He turned to Armstrong. "It's him. We need to have Secretary Collins update the President and push for a 'go' order," he said. "We need to get him out of there."

Armstrong paused, rubbing his chin. "I agree. But what do you make of what he said? I'm playing it over in my head, and none of it makes sense."

"I don't know, either," Dunlap concurred, "but given the circumstances, I see that as secondary. We need to have Collins call that meeting with the President and get Second Squad ready for insertion. As soon as we've pinpointed his location, we're going in."

48

Several meters above the rocky desert floor, he sailed through the cooling night air before coming to another landing, then leaping into the air once again.

Despite the exertion he felt from first running – and now leaping – across the massive, uneven landscape, his heart rate had begun to slow, his breathing returning to normal. The violent urges within him had gone. He could once again focus on finding help – to understand where he was, and eventually find someone who knew *who* he was.

He landed on the desert terrain and leapt into the air once again, his powerful leg muscles flexing as he pushed off. At the apex of his leap, he could more clearly see a structure that he'd noticed in his last few jumps. It was an enormous compound with high walls and what appeared to be towers. It appeared to be just a few miles away.

He had no idea who was inside, or how they would respond to a stranger … but it was the biggest sign of civilization he'd seen, so he decided to approach it. Cautiously.

Several moments later, he had reached the outer wall of the compound. He began walking around the high wall in search of a door of some sort. As he went along, the enormity of the structure dawned on him: the wall itself had to be twenty feet high, maybe twenty-five, and it appeared to be at least a few hundred meters from end to end.

What in the world was inside this place? he wondered.

He reached the corner and caught the faint smell of smoke. His gaze moved away from the wall onto the landscape, and he could see the source of the smoke: it was a large object of some kind, twisted into a black, gnarled heap, about a hundred or so meters away. He could see a few small, faint trails of smoke rising from it against the night sky, too faint to have been seen from afar. Whatever it was, it had been burning before, but no longer was.

As he neared the blackened mass, he realized that it was not one object but two.

The darkness had made it harder to make out, but when he was about twenty meters away, it became clear that the two piles of wreckage had been helicopters. Even though the blades were gone, he recognized the basic structure of the machines: the long, sleek shape, the rotor up top, the remnants of the tail.

But what had happened to them?

He reached the first helicopter. The cockpit was completely destroyed, obliterated by what must have been a direct hit by something big. His eyes moved to the second helicopter and saw the same. They had been shot down, beyond a shadow of a doubt.

Then he heard a faint sound in the distance.

He looked to the northeast and saw headlights appear, coming around a hillside, headed in his direction.

He ducked behind the helicopter for cover, watching for a moment as the incoming headlights bounded along the uneven terrain.

He glanced up at the compound's high walls once more. He was confident that he could reach the top with a running start, but without knowing how he would land on the other side, it was a risk he wasn't willing to take.

No. If he was going to get inside those walls, that vehicle would show him the way.

49

From deep inside *Santa Maria*, Javier Escondido Oropeza continued to plan. Despite having retrieved the gringo, the allegations of his nephew's involvement troubled him. There was no way the boy could possibly betray him.

And then there were the reports of the growing threat spreading throughout his desert, this menace whom many of his men had called the "devil in black." Oropeza refused to believe that one man – acting alone – had taken out over twenty of his best enforcers, but the four survivors of the Garage attack had all told him they had only seen one man. And none of the men who had encountered the threat had survived to counter that claim.

One man or twenty, this was far too important a night to have such a glaring loose end. Between normal shipment activity and tonight's larger mission, not to mention a full-scale manhunt, his vast resources and manpower were already being tapped. And with this "devil" roaming the desert and taking out his men, his numbers were dwindling rapidly. He had to put a stop to it.

Furthermore, there was the looming threat of the Americans' return. Though he had thwarted their first attempt on *Santa Maria*, he knew that they would be coming for him again, no doubt with a greater show of force. And he could not count on another heads-up from his mole the next time around: the Americans had surely learned their lesson.

At least he already had plans in motion for their return, whenever that would be.

But back to his immediate concern. What he did not understand was where this "devil" had come from, or what was the motivation behind his attacks. The survivors at the Garage had described him as looking like a gringo, but with all of the soot and blood covering him from head to toe, none of them was certain. All had said that he was a smaller man, wearing torn, black clothing.

Why had he spared the packagers after killing all of the enforcers?

Could he have been from a rival cartel? No; Oropeza didn't think so ... not acting alone, at least. Rival cartels quickly identified themselves, to show their prowess. Furthermore, his organization had dismantled every competing cartel in the region. And he would have known if a new one was budding up. On top of all that, rival cartels usually stole from each other's warehouses. Not a single item had been taken from the Garage.

And there was no chance that the man was one of the Americans who had come to attack him, either: he had watched the live feed from the tower cameras. His lookouts had hit both aircraft multiple times with RPGs, resulting in explosions that consumed everything within a ten-meter radius of the helicopters. No one could have survived that.

The man's identity and motivation aside, Oropeza could no longer deny the fact that his current strategy was not working: on two different occasions, his men had the target surrounded and outnumbered. And on both occasions, the man had escaped, killing every single one of his enforcers in the process. He had no idea how the man was able to do this, but the fact remained that he was *doing* it. So a new strategy was needed.

He began to think about each of the encounters that his people had had with the target, piecing together what little detail he had about each. In those details would lie his answer.

His short-range handset beeped. One of his tower lookouts.

"What?" he spoke into the walkie-talkie.

"Aguilar, Tower B, Jefe," the lookout's voice returned, "motion-sensors picked up movement near the downed 'copters. Night-vision scope confirms visual of a man down there. Matches description of our target."

"What is he doing?" Oropeza said.

"Just walking through the wreckage," Aguilar replied. "Almost wandering. And ..." the voice trailed off.

"And?" the Jackal demanded.

"I don't know if this matters, Jefe," the lookout's voice came back pensively, "but from what I'm able to see ... the target looks ... lost. Like he's looking for something."

To Oropeza, that didn't matter. One bullet to the head would end this threat now.

"Do you have the shot?" the Jackal said.

"Yes," Aguilar answered. "But ... one second ... we have visual of an inbound vehicle. Target has taken cover behind one of the downed aircraft."

"Do you still have the shot?" Oropeza asked.

"No. Neither does Tower A," Aguilar replied.

At that moment his satellite phone rang. Alejandro.

"Is that you coming up?" he answered the phone in his other ear.

"Si, Jefe," came Alejandro's voice through the earpiece.

"Slow down, do not call the gate," the Jackal ordered him. "I will handle that. Target is not far from your position. We have a bead on him."

"He is *here?*" Alejandro said, surprised. "Where?"

"I will handle it," the Jackal snapped. "Just follow orders."

"Yes, Jefe," Alejandro replied. "About the target."

"What is it? Speak quickly," Oropeza demanded.

"Something doesn't add up," Alejandro began. "He had an exchange with Nava earlier ... he seemed to know nothing."

"What are you talking about?" the Jackal said impatiently.

"He asked Nava where he was, even *who* he was ... it was like he didn't know," Alejandro said. "Like he'd lost his mind or something."

Oropeza said nothing, just sat back in his chair, absorbing what Alejandro had just told him. Suddenly, the pieces of the puzzle began to fall in place: the target's demeanor by the wreckage ... his questions to Nava ...

He switched to the walkie-talkie. "Keep a bead on the target, but hold your fire," he told Aguilar. "I have an idea."

50

He kept low, staying behind the downed helicopter as the vehicle drew closer.

He glanced along the wall behind him and saw the massive gate about twenty meters away. When the gate opened, he would follow it in, low and close, allowing the bright glow of the headlights to obscure his entry. Once inside, he would find cover.

When the vehicle was about a hundred meters away from the gate, it slowed to a crawl. He could hear the crunching of pebbles and dirt beneath the truck's huge tires.

Thirty meters. A loud clacking noise rang out, followed by the low hum of motors churning to life. The lock had disengaged, and the massive gate began to roll to its left, yawning wide to allow the incoming vehicle to enter.

Ten meters. The wide beams of the truck's headlights had narrowed to the width of the gate, leaving the rest of the wall in darkness.

This was his chance.

He launched into a full sprint toward the gate, reaching the rear of the truck just as it passed through the gate, the massive door starting to roll back to a closed position.

Once he was inside the walls, the first thing that hit him was the bright lights. The tops of the walls around him were lined with strobes, all of them switched on, making the inside of the compound as bright as day.

Unexpectedly, the truck accelerated forward, leaving him exposed. Before he could react, a sharp voice cut through the night air, bouncing off the high walls of the compound. It was speaking clear English.

"Stay where you are," the voice boomed, "and no one will shoot."

As those words were issued, he looked around to see that he was surrounded. At least twenty armed men stood, covering him from every possible angle — many from elevated positions — all pointing automatic rifles directly at him.

Then he saw a man walking toward him, with what appeared to be an AR-15 slung over his shoulder. He was flanked by two men, both carrying rifles as well. He held a megaphone in his left hand. He was tall, with dark hair pulled into a ponytail, and a long goatee that ran wild from his chin. He was dressed in a long black leather coat draped over a white t-shirt and camouflage cargo pants, with heavy black boots.

From the corner of his eye, he saw two men emerge from the truck he'd followed in, followed by a third man, who then heaved a large body from the rear seat and began dragging it across the ground by the arms, toward a nearby building.

He turned his eyes forward again to see that the goateed man had stopped about ten feet from where he stood, regarding him with a curious eye.

"You've created quite a legend for yourself in these lands," his host began, "in just one night. That is no small feat, especially in a region as dangerous as this."

He said nothing in return, keeping his gaze locked on the man before him.

"A man doesn't run rampant through bloodlands such as these unless he is on a mission of some sort ... or in search of something," the man said. "So tell me, senor, what is it you seek?"

He stayed silent for a long moment, then: "Start by explaining why your men were trying to kill me."

The man rubbed his chin. "Yes. Well," he began, "one can never be too careful in my line of work. Enemies, threats at every turn. But I've come to realize that you are not the threat I mistook you for. Which is why I have welcomed you into my home."

"I let myself in."

"Clearly, I was expecting you," the host replied with a broad smile, gesturing to the gunmen surrounding them.

"If you just wanna talk, then why all this?" he said, glancing around as well.

"Your point," the man acknowledged, then glanced around at the gun-men. "Stand down," he commanded them. The men promptly lowered their weapons.

"Better?" the host turned back to him, again a smile upon his face.

"Who are you," he said in return.

"My name is Javier Escondido Oropeza," the man replied. "I own these lands. And you are?" he asked the question in an expectant way, one that suggested that he somehow already knew the answer.

He had no answer, so he offered no response to his host.

Oropeza waited, then nodded slowly. "You see," he finally said, "I believe you don't *know*. Something happened to you. So you must have *many* questions. Yes?"

He stayed silent for a long moment, then simply replied, "Yes."

"Perhaps we can help each other, then," Oropeza said, extending his arms.

"And how would that be?" he said.

"Why don't we step inside and talk," Oropeza gestured to the large structure behind him. "I think ... there are many things we can do together."

51

A black hood had covered Enrique's head seconds after he'd gotten out of the truck. Now that it had been removed, he knew exactly where he'd been taken.

The room itself was exactly as he'd remembered it: a red stone tile floor with red rug at its center, upon which he was kneeling now. The torch-lights burned along the stucco walls, their orange glow illuminating the small room, flickering intermittently, casting moving shadows that filled him with dread. The windows revealed nothing but blackness outside, as if confirming his fear that he would never see anything outside of these walls again. For directly across from him was the large wooden chest, inside which waited a hundred terrible deaths.

His entire body retched. But all that issued from his mouth was hot breath and spittle; his stomach had been empty for several hours now.

"Shut up," the voice snapped from across the small room. He looked up toward his left to see one of his uncle's armed goons standing by the doorway.

He turned the other way to see Otis slumped against the wall. He had begun to move; he was coming to. His wrists were now bound by handcuffs instead of twine.

He looked down at his own wrists to see that the twine around them had been cut, but no shackles had been put on in its place. He could move his arms freely about.

They were mocking him; telling him that he wasn't even worth taking the necessary precautions for.

At that moment, the door opened, and Alejandro strode in. He was accompanied by the other man from the truck: Hernandez, he remembered Alejandro calling him.

Hernandez remained by the door while Alejandro advanced on him.

"I have to admit, boy," Alejandro shook his head, "that your disloyalty has surprised even *me*. Foolhardy as it was, your uncle trusted you. Everyone else knew that you would fail, for lack of a spine, for stupidity, whatever the reason. But *choosing* to fail your uncle? To betray him? You are far more stupid than even I could have imagined."

"Where is my uncle?" was all Enrique could bring himself to say.

"Your uncle has found someone more interesting to talk to," Alejandro said. "But I would be in no rush to see him if I were you. What you have done will not only cost you your life, but also your mother and sister."

"No," Enrique said. "He could never do that. They are innocent; they had nothing to do with this."

This made Alejandro laugh out loud.

"You," he said before another laugh interrupted him, "have no idea who he is, do you? After he's finished with the gringo here, he will do your family – right here, in front of you, before he turns his attention to you."

Without thinking, Enrique lunged at the wooden chest, only to be struck by Alejandro's backhand. His neck snapped back; his head hit the hard stone floor, sending him into a daze. He could taste the blood in his mouth; he'd bitten his lip.

Alejandro stood over him, shaking his head, before kicking Enrique in the midsection. Then a second time, even harder.

"I thought Jefe wanted him unharmed," Enrique heard Hernandez say.

Ignoring Hernandez, Alejandro stood back up and disappeared from Enrique's view, leaving only the white stucco ceiling before him, fading in and out with each wave of intense pain that washed over him.

The door opened, and Enrique could hear Alejandro issuing harsh words to Hernandez, then an order to the guard, before it slammed shut.

52

The clock read 2:15 A.M. on the eastern seaboard when Dunlap heard the distinctive ring of Armstrong's secure line.

Armstrong answered. "Yes, Sir. All right, Sir," was all Dunlap heard him say.

Armstrong hung up, then turned to face Dunlap.

"We have a 'go' order," he said. "The President said he would deal with Vincennes once he knows his status. He wants birds in the air as soon as we've pinpointed the Specialist's location."

"All we needed," Dunlap replied, picking up the phone to call General Norris.

As he hung up, Stewart suddenly approached them.

"Sirs," he said urgently, "we've found him."

"Where?" Armstrong turned to Stewart.

"We just processed a transcript from Oropeza's own mobile unit," Stewart answered. "It confirms that the Specialist is presently at Oropeza's main compound."

"The original L.Z.?" Armstrong said.

"Yes, sir," Stewart replied.

"He's going in to finish the mission," Armstrong concluded.

"We don't know that yet," Dunlap argued, picking up the phone again to call Norris. "But regardless, let's get some boots on the ground and get him out of there."

"And the mission, Jack?" Armstrong said in an assuming tone.

"It's like you said before, Edward," Dunlap replied, "we are still in play."

53

He was led into the structure through a large set of metal doors, which closed automatically behind him once he was inside. A massive steel bar slid across both doors.

Whatever this place was, he thought, it was designed inside and out to withstand even the most comprehensive attack: there were the high walls, the watchtowers, the weaponry all around, even the heavy doors to each of the buildings.

Another thing about the place was certain: even though it was surrounded by a harsh, unforgiving landscape outside, it had every possible luxury on the inside. As he walked with his host, ten armed guards in tow, he noticed the marble floors beneath him, the sculptures and fine art along the walls, the indoor gardens boasting exotic flora and fauna.

They rounded a corner and walked through a doorway, leading them into another large room. The room itself had high ceilings like the others he'd been in thus far, but the first thing he noticed were the guns and weaponry: literally hundreds of firearms, of all shapes and sizes, ranging from small, jewel-encrusted pistols to Gatling guns and RPG launchers. The smaller guns hung on the walls or were mounted inside glass display cases; the larger ones had their own mountings that rose from the marble floor.

It was clear to him that this was nothing more than a massive armory, but the room had more of a museum feel to it: a shrine.

However, when he saw the enormous shooting range at the far end of the open space, he knew that the room served more than just that one purpose.

"My trophy room," his host cut into his silent observation. "Do you like?"

When he didn't respond, his host went on: "The gun is the instrument of many things. Of death. Of life. Of liberation. Freedom. Livelihood. Of victory, of defeat.

"Each of these instruments served a different purpose," he continued. "Each has its own story. Each one of them played a role in where my people and I are today."

"Your people," was all he said in response.

"Si," the host nodded. "The people who depend on me to support their lives, the region, and the greater good of Mexico. My product is the lifeblood of my people."

"Why are you telling me all this," he said.

"Come, first," the host said. "I have yet one more thing to show you."

He followed the man through the armory and into the firing range, at which point the walls, ceiling, and floor abruptly turned from marble and plaster to cold, gray concrete. The ceiling had dropped to normal height, no more than nine or ten feet. The length of the room was about one hundred yards or so, and as he went further along in the dimly lit space, he could see no conveyors or hooks for hanging targets. In fact, there was no evidence of targets whatsoever. In the low light, it was hard to see much of anything, but he began to notice a faint hue of red covering the floor. He looked up and could see swaths of it along the ceiling as well, and he understood immediately.

This wasn't a firing range; this was an execution room.

He then noticed the large cut-outs in the floor, which looked like over-sized manhole covers: there were five of them in total, each of them about one meter across, each separated by about five meters. He considered them for a moment as he walked, then turned his gaze forward once again.

They reached the far end of the range; the back wall was pocked heavily throughout, the result of being fired upon countless times. But there was no debris, no fallen chunks of concrete from the barrage of bullets. And just like the floor he had walked across, there were only traces of blood having been there. The room had clearly been wiped clean after each execution.

Once at the wall, his host stepped aside, and two of the gunmen went up to it and began pushing against the concrete surface. He could see the wall begin to move, heavily inching inward on the side the two men pushed. He then saw the other end of the wall section begin to move out toward them. The wall section was actually a door, about two meters wide, built on a large swivel at the center.

They walked through the opening, the host leading the way, the gunmen following close behind.

He realized what his host was doing: drawing him deeper and deeper into his compound, into ever closer quarters, surrounding him with what he had to assume were his best-trained fighters, ready to attack upon even the slightest of orders.

The order itself could even be a code word or phrase, he presumed: something designed to give him no indication of an ambush. He had no idea how he knew this; perhaps it was clarity of mind given the danger around him, perhaps there were echoes of knowledge from his former, unknown life.

There was no question that his host was a force for great evil: he had no doubt that countless atrocities had been committed by this man.

Perhaps his host was the reason he was in these lands in the first place. The more time that passed, the more that emerged as the most plausible explanation.

So perhaps he was given a second chance, to do whatever it was he was sent down here to do. And in his gut, he knew what that was.

But the timing would have to be right. He would wait for his opening.

In the meantime, he felt compelled to follow his host along, to play his game.

And if he was able to uncover some answers about himself in the process, it would be all the better.

Once past the wall, he was led into a short, wide corridor, again with concrete walls, floor, and ceiling. Long flatbed carts neatly lined the right-hand wall, at least twenty of them, leading to a massive, round stainless-steel door.

A vault.

The host reached the door and punched in a numeric code, then placed his thumb on a small touchpad. There was a loud, echoing click, and two of the gunmen came forward and began turning the handles of the large wheel at the center of the door.

Seconds later, the gunmen pulled open the enormous door, and the host approached the threshold.

"Come," the man turned back toward him. "I have something to show you."

He stepped inside, and took in the largest collection of riches he could imagine. He immediately realized that it was not a vault, but rather an enormous, sealed room, as massive as the armory he'd just seen. It contained neatly stacked mountains of cash, shrink-wrapped and piled high on rows of pallets, lining both the far wall and the one to his right. There had to be dozens of pallets.

But it didn't stop there: along the left-hand wall were rows upon rows of gold bars, set in interwoven stacks at least ten to twelve feet high. And nearest to him on the left were several wooden crates, their open tops revealing countless diamonds, rubies, emeralds, and other precious stones gleaming brightly under the fluorescent lights that ran along the ceiling.

His host came up alongside him. "The end that justifies the means, some would say," he commented. "But to me, it's only part of the equation."

"And what's the rest?" he said.

"When a man has conquered money, what comes next?" the host said.

"Power," he answered.

"Exactly," the man confirmed. "I could destroy every ounce of currency, metal, and stone in this vault, and still have enough capital to buy entire towns, regions, perhaps even a small country if I choose. So money is no longer an object for me. But the ability to influence – to *control* – things like commerce, people, even governments … that is power that no amount of money can truly buy."

"And how do you expect to do that," he said.

"I have plans," the man answered. "Some of which will be put into play tonight."

"Again," he said, "why tell me all this?"

"Through the eyes of my men, I have seen what you can do – what you are capable of," the host replied. "It is sheer brilliance. The likes of which I have never seen before. You would be an extremely valuable asset to me, for all that is to come."

"And what would be in it for me," he said flatly.

"Besides *this*," the man gestured to the room full of riches around them, "I would find you the answers you seek. About who you are."

"And what if *you* don't like what you find," he said.

The host smiled. "Then I would make the life you have known before this moment *irrelevant* to you. Your new life here would be so much better, so much more rewarding – you would have your every desire fulfilled."

He said nothing in reply, taking in the words that his host had carefully laid out for him. There was no chance that he would take the man up on his offer: he didn't know who he had been before, but he knew he could never be part of anything like this.

And he knew what he needed to do now: he would have to take this man – this entire operation – down.

And based on what his host had just told him, it would have to be soon.

But this was not the moment. He would have to wait for an opening.

"So, amigo," the man finally said, "what do you say?"

He hesitated, then finally said, "I'll have to think about it."

"I see," the man said, nodding once slowly. "Then come. There is still much to be done tonight. Gustavo will show you to a place where you can think things through."

They exited the vault and went back through the wall opening to the firing range. As the massive concrete section closed behind them, several bright spotlights switched on before him. He stopped in his tracks, blinded.

As he shielded his eyes from the intense light, he saw that he was once again surrounded by as many armed men as when he'd first entered the compound. He could not see where his host had gone, but it was clear that he had been prepared for whatever this was and had scattered. He stood alone and exposed.

"I am sorry, amigo," the host's voice came from afar. "A man in my position cannot afford not to hedge his bets. I knew your answer the instant you hesitated."

Gustavo, he realized. That must have been the code word. The host had had gunmen set up outside while they were in the vault, in case he refused the offer.

"A shame, truly," the voice continued. "We could have done wonderful things together."

He could hear footsteps walking away, then: "When ready," the host's voice said.

There was no warning. Gunfire erupted all around him, echoing loud in the low-ceilinged space. He instinctively dove to the floor, his fingers finding a grooved metal surface. One of the giant manhole covers. Tearing fingernails off as he tried to wrench it from the concrete floor, it finally came free, and he held it up, shielding him from the barrage. But it wasn't enough cover: bullets tore into his sides; he had no choice but to dive into the opening that yawned below him.

Knowing it was his only chance, he plunged into the black abyss.

A full second later, he crashed to a hard landing; whatever broke his fall cut into his flesh in several places. He lay there, stunned for a second, and then saw the guns appear in the opening above him. With all the strength he could muster, he leapt away from the spot as far as he could as another array of bullets sprayed in his direction. He rolled along the rocky, grooved surface until he crashed into another cluster of the hard, prickly things that had cut him up when he'd first landed.

Then the firing ceased. He could hear voices above him faintly. Then he heard the rough, scraping sound of metal sliding across concrete.

As he began to succumb to the pain from his bullet wounds, the manhole cover closed above him, plunging him into complete darkness.

54

Otis slowly waded back into consciousness.

He was propped up against a wall, his wrists bound tightly behind his back.

He decided to open his left eye a sliver, to survey the room. In his limited view, he could see Enrique sitting on the floor a few feet away, his head down.

At that moment, the door opened and Alejandro strode in, followed by the other man who had taken them prisoner. There was also a third man whom he immediately recognized from CBP file photos and the TV news: Javier Escondido Oropeza, head of the *Diablos del Rio* cartel, known throughout Mexico as the Jackal.

The drug lord did not even acknowledge Otis as he pulled a chair from the corner of the room, turning it backwards and taking a seat in front of Enrique. He began speaking to him in Spanish.

"Enrique," he spoke solemnly. "My ears must deceive me, my son. I have heard things tonight. Things that cannot be true. Things about you.

"These things cannot be true," he went on, "because you are someone I trust. And I know that you would never betray me. But I have *heard* them from someone I *also* trust. So someone very close to me is lying.

"Alejandro," he barked, keeping his eyes on Enrique. "Bring her in."

And with that, Alejandro left the room. He returned a moment later with a young Mexican girl, who Otis guessed was no more than twelve years old.

"Juanita!" Otis heard Enrique cry out. He watched as Enrique jumped to his feet, only to be restrained and set back upon the floor by the other man who'd taken them prisoner. The man then removed a pair of handcuffs from his pants pocket.

"Hernandez, no," the Jackal barked. "There's no need. He will stay where he is, if he knows what's best for his young sister. Isn't that right, Enrique?"

Enrique did not respond. He began to sob on the floor.

"Hernandez, hold the girl," the Jackal ordered. "Alejandro, stand next to me."

Hernandez moved behind the young girl. Alejandro came to the Jackal's side and stood facing Enrique, a gluttonous grin spread across his face.

"Hold out your right hand," he ordered Alejandro.

Puzzled, Alejandro did as he was told.

"Now, as I had said," the Jackal said briskly, removing a small silver instrument from a coat pocket, "because both of you are men I trust, and one of you is lying, one of you must be punished. But I must understand *who*. And Enrique, because you are family, *you* will have the opportunity to clear this up first."

With a lightning quickness, he took the silver instrument, which Otis could now see looked like some kind of giant cigar cutter, and placed it around Alejandro's extended hand. Otis knew exactly what would happen if the Jackal pushed the metal switch on the instrument: all four of Alejandro's fingers would abruptly drop to the floor.

He saw Alejandro's eyes widen in surprise, but he did not object, did not move; he merely remained still, obedient as a trained dog.

"This will be the test," the Jackal explained calmly, "to make clear who is telling the truth, and who has betrayed me. Enrique, I will ask you a question, and you will answer me. I will be able to tell if you are lying. I can always tell.

"If you are truthful," he went on, "only whichever of you has betrayed me will be punished – you or Alejandro. But if you are lying, your dear, young sister will pay the price. Are you ready?"

Enrique did not respond; his body lurched forward, accompanied by a horrible retching sound.

"Here is the question," the Jackal said. "The gringo here. Did you set him free?"

Enrique hesitated, then finally said: "I ... I did."

The Jackal seemed surprised by this answer, despite all the evidence that supported it. Keeping his eyes on Enrique, he slowly withdrew the cutting instrument from Alejandro's extended hand. He leaned back, his long fingers cupped over the chair back, seeming to slowly take in his nephew's response.

"Why would you do such a thing, boy?" he finally uttered.

Enrique said nothing, just remained still on the floor, clearly bracing himself for some kind of outburst from the drug lord.

"This ... hurts me," the Jackal said quietly, standing up and beginning to pace the tiny room. "Despite all that I have done ... the one thing I have held dear ... has been family. We are family, Enrique. I had taken you in like my own son. I had thought that you would play a role in our future here. A future that will begin now. With my biggest undertaking yet. It will make what happened two weeks ago seem as nothing."

Otis saw Enrique raise his head to look up at the drug lord. "The attack ... that ... that was *you?*"

The Jackal laughed. "Boy. You are more naïve than I thought. Of course it was. Who else in Mexico could have pulled off something of that scale?"

"But all ... all those people dead ..."

"The lives and deaths of others," the Jackal waved off Enrique's comment as he sat in the chair again, "nothing more than a means to an end."

Otis felt his stomach turn, his mind's eye showing him all the faces of those who had died in the attack.

"But ... but why? How could ... how could you ... do this?" Enrique said.

The Jackal leaned forward. "To set an example. We had an arrangement, the Americans and I. Then things changed. So, there had to be consequences.

"But," he added, cocking his head, "I also needed to see if such a thing could be done. Once I had seen that it could be, I began planning something even bigger."

"What are you going to do?" Otis heard Enrique ask.

The Jackal chuckled as he stood from the chair and went over to the window. "I suppose you won't be alive long enough to tell anyone," he said thoughtfully, staring out into the black night beyond.

"It's a simple plan, really," the Jackal began, turning back to Enrique. "There are two trucks outside, full of explosives. In a few hours they will be leaving, headed to the main border crossing in El Paso. When the trucks reach the crossing, they will blow. It should be enough to take out their headquarters just beyond the crossing."

Otis felt numb. He had dealt with enough IEDs during his tours to know how much explosive power could be packed into the trunk of a car, or even something small like a backpack. Two armored trucks filled with even mid-grade explosives would wipe everything out within a thirty-yard radius; probably more. Hundreds would be killed or injured.

"But — but that's —" Otis heard Enrique say. "So many people will die."

"Exactly the point!" the Jackal exclaimed.

"But the Americans ... they will never let you get away with it," Enrique said.

"Hmmh," the Jackal said dismissively, "they will certainly try. But, as always, I come prepared. I have many, many safe houses. Disguises. Body doubles. Allies and servants alike, in places you could only imagine, all ready to lay down their lives for me.

"And it won't end there," the Jackal continued. "It will set things in motion for a much bigger scheme. The Americans will retaliate, yes. More so than the Mexican government will want them to. Then there will be questions. How did our government allow this to happen. There will be a loss of trust between leaders. The people will see the Americans here, in our lands, hunting for us, and will feel violated. Occupied. There will be changes in public opinion. Then changes in power in Mexico City. A more defiant stance against the Americans. The Americans will be vilified and forced out.

"This is a chance to be part of history," the Jackal went on. "A chance to shift our country's direction. Mexico has always played to the Americans' needs, whether it be for their entertainment on our side of the border, or for our labor on theirs. We take their dollar for these things, but they drop it on the ground just to watch us pick it up. That is what we are to them. The Americans have always pushed, and we have taken it. I am simply giving us a chance to push back."

Otis remained still with eyes closed, absorbing the Jackal's diatribe. It was no doubt far-fetched, but nonetheless, it was plausible. He had seen similar shifts in public opinion during his tours in Iraq and Afghanistan: one day, the Americans were hailed as heroes; the next, they were the root of all evils. He had no doubt that this man had the intelligence and resources at least to give such a crazy plan a legitimate chance.

So he had to figure out a way to stop it before it even went into play.

"And now ... comes the task of what to do with you," the Jackal began again.

Alejandro chimed in quickly. "Let me end the gringo, Jefe. He has been a thorn in our side all evening. I know just the right tool." And he began making his way over to the large wooden chest.

"No," Oropeza cut in. "I wanted to keep him for questioning, but there isn't time right now. I have a better idea on what to do with them. One that will be much more entertaining."

"Are you saying —" Alejandro began.

"The Pit," the Jackal interrupted him. "You and Hernandez will take them both. We'll see how they fare with our other guest down there. If they survive the drop."

"The devil in black …" Alejandro said.

"Exactly," the Jackal confirmed. "Go now, there's still much to do."

As Alejandro gestured to Hernandez to pick Otis up, a beeping noise sounded, and Otis heard the Jackal answer his mobile phone: "What. All right. I'll be up."

He then addressed Alejandro. "There is a change of plans; our President has finally come out of hiding. He is communicating with the Americans. Hernandez, you and the guard take these three to the pit. Alejandro — you come with me."

And with that, the Jackal and Alejandro left the room, leaving Otis, Enrique, and the young girl alone with Hernandez and the guard.

55

As he came to, the pitch-black space felt like an invisible noose around his neck, tightening with each second that passed.

He squinted, hoping for even the faintest source of light that he could use to adjust his vision. But there was none.

Several odors confronted his senses: rotted meat, feces, and some others that he couldn't place but were much worse.

He tried to move, but his entire body rocked with pain. He'd been shot several times along both sides of his body, and his flesh tore against itself with even the slightest movement. Whatever had healed his wounds before would surely kick in soon – but he didn't have the luxury of waiting for that to happen. He had to find a way out.

He began feeling around the floor, away from the cluster of jagged protrusions that he found himself against, in search of some sort of pathway. The sharp objects had a somewhat familiar feel to them. He reached out and touched one. It moved slightly at his touch, so he pulled at it, and it came free. He held it in one hand, his other hand moving along its smooth, curved surface.

It was a bone.

Startled, he dropped the bone to the floor.

What was this place?

He reached out to the pile next to him once again, his fingers cautiously feeling along, but he felt only more bones: ribs, fibulae, joints, hands, feet.

Then a skull. And another. And no trace of flesh on any of them. They had been picked clean.

He had been dropped into some kind of mass grave.

Then he heard movement.

It was faint at first, a soft ticking. Like the second hand of an old clock, but quicker, duller, without consistency. Like a tapping of fingernails. Then the ticking increased, swelling into a chorus around him, until the sound filled the room. It was closing in. Before he knew what was happening, he felt a strange, tapping pressure on his boots, then a tugging at his pant legs: there were things crawling on him, then more things, then there was a terrible squealing as the crawling and tugging made their way up toward his torso, inching their way up his body.

In that instant, he understood: he was being swarmed by hungry, crawling rats.

With a roar, he violently shook the things off him, then reached out to the cluster of bones, searching for something to fight with. He found a skull, which he promptly hurled into the floor before him, smashing it to bits, hoping to take some of the vile creatures with it. He then reached back into the pile and got hold of two larger bones, and he began thrashing about with them, connecting several times with scurrying rats, sending them flying about in all directions. He roared again and again, louder and louder with each swing, each terrible roar echoing throughout the chamber.

He could hear, could feel, the rats scattering around him, running away in a panic, receding into whatever cracks and crevices from which they'd come, leaving him alone once again.

The pain returned, and he dropped to the floor. Despite his efforts, he could feel that he'd been bitten in several places. As with the bullet wounds, he hoped that his unexplained healing abilities would protect him from whatever terrible things the rats happened to be carrying.

The room fell silent once again, enough that another ticking sound became clearly audible. This one was different: consistent, even, precise. A wristwatch.

He moved cautiously toward it, doing his best to not trip over any bones in the darkness. Each time he did, he was forced to wait until the room fell silent once again to track the soft, subtle sound.

Then he came upon it. Dropping back down to his knees, he reached out, his fingers feeling along the floor until they touched its metal surface. He felt around the watch; it was still being worn by its deceased owner, wrapped around the bare wrist bone. The rats had apparently picked the body clean, as they had likely done with all the others in the room, leaving the watch intact on the wrist.

He removed the watch, feeling around the sides of it, in hopes that it would be the kind with a light-up face, to provide even the smallest amount of illumination. It was not.

Snarling in frustration, he flung the watch away, where it crashed against something with a sharp clanging noise.

Puzzled, he turned toward the direction of where he'd thrown the watch.

The sound was distinctly that of metal-on-metal.

He carefully began moving toward the source of the sound, and it dawned on him.

He was able to breathe down here. The place was ventilated.

Perhaps the metal he'd heard was an air vent.

If he could find the vent opening, maybe it would be his way out.

Once he reached the wall, he put his hands out and felt around the rocky surface. As his hands made their way down to the floor, his fingers came across not metal, but another familiar surface: denim. Blue jeans.

Some of the victims' clothes were still intact. From the volume of bare bones that he'd encountered thus far in the room just by touch, it was clear that the rats had eaten through most any clothing to get to the flesh of the victims … but not all.

He took hold of the pant leg, found a pocket and dug around, then moved to the next. In the right back pocket, he found a lighter.

He flicked it on, and in the flickering light, got his first glimpse of the room.

He couldn't see far in the tiny glow of the lighter, but the room appeared to be massive. His eyes moved first to the ceiling, which loomed high over him, at least thirty feet up. He could see the five round, covered openings spaced evenly along it. There were also four steel support beams that held it up, placed evenly between the covers.

He shifted his gaze to the floor around him. The piles of bones seemed endless, filling the room. There had to be several hundred victims down here, maybe a thousand. But the bones were all that remained of them, along with a smattering of clothing here and there. The rats and who-knows-what-else had completely devoured the rest.

Now that he could see what this place was, all the pieces began to add up: the firing range above, this giant pit beneath it. Above was where the drug lord would kill his victims, and down here was where he would deposit the bodies, an enormous nest of rats waiting to pick the bones clean, keeping themselves well-fed in the process.

The drug lord had set up an entire ecosystem down here.

He turned the lighter toward the wall next to him, in search of the metal surface he'd heard a moment ago. He found several.

It was as he'd assumed: the place was in fact ventilated, but instead of one large vent or return, the wall was pocked with about ten small, circular vent covers, no more than a foot across. There were also two cameras mounted near the top of the walls, one at each end of the room. Keeping the lighter trained on the wall, he walked around the perimeter of the room, looking for any sign of something he could use for an escape.

After he'd circled the room twice, he realized there was nothing.

The only way out was up.

His eyes moved once again to the round covered openings above, then to the enormous support beams. He could tell that even if he were to scale the beams to the top, he would not be close enough to reach any of the openings, nor would he have enough leverage or momentum to dislodge the heavy covers if he made a leap to any of them.

The lack of a way out meant that there was also no other way in, which meant that the drug lord's henchmen would not be coming for him after all.

He had been left down here to die.

The lighter's flame went out, and he could hear the ticking begin once again in the darkness.

56

Enrique watched Juanita walk ahead of him as they were led down a long corridor. She had stopped crying and was walking silently with head down.

He wanted to reach out and hold his young sister, to comfort her; but when he had made to approach her as they left the clubhouse moments before, the guard had roughly separated them, warning them both to walk separately.

He looked to his right to the American, Otis, who was clearly taking in their surroundings as well. He hadn't said a word since being roused in the clubhouse moments ago. It was as if he was deep in thought.

They rounded a corner and entered what looked like an armory. Beyond it was an enormous shooting range. He, Juanita, and Otis were led straight there. As they went on into the room, he noticed traces of dried blood along the floor.

Then he saw what appeared to be manhole covers in the floor just ahead of them. What they were for, he had no idea.

At that moment, a deep rumble sounded nearby, accompanied by a dull shock. It was muted, as if it had come from outside. It didn't have the feel of an earthquake; it resembled a tremor at most, but it was clearly noticeable. Enrique looked around for its source but couldn't pinpoint it. The others had clearly noticed it as well.

Then it sounded again.

A moment earlier, several floors up, Oropeza and Alejandro walked into *Santa Maria's* command center. "Give me the situation," Oropeza ordered his intel officer, Nunez.

"Several situations, Jefe," Nunez replied in an urgent tone, "all stemming from Vincennes resurfacing moments ago. Our source tells us he is communicating with the Americans."

"And?"

"Source confirms that another attack is headed our way," Nunez said.

"How long?" the Jackal demanded.

"No specific window was given," Nunez said.

"But we have to believe they are coming soon, Jefe," Alejandro said. "We have to be ready."

"Jefe," came another voice from across the room, followed by a stout man making his way towards Oropeza as quickly as his short legs would carry him.

"What is it, Gutierrez?" the Jackal turned to the stout man.

"You asked me to keep watch of the pit, record the activity down there," Gutierrez began.

"And?"

"Both the cameras went dead a moment ago," Gutierrez said.

"Fix it," the Jackal snapped.

"I am trying," the stout man pleaded, "but it looks like they were each taken out."

"Destroyed?" the Jackal questioned.

"The very last second of each feed shows something being thrown directly at the camera, then the feed immediately goes black. Something round. Like ... skulls."

"It's time to put an end to this game, then," the Jackal snarled. "Alejandro. Order twenty enforcers to the pit to execute the gringo, my nephew, and the girl. Then have them use any means necessary to kill the devil in the pit. *Any* means necessary. Do you understand?"

"Yes, Jefe," Alejandro replied and immediately headed for the door.

"Jefe, there is one more thing," Nunez broke in. "Our source also gathered the intel you'd asked for. He confirmed we have a traitor inside *Santa Maria*."

The Jackal stood up at this.

"Who?"

Enrique and the others were halted beyond the furthest manhole cover as yet another shock rippled throughout the room, this one more powerful than the first two. The guard's eyes moved left to right, but he kept his full attention on his three prisoners.

"What is that?" the guard asked Hernandez.

"I don't know," Hernandez replied, "but there's been a change of plans."

And with that, Hernandez drew his firearm and swiftly shot the guard straight through the side of the head.

Enrique gasped in horror as the shot echoed throughout the range. Juanita screamed. The guard dropped to the floor in a bloody heap.

"We don't have much time," Hernandez turned to them, keeping his gun trained on them for a moment. "But I can get you out of here — if you do as I say."

"What is happening?" Enrique said, holding Juanita tightly.

"Cut me loose," were the first words Otis said. "I can help you."

"I don't have the key," Hernandez said. "Hold up your hands, above your head."

Otis did so, and Hernandez raised the handgun, firing at the short chain that stretched between his handcuffs, shattering it.

At that moment, another shock hit the room, again shaking the floor harder than the one that had come before it.

"We gotta get outta here before we find out whatever in Sam Hill that is," Otis said.

"Follow me," Hernandez ordered them.

But before they could take two steps, the doors slammed open at the far end of the armory, and a large group of armed men spilled into the room.

"Christ. Is there a back door you know of?" Otis asked Hernandez urgently.

"No," Hernandez replied, laying his gun on the floor. "I'm afraid not."

"Hernandez!" one of the men shouted. "You must have known that the Jackal would figure you out before long."

Enrique saw ten of the men step forward, all with automatic rifles pointed. The others remained behind them, carrying larger weapons, including grenade launchers and what looked like a flamethrower.

"On my order," the leader told the others.

Enrique closed his eyes and held Juanita tight. She was trembling uncontrollably. He could not save her; couldn't even protect her. He fought back tears as he whispered calming words into her ear, waiting for the end.

Upstairs, the Jackal had begun planning for the Americans' arrival. The *Santa Maria* had an ample amount of weaponry and skilled fighters to hold off any sort of incursion; however, he had no doubt that the Americans would double down their efforts this time around, considering their complete and utter failure in their first attempt.

"Alejandro," he said, "how many more enforcers do we have available?"

"Eighteen," Alejandro replied.

"Assemble them all here in the main tower, on the second floor," he ordered. "Set up a line of defense, in the event that the Americans are able to get inside.

"And the moment the others have finished in the pit," he continued, "get them to all entry points inside our walls. Automatic rifles and grenade launchers."

"The towers —" Alejandro began.

"They will be ready for that this time around," the Jackal replied.

"Yes, Jefe," Alejandro replied.

In that instant, a tremor shook the floor, causing everyone in the room to stop and take notice.

Turning back to look at the Jackal, Alejandro said, "What was that?"

"The Americans," the Jackal surmised. "They are here. This changes things."

He then picked up his walkie-talkie. "Mondelo," he said.

"Yes, Jefe," came the voice from the other end.

"There's been a development," the Jackal said. "We have to deliver the packages early. Get the trucks ready. Send them as soon as they are."

At that moment, Gutierrez hurried over to him once again. "Jefe," he said, panting. "Something has just happened in the range. The prisoners ..."

The Jackal turned to him. "What is it now, Gutierrez?" he snarled.

"I cannot describe what just happened," Gutierrez admitted fearfully, "please. You must come see for yourself."

He followed Gutierrez to the array of monitors, Gutierrez pointing out the two screens capturing the video feeds from the shooting range, where his nephew was to be executed.

His mouth fell open.

"Call every man in, now," he ordered the room, unable to take his eyes off of what he was seeing. "Every single enforcer who is not at *Santa Maria*, I want here. Do it, NOW."

Seconds earlier, Otis looked on as the gunmen organized into a firing line. He saw Hernandez, their would-be savior, out of the corner of his eye, both hands still in the air. He looked down a few feet in front of him to see Enrique holding the girl tightly, trying his best to comfort her, both of them shaking.

He wished he could think of some kind of angle to at least save the girl, but he knew better: men like these could not be appealed to or bargained with. And he had nothing to bargain with in the first place. His stomach turned at the thought of not being able to save her.

Otis himself had faced death before, at least twice on each of his tours, during the most dangerous missions. Each time he did, the feeling became a little more familiar to him. It came back to him in this moment, and he took a deep breath at the sameness of it, the icy flow through his veins, the dry mouth, the weak limbs, the cold sweat.

If anything, he figured he would die overseas, during a tour, in the line of battle. If someone had told him that it was going to happen this way, in some Mexican drug lord's basement by firing line, he would never have believed it.

The worst part of it was, Silas and Annie would never have any idea what had happened to him. His death would be an unsolved mystery, one for which Silas would never give up trying to find answers. He knew it would haunt his father for the rest of his life.

The thought of them not knowing made his legs buckle a bit as if the weight of his parents' future was pushing down on him. But he fought it, fought to remain standing. He would not die on his knees.

He decided to distract himself with other thoughts, the most pressing of which was what he had noticed about the firing line in front of them. Why have twenty heavily armed men for an unarmed group of four? And why did some of the men have much heavier weaponry? What were the RPGs for? And the flamethrower?

Something else must have been going on — a much greater threat, no doubt. But he had no idea what that could be.

At that moment, another powerful shock struck the room, this one strong enough to send dust and tiny bits of concrete from the ceiling down onto them.

The leader paused, looking around, puzzled. Then he glanced back toward his men, making sure they were all still focused on their target.

Before anyone could react, yet another tremor hit, far stronger than any of those before it, sending a few of the men staggering. Then, without warning, a large section of the concrete floor gave way completely, opening up in a massive hole beneath the gunmen, swallowing them, a cascade of bodies falling into nothingness. Only two men held on to protruding chunks of the concrete floor, their weapons having fallen into the maw beneath them, shouting as their tenuous grip gave way, then disappearing into the enormous opening themselves.

More screaming sounded below, echoing up in a terrifying chorus, filling the room. It was as if whatever the gunmen had fallen into was one hundred times worse than the fall itself.

Otis forced himself from the utter shock of what had just occurred, back to their own predicament. He realized that every single one of the gunmen had been swallowed up by the hole; now, nothing stood between them and their escape.

"Come on," he said urgently to Hernandez, offering a hand to Enrique. "If we're gonna go … now's the time."

"Si … si," Hernandez agreed, clearly stunned by what had just happened.

"What happened?" Enrique said as he helped the girl up. "Earthquake?"

"I don't know," Hernandez answered him as he picked up his gun. "But we need to move. The rest of the floor could give way at any moment."

At that moment, the screaming stopped, and the room fell silent around them.

Otis and the others had just begun to run when something shot out of the gaping maw, landing several feet to the side of it, directly in their path. It rose and stood before them.

He was covered in blood, both dried and dripping from him. He wore what appeared to once have been fatigues, all black, now shredded and torn and hanging loosely from one shoulder, both of his thick, muscular, blood-covered arms fully exposed. Otis was suddenly hit by a sense of déjà vu; the man's short stature, black fatigues, and something else about him made Otis believe that he had encountered this man somewhere before.

Then, when he saw the man's eyes, the blackness of them, deeper than the darkest depths of midnight, a wave of recognition washed over him.

"Christ Jesus," was all Otis could bring himself to say. "It's you."

The bloody man seemed taken aback by this statement. But before Otis could register a thought, he found himself pinned high against the concrete wall, the man's right hand squeezing his throat, his left cocked into a fist, ready to strike.

He heard Enrique and the young girl cry out; saw Hernandez draw his gun and point it at the man, shouting something warningly.

The man leaned close to Otis, his snarling filling Otis's ears, the hot breath blasting against his face. The man's black eyes studied him, the raw fury pouring forth from them, but also something else Otis couldn't place. Almost … an emptiness.

Then came the harsh, raspy voice he had last heard all those months ago. But this time, all that issued from the man's lips was one quiet, desperate word:

"Who."

57

M oments earlier, the rats had begun to swarm him a second time.

He backed into one of the steel support beams to fight them off, and his foot caught in something at the base of the beam. Grabbing bone, skull, and rib-cage from around him, he fought them off, crushing them, throwing them in all directions, until he had rid himself of them once again.

He flicked on the lighter to see his foot wedged in a deep, wide crevice that went under the base of the beam. He looked closer to see that the rock had some-how eroded under the beam, leaving much of the base separated from the floor.

His eyes moved up along the beam, all the way to the ceiling. He knew he had the strength well beyond that of any ordinary man, maybe even that of a hundred men. But he was certain that a two-inch-thick steel beam was well beyond what he would be able to break, smash, or move.

But if the rock surface below it had been weakened … maybe he could somehow dislodge it from the floor, and then use it as leverage in some way.

Exactly how he would be able to use it, he wasn't sure … but it would be something more than what he had now.

He found a good foothold on the floor, leaned next to the beam, and be-gan to push with all his might. Nothing.

He tried again, getting lower to the floor, throwing a hand and shoulder into the wide gap of the beam itself, driving with as much power as his legs could muster.

But the beam didn't budge.

There has to be a way, he thought.

He flicked the lighter once again, looked between the piles of bones and debris, and saw a clear path from the beam all the way to the far wall.

He walked to the far wall, eyeing the metal vent covers.

Then he glanced up a bit further and remembered the cameras.

If he was going to escape, he would need to conceal his means of doing so.

He grabbed two skulls from the nearest heap of bones. He threw one at each camera, hitting each on the first try, taking them both out.

Then he turned back to the matter at hand.

He jumped up and grabbed hold of one of the metal vent covers, tearing it from the wall. Then a second one.

He removed a shirt from one of the skeletons. He tore it into long strips, then wrapped the strips tightly around the vent covers and his upper right arm, tying them together. They would serve as a makeshift form of armor for what he was about to do.

He would have to do it blindly; even if he were to hold on to the lighter, it would never remain lit at the speed he would be moving. But to his luck, the pathway he was on led directly to the beam – a straight shot. He would need to hit it square, though.

He knew one thing for sure: this was going to hurt.

He backed up against the wall. He flicked the lighter one last time, surveying the path in front of him. He was as ready as he was ever going to be.

Leading with his covered shoulder, he launched into a full sprint and rammed the beam with everything he had. Upon impact, he bounced off the beam violently, feeling the concussive force of the massive stationary object hitting him back, a small body of flesh against ten meters of thick steel bored into bedrock. He landed hard in a pile of bones, then tumbled to the rock floor. He rolled over, writhing in pain; he felt as if he'd fractured his arm, shoulder, or both.

But he had felt the beam move.

It hadn't been much, maybe an inch at most, but there was no question about it.

He forced himself up, fumbling around in the dark to find the base of the beam. When he found it, his fingers moved around the rock floor; he felt the loose stones that had not been there a moment ago.

He had moved it.

It would take a few more tries at least, but now he knew there was a chance.

Every few moments, he would repeat the attack, every time breaking his body a little bit more, knowing full well that he wasn't allowing himself enough time to heal between each try. He understood that time was a luxury he did not have; he had to assume that as soon as he'd taken out the cameras, the drug lord had sent men on their way to kill him.

Then, on the fifth try, it happened: the beam broke loose from the floor. He felt the chunks of rock and debris begin to separate from the ceiling, the bits and pieces falling all around where he stood. He pushed with all his might against the beam, hitting it again and again, using its length as leverage to try to break it away from the concrete ceiling, when suddenly an entire section of the ceiling gave way, forcing him to dive away from where he stood with whatever strength he had left in his legs.

As he landed, he turned to see the bright shafts of light pouring into the pit, and in that light he saw that giant sections of rock were not the only things crashing down before him: several bodies were falling in as well, arms and legs flailing amid cries of terror.

Then he saw the guns, and he understood why they had been in the room above.

He wasted no time, allowing no one the chance to recover. All had suffered some kind of injury in the fall; some had been impaled by shards of bones. Those, he considered mercy killings.

Within seconds, it was all over.

As he felt his body gaining strength, felt the urge once again building upon itself, he glanced up at the enormous opening above and hoped that there would be more enemies waiting for him up there.

It took only one try to reach the level above, his legs propelled by the insatiable need inside him. And by the hope of a greater challenge than what had been served up to him in the pit.

The instant he landed, he saw them: three men, two of them armed. A large man flanked by two others, all moving in his direction.

He turned toward them, and all three men stopped short. They didn't raise their weapons, didn't make any kind of threatening move at all. In fact, they all seemed shocked at the very sight of him.

Then, the large man addressed him in a way he would have never expected:

"Christ Jesus … it's you."

He stopped in his tracks, not understanding at first, then it hit him.

This man knew who he was.

Without a thought, he was upon the man, pinning him hard up against the wall, hand closed tightly around his throat, ready to squeeze the truth from him.

"Who," he snarled, spittle flying from his mouth like a rabid dog.

The large man could not respond, could not breathe in his terrible grip, only spluttered nonsense as he tried to wrest his fingers free from his throat.

He understood that this man had the answers he needed, but the urge was teetering beyond his control. He wanted to tear the man's head from his body, rip him to shreds. His vision began to blur as the urge began to overtake him.

Then he heard the cry from behind him.

It was simply a wail at first, then the words, "No, no, no, no, no, no, no ..."

He turned to see a young girl being held tightly by the smallest of the three men. She was crying. Frightened. At first, he thought that the small man was harming her, and he was ready to act, when he realized: he was covering her eyes, shielding her.

Protecting her.

Then it hit him like a wave, a flood within his mind.

It was a single memory; but the clarity of it, the vividness, took him out of the moment that he was in, transporting him back to that world, to that exact point in time.

A young girl, just like the one in the room with him now. Sobbing. A village. Burning; fire all around them. He could feel the intense heat. Men with guns. The loud roar of gunfire. Other men shouting, yet still others – men, women, children – screaming, running, falling.

She was holding something – no, someone – a small child. Lying limp in her arms. He saw the arm, the tiny hand, palm up from the ground, shaking slightly with each sob. Lifeless.

He looked down to see a man in his own grip, dead as well. He dropped the body and went to the girl.

She looked up to see him, and her cries of sadness turned to anger. She held out a hand to halt him. "No. You. No, no, no, no ..." then turned her eyes away from him.

His eyes moved from the girl to where she was now looking. The smashed motorcycle. Two gunmen, now pinned to a wall, crushed beneath it, their bloody legs protruding out from the wreckage.

He hadn't seen the child.

He kneeled before her. The war zone vanished around him; only the girl, the child, and the murderer remained.

Then the voice came from behind him, the hand grasping his shoulder. He turned. A soldier, barking orders in his ear.

"Target down," the voice said. "Time to go. Head to the L.Z. *Now.*"

But he didn't go. He was unable to turn away from the girl, the child — the one life, he had ended; the other, he'd changed forever.

"Specialist, that is an order!" the soldier stood over him.

Then a bullet slicing through the air, the dull *splut* of it piercing skin and bone, and the blood popped in spurts on his face, his clothes. The soldier dropped dead in a heap between him and the girl.

Then, as abruptly as it had appeared, the memory vanished, pulled away from him as if stolen, bringing him back to this moment.

He looked around him to see the large man still in his grasp, the young girl being held tightly by the smallest man, and the third man pointing his handgun at him. He had no idea how long he had been gone; it couldn't have been more than a few seconds, but it felt much longer. It was almost as if he'd been transported to another life, then brought back to the present after years of being away.

"Let him go!" the man with the gun ordered, his voice finally audible.

He turned back toward the large man, letting him down easily. The urge was gone, extinguished by the vivid, terrible memory of the child, the girl. He looked back at the young girl again, needing to confirm that she was still there, that she hadn't been an apparition of the one memory he now possessed.

He turned his focus back to the man before him.

"Who," he said calmly. "Who am I?"

Clutching his own neck, the man tried to regain his breath. He studied him for a second, as if trying to decide something, then said in an urgent tone, "Listen, mister. I don't know your name. But I know you from before. You saved my life. So I'll tell ya everything I know. But right now, we gotta get outta here. Somethin' terrible's about to happen, and we gotta find a way to stop it. Will you help us?"

He stared back into the man's eyes, the decision already made in his mind. If he was going to find out who he was, he was going to have to keep this man alive.

"Let's move, then."

58

The MH-60s flew low above the rocky northern Mexican terrain as Captain Carter "Chuck" Johns scanned the latest satellite images of the target's compound.

Captain Johns had led the initial First Squad for the mission to take down Oropeza after the border checkpoint attack. When one of his soldiers went down with a broken arm during training, the entire unit had been swapped out for Stevenson's Second Squad.

Upon word that Stevenson's unit had just been KIA in a surprise ambush, Johns had ordered his men to be ready for their own deployment at any given moment.

Now that the order had come, he surveyed the five men under his command: Crane, Milcher, Baarton, Gallo, and Wahler were among the best the SEALs had to offer; all were seasoned warriors with whom he'd run many missions.

The mission would be an insert-and-kill mission for the target; it would also be a rescue mission for the Specialist, the apparent lone survivor of the mission's first run.

This time around, the helicopters would drop the unit directly into the maw of the compound, from where they would rappel down from a height of thirty meters. The DoD didn't want to risk another MH-60 being blown out of the sky; the chances of that happening greatly decreased inside the compound's walls.

Based on intel that he'd just heard, they knew that they could be walking straight into a trap: sources had confirmed a mole within the Mexican presidency who may have leaked the insertion plan to the target, as was believed to have happened earlier.

In addition to the known and unknown dangers, Johns's squad had to contend with another unknown: the exact whereabouts of the Specialist. Pentagon brass had intel on him being alive and in the vicinity of the compound, but they knew nothing beyond that.

First, they would need to deal with the four lookout towers. Stevenson had used infrared to detect any heat signatures or movement within the towers, but there were a few known ways to throw the scanners off: the type of brick used in the structure, heated glass, clothing worn by the lookouts, to name a few. That underestimation by the Pentagon had proven to be fatal for Stevenson's unit.

They would not take that chance this time around.

As they approached the compound, Johns gave the order: "Proceed with clearing the towers."

Two short-range missiles were fired from each MH-60; Johns looked on as each missile struck its target, taking out all four towers in a fiery blaze.

"Accelerate your approach on the structure," Johns ordered the pilots. "Plan for drop in T-minus ninety seconds."

59

Moments later, Enrique held Juanita tight as Hernandez and Otis loaded up with guns in the Armory, while the small, bloody man kept watch of the door.

"You should grab something," Hernandez called over to the small man, then turned to Enrique. "You, too. We're going to need all the firepower we can get our hands on."

"I don't need anything," the bloody man growled in reply, seeming angry that Hernandez had even suggested it.

"Thank you for savin' us," Otis turned to Hernandez as he loaded a magazine into an automatic rifle. "But I gotta ask — why're you doin' this? You just put a huge target on your back."

"I was a police officer in a town south of here," Hernandez said, slapping a clip into a handgun. "My captain decided to take a stand against *Diablos del Rio*. We captured shipments, raided safe houses. It lasted one week. The Jackal had him kidnapped and brought to the school where his children went. As my captain watched, the Jackal and his men beheaded his twin daughters right in their classroom. The teacher, she tried to stop them from doing it. Pleaded for the children's lives. The Jackal had two of his men stab her to death."

Hernandez paused, seeming to gather himself, then went on: "The teacher — was my wife."

Otis said nothing. His eyes dropped to the floor solemnly.

"Since that day, I vowed to avenge her," Hernandez continued. "But I decided it wasn't enough to kill him. The Jackal's reign of terror — it had to be stopped. All of it.

"But I could not convince anyone to help me," he went on. "So I went off alone. I joined the cartel, and I have been waiting for the right chance."

His eyes moved from Otis to the man in black. "I believe tonight — with you, with him — is my chance."

Otis glanced back up at Hernandez. "Okay," he nodded.

Otis then went over to Enrique. "Hang onto this," he instructed, handing him a small handgun. "The safety's here. Fully loaded magazine inside. It's automatic, easy to use as they get. Just disengage the safety, and shoot.

"We'll do our best to keep her safe," he added. "But if things go south, you run. Get her as far away from here as you can."

Enrique nodded.

Once Otis and Hernandez were both doubled up with guns and ammunition, a series of low booms could be heard outside.

"What in the world was that?" Enrique said.

"I don't know," Otis replied. "But it's time to go. Now."

Hernandez pointed to the lone set of doors that the small man had been watching. "That's the only way out of this room. Then the building itself has two entrances, one in the front and one in back."

"Path of least resistance?" Otis asked.

"No such thing tonight," Hernandez replied. "We just have to move quickly."

"Okay," Otis acknowledged. "Let's just try to avoid getting into a firefight if we can. Any way you look at it, we're guaranteed to be outnumbered."

With that, the five of them headed for the lone set of doors to exit the room and proceeded cautiously down the hallway, toward the front doors. The bloody man insisted on leading the way, followed by Hernandez and Otis, with Enrique and Juanita bringing up the rear.

"An' you're sure you know where these two armored trucks are bein' kept?" Otis whispered to Hernandez as they moved along.

"Si, *Santa Maria* has a south entrance that is used for deliveries," Hernandez said. "I saw the trucks being prepared there earlier tonight."

"You know anything about diffusin' bombs?" Otis asked.

"No," Hernandez answered. "Assuming you don't, either?"

"I know some, from past tours," Otis said. "But not enough to disable a whole truck full of 'em."

"Then we gotta disable the trucks themselves," the small man chimed in from the front, "so they can't even leave."

"I s'pose that'd be a bit easier ... and less dangerous," Otis considered.

"When we get there, leave it to me," the man said.

Once outside, they followed Hernandez's lead, staying in the shadows, making their way toward the trucks. As they rounded a corner, at least fifteen gunmen popped up from cover positions around them, all of them pointing guns at the group.

"Drop your weapons. Hands in the air!" a familiar voice ordered them.

Enrique turned to see that it was Alejandro, his rifle pointed directly at Enrique's head.

The man in black watched as Otis lowered his rifle to the ground, raising his hands as the drug lord's lead henchman came before them. He saw the others quickly follow suit.

In that instant, he heard it: the low hum of a helicopter, coming from beyond the walls. Then he saw them; there were two helicopters, appearing over the high wall, flanked by what used to be the watch towers, which were now in smoking ruins. Each helicopter shone a spotlight that swept the ground, ultimately finding them.

Then he saw the silver canisters hit the ground.

Before anyone could react, the canisters went off, a loud popping sound momentarily taking everyone's hearing, a blinding white light taking their sight.

Stun grenades. He'd somehow recognized them just in time. A split second before detonation, he covered his ears and shut his eyes tightly, trying to minimize their effects on him. As he opened his eyes long seconds later, the sheer whiteness still penetrating his corneas, the shrill sound stinging his eardrums, he could see all those around him covering their eyes, reeling backward from the effects of the multiple detonations.

Chaos ensued. Gunfire erupted from blinded, stunned gunmen, bullets slicing through the air in all directions, one of them tearing through his shoulder. He dove for the girl, grabbing the brother in the process, and all but threw them behind a stack of crates near a wall. He leapt toward the two gunmen nearest him, turning their necks in one swift motion. Then he saw the soldiers exchanging fire with the henchmen. They were picking the gunmen off one by one, with single shots to the head. He could see Hernandez and Otis taking cover on opposite sides of the clearing, hands over their ears, eyes tightly shut.

Within a matter of seconds, it was all over. The soldiers approached them, weapons still raised.

He clenched his fists, readying himself.

Captain "Chuck" Johns approached the scene, surveying the array of bodies strewn about the ground. He ordered his men to look for survivors.

It was clear to Johns that they had walked in on an impending execution. Amongst the gunmen that lay dead around them, Johns noted the would-be victims: a young man, a girl, a second man – all of them Mexican, all dazed by the flash grenades.

He ordered Baarton and Wahler to tend to the three and sent Crane and Gallo to clear the area, taking out any cameras in the process.

But before he could register another thought, a short, bloodied man in shredded black fatigues approached him. The Specialist; they'd found him. Behind him was a much larger man, clearly still stunned by the grenades.

"Glad to see you're alive, Soldier," Johns nodded to him. "We have twelve minutes 'til we need to be back to the L.Z., so let's finish the mission."

"I'm going to need answers from you," was all the Specialist said in reply. "But there's no time. We have to stop it first."

"Stop what?" Johns said, confused by everything the Specialist had just said.

"The trucks," the larger man interjected, his eyes still somewhat out of focus. "He's sendin' trucks ... with bombs in 'em ... up to the border ... gonna hit us again ..."

"Where are they?" Johns said urgently.

"Sergeant Otis Brown, USMC, Third Division, Sir," the man addressed him, then continued: "we think they're ... still here ... in the compound."

He then pointed to the Mexican. "Hernandez there ... knows where."

Johns looked at Otis, then turned to Hernandez. "Where?" he demanded.

"I'll take you," Hernandez replied.

Johns had no choice but to break radio silence. He reported into Central Command: "Comm," he began, "Delta-Two. Specialist acquired. Need to push back L.Z. extraction. Code-Two-Two is active. I repeat: Code-Two-Two is active. Will radio in for updated L.Z. timeframe. Copy."

"Copy that," came the reply in Johns's headset.

Johns addressed Otis once again. "I'm going to need some answers as to why we'd find a Marine Sergeant in the middle of our op," he said. "But we've more pressing matters at the moment."

"Yes, Sir," Otis said.

Code Two-Two had been set into the insertion plan as a contingency, in the event that any new threats were discovered and needed to be dealt with immediately. With this development, they would need to push back their pickup and neutralize the new threat.

At that moment, Gallo returned from clearing the area. "Six cameras down. No other survivors, Sir," he said.

"All right," Johns said, then turned to Hernandez. "You. Lead us to those trucks."

Enrique took Juanita by the hand as they began making their way toward the south end of the compound. As they moved, he took one last look at the group of bodies on the ground.

He did not see Alejandro among them.

60

From the Pentagon War Room to the White House, the news spread immediately: Johns's squad had confirmed a visual on the Specialist. He was alive.

Then, unexpectedly, Johns had issued the Code Two-Two: two trucks containing heavy-grade explosives were about to be deployed to the CBP checkpoint at El Paso. A second wave attack. New priority was to prevent the vehicles from leaving the compound.

Dunlap and Armstrong stood at the map table when Stewart hurried up to them.

"Sirs," he said urgently, "another development."

"Go ahead," Dunlap nodded.

"Satellite images confirm two vehicles headed northbound from target's location."

"Jesus," Armstrong said. "They're already en route."

"Location at present?" Dunlap asked Stewart.

"About fifteen clicks from the border checkpoint, currently," Stewart answered. "Vehicles proceeding at approximately twenty-five miles per hour. Chatter we've intercepted suggests that these may be a part of some second-wave attack."

"Have we confirmed that the cargo is in fact a threat?" Armstrong questioned.

"We haven't verified what's in the trucks," Stewart said. "But as I said, we have audio from multiple sources that leads us to conclude that it is very likely a threat."

"Without verification of an imminent threat, we can't go in and intercept the vehicles without proper clearance from the Mexican government," Armstrong commented. "Nor can we eliminate them on Mexican soil without that same clearance."

"But this would call for an exception, Edward," Dunlap argued. "We have enough evidence from Johns's squad, as well as this intel. There are American lives potentially at stake."

"Sirs," Stewart cut in again. "There's more."

"Go ahead," Dunlap waved him on.

"We also have chatter of enemy reinforcements inbound to the target compound," Stewart said.

"Reinforcements?" Armstrong said. "How many?"

"In excess of one hundred, potentially one-fifty," Stewart answered. "ETA appears to be staggered, but all should be arriving within a thirty-minute window."

"This — along with the trucks — can only mean that the target knew about us coming in," Dunlap said.

"We need to call in a QRF," he went on. "Our men are sitting ducks in there."

"Quick Response Force is secondary, Jack," Armstrong argued. "We need to inform the President of the inbound threat to our border. He'll have to make the call on what to do."

"You do that," Dunlap said, picking up the phone to call Norris.

"What are you doing?" Armstrong questioned.

"Anticipating you'll get a 'yes'," Dunlap said. "There's no time to assume otherwise."

"Jack, you can't proceed without White House clearance!" Armstrong exclaimed.

"Which is why you need to get it, for both — now," Dunlap shot back. "We can't allow those trucks to get within range of our border. So get approval for that, *and* the QRF, so we can get our men out of there alive."

61

Near the south entrance of the compound, the group had just taken cover when Johns got the intel from his comm unit.

"There's been a development," he addressed them. "The trucks have already been deployed. CentCom also received reports of enemy reinforcements inbound."

"What's our plan, Sir?" Milcher said.

"Our two birds are inbound right now to do the extraction," Johns said. "We're going to intercept the trucks before they get to our border."

"ETA?" Crane inquired.

"None yet," Johns answered. "CentCom will be sending us coordinates for the L.Z. momentarily."

When the orders came in, a new mission had been assigned to Johns's squad: the two MH-60s would immediately proceed to the trucks' position and intercept both en route. Two men would rappel down from each helo onto the roofs of the vehicles, taking control of them by any means necessary and turning them back from the border.

Though CentCom had its doubts on whether the drivers of the vehicles even knew exactly what their payloads were, the trucks needed to be stopped long before they reached the border. The helos were their only chance.

As they neared the L.Z., the first of the two birds appeared over the wall, followed by the second.

The two helicopters descended quickly, both landing several meters from one another. As the first group of men approached Helo One, a sound erupted above them, and suddenly the tail of the chopper exploded, sending it rocking forward and bursting into flame.

"RPG!" yelled one of the men.

With one MH-60 gone, Johns knew that they would not be able to extract everyone.

The squad immediately began returning fire in the direction of the attack, and Johns began barking orders to the men around him.

"Baarton, Wahler," he shouted, "keep fire on the enemy — protect that bird! Milcher, Gallo — you're coming with the Specialist and me to retrieve those trucks. Crane — take the civilians to cover. Hole up — keep the enemy off your position.

"Godspeed, men," Johns finally said, stepping into the MH-60. "Just keep yourselves alive. We'll be back for you."

62

As Helo Two cleared the wall, the man in black looked out at the vast expanse of land beneath them. Dozens of vehicles were approaching the compound.

The pilot ascended rapidly before veering to the left — away from the incoming convoy — then accelerated to maximum speed. They were clear of the convoy in a matter of seconds.

Though he still did not know who he was, he understood that he had somehow been involved in operations such as this one, with soldiers like the ones before him. He assumed that his unique abilities were the reason for it, and moreover, why the leader, the man named Johns, had taken him to intercept the trucks.

He somehow knew that he hadn't liked taking orders in his life before, but there was no time to question authority now. Nor was there time for answers about who he was. There was only the mission. Everything else would need to wait.

"T-minus two minutes to contact," the pilot informed them.

"Milcher. Gallo," Johns addressed the two soldiers. "You two will apprehend the first vehicle. You know the drill: rappel down and take control, incapacitate it, and retreat before it gets within range of the border. The enemy can and will detonate the payloads remotely."

Then the C.O. addressed him. "You and I will do the same for the second truck."

"And what if that truck gets too close to the border," he said.

Johns returned his knowing glance. "Then we are to steer the vehicle away from the border and proceed in the opposite direction until a safe distance has been reached."

"We have visual on the trucks," the pilot informed them. "T-minus thirty seconds to acquisition."

Everyone understood the danger involved: rappelling down from one moving vehicle to another carried risk enough. Once those inside the trucks became aware that they were being boarded, they would no doubt resist — swerving to shake them off, firing upon them — at which point the danger increased a hundredfold.

"Go time," Johns informed them. "Milcher, Gallo. Take positions."

He looked on as the two soldiers adjusted the night-vision glass on their helmets, then took position at the rope firmly stretched from the top to the bottom of the helo's open side. Milcher went first, dropping immediately from view. When the co-pilot confirmed Milcher's successful landing, Gallo took position and disappeared as well.

The co-pilot gave a signal that both SEALs had now boarded the first truck.

The MH-60 advanced on the second vehicle. The C.O. nodded to him, and he moved into position.

As he began to make his way down the rope, he saw the two flashpoints in rapid succession from inside the first truck's cabin. Milcher and Gallo. He saw the truck begin to slow, then make a u-turn before stopping at the side of the road.

The night wind whipped through his torn fatigues as he rappelled down the swinging, jerking rope, sliding rapidly down toward the roof of the moving truck.

He was about five meters from touching down on the vehicle's roof when the truck jerked hard to the right, taking his landing spot out from under him. He tried to swing himself toward the vehicle, but he could not gain any momentum. Then the truck swung to the right once again, and as the MH-60 moved to get him into position once more, machine-gun fire erupted from below him. At first, he thought that they were shooting at him, then he thought they were firing at the helicopter; but then the rope twisted, snapped, and he fell straight to the ground, crashing in a heap on the hard rock and sand below. Several meters of rope cascaded down upon him, landing like a giant, curled snake. They had hit the rope high, essentially taking the C.O. out of the equation.

He would have to do this himself.

He had fallen at least seven or eight meters, landing hard on his right leg and arm. He felt the cuts from where the jagged rock had pierced his skin; he could feel the fractured bones in his right arm and leg.

But he couldn't give in to the pain; the lives of so many were on him now.

He forced himself up and began to run, pursuing the vehicle with all the strength that remained in his injured legs.

63

The evacuation order had been given at the El Paso Customs and Border Protection checkpoint.

Roadblocks had been set up two miles north of the station, and all southbound traffic was being re-routed to other border crossings. But even with this contingency plan, there was no way to stop the northbound flow of traffic coming into the U.S.; the Mexican border authorities were not nearly prepared for any such emergency, despite the CBP's warnings. There was no way to ensure the safety of hundreds still inbound from Mexico.

General Jack Dunlap stood watching the massive monitor array as the lone remaining vehicle edged ever closer to the El Paso CBP checkpoint.

He and Armstrong had been monitoring the vehicles' progress for the past several minutes via surveillance drones, along with the cameras mounted to each of the SEALs' helmets, which gave a more close-up view of the ongoing situation.

The only one not equipped with a helmet was the Specialist. This had been protocol in all previous missions as well; but on those occasions, he had always been in close proximity to others equipped with comms equipment, so keeping him on a tight leash had never been an issue.

As Dunlap watched the sequence of events unfold — from Milcher and Gallo taking out the first vehicle, to the second vehicle opening fire on the helo, severing the rappel line, cutting the Specialist off from Johns' command — he realized that they no longer had any line of communication to the Specialist, no control over his actions.

The drones maintained an aerial view of the situation as the Specialist dropped suddenly to the ground, crashing in a dusty heap. He quickly recovered and began pursuing the truck, but it was clear that he'd sustained injuries from the fall: he was hobbling badly, all but hopping on one leg as he moved.

But he needed to make up ground, and quickly. There were only moments until the remaining vehicle got within range of the border crossing.

Suddenly, he heard Armstrong's voice from behind him: "Jack," Armstrong began, the tension in his voice clear, "we have an update from the President."

Dunlap turned to Armstrong. "This had better be a 'go' on my QRF," he said impatiently. "The President doesn't seem to get that our men are sitting ducks down there."

"Jack," Armstrong said. "You know you can't authorize a QRF on an ally's soil; that level of order can only come from the President himself. Norris knows that."

"It's bullshit, is what it is," Dunlap argued, then sighed, "What's the update?"

"The President and Vincennes have agreed on a failsafe measure for the trucks inbound to our border," Armstrong said.

"A failsafe," Dunlap repeated. "What kind of ... oh Jesus, no."

"A missile strike was ordered not one minute ago," Armstrong confirmed. "The drone is getting airborne as we speak. The instant that truck gets within one-quarter mile of the border, the drone will deploy two short-range MD-22s to detonate the vehicle's payload."

"Christ," Dunlap said.

"The president's directive is minimal casualties, both Mexican and American," Armstrong said. "And right now, that remaining vehicle is still on side roads, not a main road, so there is very little inbound traffic around it. Vincennes agreed to the plan – again, as a failsafe only – on condition that we'd prevent as many Mexican casualties as possible, as well."

"And what about Johns? And the Specialist?" Dunlap argued.

"Norris has already issued the pullback order for the helo," Armstrong said. "There's nothing more it can do from there. Captain Johns will be safely out of the blast radius, and the drones will keep an aerial view of the situation until it's been resolved."

"And what about *him*," Dunlap pressed, becoming angry.

Armstrong glared back at him. "How do you expect me to answer that, Jack?" he said. "We have no way of communicating with him; we've never been able to wire him up because of his … tendencies. There's no contingency plan for this."

"Unless he turns that truck around," Dunlap argued. "Then what."

"Then we put the call in to not fire the missiles," Armstrong said plainly.

"In time?" Dunlap maintained. "We're the only ones seeing this real-time. He turns that truck around with no time to spare, there's no window for the President to call it off. We need command of that drone."

"You know that's not going to happen, Jack," Armstrong shook his head. "This is the President's call; only he can call off the launch."

"He's going to stop that truck," Dunlap said. "You know it and I know it. And he's going to get blown to hell for it."

"But the President doesn't know it, Jack," Armstrong said. "And you know he's not willing to bet the lives of hundreds on it. Nor could he. Let's just hope the Specialist can get there in time for us to make the call to the President."

Dunlap said nothing, just turned back to the monitors and watched as the Specialist struggled to catch up with the truck, unaware that he was in pursuit of his own certain doom.

64

In the command center at the top of *Santa Maria's* tallest building, the Jackal looked upon an array of monitors, watching events unfold.

He had watched as his nephew and the others emerged unharmed from the firing range. Hernandez had betrayed him, and when he sent a team of enforcers down there to execute them all, the Devil somehow found a way out of the Pit, killing all of his men in the process.

He had seen the Americans' second wave of helicopters land inside his home, moments after blowing all four of his watchtowers from the sky. He saw the five soldiers emerge and begin taking down yet another squad of enforcers he'd sent to kill his nephew and the others, once again saving them from execution. Only Alejandro had made it out alive, retreating to the command center to join him not moments ago.

He had looked on as those same helicopters landed in his home a second time, and he ordered yet a third team of enforcers, this time armed with RPGs, to destroy them. They were successful with the first helicopter, but the Americans quickly returned fire upon his men, preventing them from taking down the second.

But he saw only four men disappear into the lone remaining helicopter: three soldiers, and the devil himself. The others had been left behind, including Hernandez and his nephew.

The two traitors.

236 | CHRIS LINDBERG

He had heard the Americans' new plan from his mole, and he had prepared accordingly, ordering reinforcements to *Santa Maria* to fight off the American soldiers, and deploying the trucks immediately to the American border, before the Americans could discover his plan and stop them. He was not about to let his largest plan fail.

With the trucks now well on their way, he could concentrate on killing the invaders inside his walls — most importantly, his nephew and Hernandez.

And he would do it himself.

They had taken out enough of his cameras, and there were enough hiding places around *Santa Maria*, that he could not find their location from the command center.

So he would flush them from their hiding place.

He walked to the far wall and opened a small panel, inside of which was a large, square-shaped button marked MAIN DOOR. He hit the button with the side of his fist.

He looked on at the monitors as the massive entry door began to slide open, and dozens of enforcers began pouring in.

He picked up his AR-15 and nodded to Alejandro, who had armed himself as well.

The hunt for the invaders had begun.

65

He felt the strength returning to his right arm and leg, but not quickly enough: as he ran, the truck kept pulling away, putting more distance between them with every second.

He was running out of time. He had to move faster, make up ground.

With a scream, he forced all of his remaining strength to his legs and leapt with all his might toward the vehicle. He landed awkwardly, stumbled but regained his balance, and kept running. Howling in pain, he once again forced his legs into a jump, soaring through the air, again landing with a jarring crash, again keeping his legs beneath him. He ran a few steps to keep his balance, then leapt once again.

It was working; he was gaining ground on the vehicle. He was only a car's length behind it now. One more jump and he would be on top of the truck.

He made the final leap and landed on the very front of the trailer's roof, almost overshooting the vehicle entirely. With his forward momentum, he slid off the trailer and onto the roof of the cabin, where he continued to slide forward on its slippery surface, finally crashing down onto the hood of the truck. The bouncing of the truck forced him farther forward, so that he almost slid off the hood and in front of the heavy tires, but he was able to grab onto the hood ornament an instant before he fell off entirely.

He looked up and exchanged surprised glances with the two men in the front seat, when the passenger raised his semiautomatic rifle and began firing. Bullets punched through the windshield at him. He was able to dodge most of them, others missing wildly with the bouncing of the truck, but two of the rounds connected: the first one sliced into his left shoulder; the second clipped the top of his right ear – it missed his skull, but it took off the top few millimeters of his ear nonetheless.

He roared in agony as the driver swerved to the left, his weakened left arm losing grip of the hood ornament, sending him pivoting back on his right arm, his neck and back smashing into the large grille. He held on with all his might, the frail grip of his injured right arm the only thing keeping him from the heavy, rolling tires beneath him. More shots fired; one buzzed the top of his head, another grazed his arm. The pain began to overtake him. He was a sitting duck; it was only a matter of time before one of the bullets went through the center of his head.

He had to act now.

He channeled his pain into anger. The fury swept through him like an electrical surge, racing through his bloodstream, filling his muscles, his bones, his very core.

In a blinding motion, he grasped the hood ornament with both hands, pulling himself into a back-flip over the hood, smashing through the punctured windshield and into the cabin. Before either man could react, he had snapped both of their necks. He promptly kicked the driver's body through the driver-side door, smashing the door off of its hinges, sending both driver and door into the black night beyond.

He slid behind the wheel and took control, swerving to keep the careening vehicle on the road, then promptly slowed it to a halt.

He'd stopped the biggest threat. Now he could get the answers he sought.

But as he leaned back on the seat, something below the dash caught his attention. It was mostly concealed by a black cloth.

He tore the cloth away to reveal a timer, its bright red numbers glowing up at him.

13:45 …

13:44 …

13:43 …

13:42 …

Count down.

The truck was going to blow either way.

Without another thought, he swung the truck around, heading back in the direction of the drug lord's compound.

66

"Done!" Dunlap thumped the map table with his fist as he and Armstrong watched the Specialist begin turning the truck away from the border. "Abort failsafe!"

"I'll inform the President," Armstrong said quickly.

"And get me authorization on that QRF," Dunlap barked at him. "The clock is ticking on our men down there."

Dunlap turned back toward the monitors. The drones continued to follow the vehicle southbound.

Moments later, Armstrong entered the War Room again and walked up to Dunlap. "Failsafe aborted," he informed Dunlap.

"Good. QRF?" Dunlap pressed.

"Authorization denied," Armstrong said. "Vincennes did not approve of a mass invading force on Mexican soil. The President didn't want to press the issue."

"And what about our men down there?" Dunlap said angrily. "How –

"I'm wasting my time here," Dunlap cut himself off, turning away from Armstrong and picking up the comm. "Norris," he said, "where is Helo 2 currently?"

Norris replied, "Refueling at Biggs."

"How quickly can you get her back in the air?" he said. "We need to do an extraction from that compound, on the double."

"Yes, Sir," Norris said. "I'll have her up as soon as soon as she's ready."

"Get Crane to the roof of that tower. Only then will Helo 2 approach," Dunlap ordered. "There'll be a lot of enemy forces on the ground. So it needs to be a load-and-go."

"Issuing orders to Crane now, Sir," Norris acknowledged.

"Let me know when they're en route. Out," Dunlap said, then switched off the comm.

He once again looked up at the monitors. Armstrong joined him. The vehicle continued to head south but had clearly picked up speed.

Stewart quickly approached them. "Sirs," he said urgently, "a report's just come in from the Mexican authorities. They sent a crew in to diffuse the bomb, and discovered a running timer in the cabin."

"My God," Armstrong said. "How much time?"

"Thirteen minutes when it was discovered," Stewart answered. "They've confirmed that they'll be able to diffuse it in time, but they're concerned that the other truck has a running timer also."

"I'll call Norris to get our men as far from there as possible," Dunlap said.

Armstrong looked back up at the monitors, staring at the aerial view of the truck headed southbound. "He knows, too, doesn't he," he mused.

"Yes," Dunlap glanced up at the monitors as well. "I think he does."

"So what is he doing?"

"Isn't it obvious?" Dunlap replied. "He's going to put that bomb right back in the target's lap."

67

In the skies above *Santa Maria*, Captain Chuck Johns turned to the pilot to assess their final approach on the compound.

"What's our ETA?" he said to the pilot.

"Under two minutes, Sir," the pilot responded.

"This will have to be a quick extraction," Johns said. "We don't know the situation down there. Could be several active shooters, and we'll certainly draw attention. We reach the roof, onboard our men, and take off, immediately. Understood?"

"Yes, Sir," the pilot responded. "Descending to L.Z. now. Two hundred meters."

Johns lowered his night-vision lens to survey the landing zone below. There was movement on the tower's roof: Johns counted four men, but they were too far to identify whether Crane had gotten all of his men up there yet.

He spoke into the comm: "Lt. Crane, what is your twenty?" he said. "Respond."

Nothing from the other end.

"Incoming!" the pilot shouted amid a sudden beeping in the cockpit. "Hold on!"

Johns grabbed onto a cross bar just as the MH-60 rocked to the right. He held on as the MH-60 straightened out and began ascending rapidly, the pilot issuing return fire from the front gun pod, barking into his comm. unit that he was under heavy fire.

At that moment, another beeping issued from the cockpit, and once again, the pilot swung the chopper to the right, yet again sending Johns to hold on for his life. But this time, the incoming fire struck its target: Johns's face smashed against the helo's side wall as the MH-60 shook in mid-air, then began spinning.

The pilot continued to issue the distress call into the comm, and Johns felt himself pulled hard from the ceiling as the pilot regained control of the MH-60. The helicopter began ascending once again, getting itself out of range of the fire down below.

"The hell hit us?" Johns shouted. "Has the bird been compromised?"

"We can fly," the pilot shouted back to him, "but we lost part of our landing gear. I can't set her down anywhere; we have to head back to Biggs."

"No," Johns shot back. "My men are in there; get low and drop me somewhere."

"We can't go back in range of that compound," the pilot argued. "There are too many guns; we'll be downed in seconds."

"Drop me outside range, then," Johns said. "I can rope down and go in on foot."

"Sir, we don't know what threats there are on the ground," the pilot said.

"I'm not leaving here without my men," Johns shouted. "Head around to the south end and drop me. Then take this bird back to Biggs. That's an order, Sergeant."

Without another word, the pilot swung the MH-60 around and began heading south, away from the compound. Once they had reached a safe distance, the pilot began descending rapidly once again.

Johns threw the rappel gear out the open side window. When they'd descended down to ten meters' altitude, he threw his rifle over his shoulder, grasped the rope, and began rappelling down to the ground.

68

Moments earlier, Otis and the others had been holed up in one of the Jackal's storage sheds when Crane got new orders on his comm.

"Good news, and some bad," Crane began. "The good is, we've got a bird inbound to extract us. And better news, both trucks have been halted shy of the border."

A collective sigh of relief came from the group.

"And the bad?" Otis inquired.

"We need to get to the top of that main tower for extraction," Crane answered. "And that's not the bad part."

"What is, then?" said Otis.

"Target has let about one hundred-fifty enemy forces into the compound to hunt for us," Crane said. "They're the reason we can't do a ground extraction. And we have to find a way to avoid them while en route to that tower."

"Not to mention, the Jackal is still alive," Hernandez pointed out. "I'm not leaving here until he is dead."

"That was our mission, too," Crane replied, "but this mass of forces changes things. We need to get out of here, stat — and there's very little chance we'll encounter him unguarded along the way."

"There's even less of a chance we get to the top of that tower alive," Hernandez argued. "It will be booby-trapped and lined with enforcers, just waiting to ambush us."

"How well do you know this place?" Crane challenged him.

"I know enough," Hernandez replied.

"Then take us the way you think will give us the least resistance," Crane said.

"There's an underground passage just beyond the shed," Hernandez said. "It leads right underneath the tower, to a hidden vertical passage. That is our best shot."

"Let's move, then," Crane said, moving toward the door. "We'll move two-by-two; Baarton, take the boy with you; Wahler, the girl."

Crane cautiously opened the door, motioning Hernandez through to lead the way.

But as they began making their way out of the shed, a voice called out to them: "Stop! Drop your weapons to the ground."

Dozens of enforcers emerged before them.

They were surrounded.

69

Bearing down on the compound as fast as the truck could go, he once again glanced down at the countdown timer.

1:01 ...

    1:00 ...

    Under one minute.

He was less than one half-mile away now. Keeping his eyes on the bumpy road ahead of him, he reached over to his right and grabbed hold of the rifle that lay on the seat. He held it tightly in his hand, waiting for the right moment. He would need to time everything perfectly, otherwise he could very easily blow himself up in the process of what he was about to do. Or miss his target. There was no room for error.

He looked down again at the timer.

0:45 ...

It was now or never.

Moving the rifle underneath the steering wheel, he slid the barrel back up along the bottom of the wheel. The wheel fit perfectly between the barrel and the scope. He then wedged the butt-end against the accelerator pedal, the length of the rifle pushing the pedal all the way to the floor. There was no guarantee that the vehicle would maintain a straight course along the bumpy road, but it would have to do.

He glanced up to the windshield; the high wall of the compound loomed just a few hundred meters ahead.

He took one last look at the countdown timer.

0:22 ...

He surveyed the fast-moving ground outside the open driver-side doorway to his left. He jumped out of the open doorway, landing hard on his feet on the rocky desert terrain before rolling forward a few times, finally coming to a stop on his back. He regained his footing and began running away from the compound as fast as he could.

The night sky lit up behind him as the roar of the explosion battered his eardrums, forcing him to the ground. He turned to see the fireball stretching upward, a cascade of rock, concrete and debris flying in the distance, the massive wall of the drug lord's fortress coming down in its wake.

70

Enrique watched as Otis and the others all threw their guns to the ground, then placed their hands above their heads. It was over; there was no doubt that they would die now.

"Take the boy and the traitor to the clubhouse," the lead Enforcer ordered two of his men. "We'll finish the rest here."

As two of the Enforcers came forward to take Enrique and Hernandez, several of the other armed men trained their rifles on the others, ready to fire.

BOOM.

The explosion was as deafening as it was sudden. The ground shook beneath them, knocking many of the Enforcers off their feet and sending several others running for cover. Enrique saw Otis lunge at the distracted lead Enforcer, ripping the gun from his hand before turning it on him and shooting him through the head. The other soldiers quickly took advantage of the situation as well, jumping a few of the Enforcers, stealing their guns before shooting them. Gunfire erupted in all directions. He saw Otis grab Juanita, and then he felt his right arm being pulled before he looked up and saw one of the soldiers dragging him back while simultaneously firing at the scrambling group of Enforcers. The soldiers had the advantage for the moment, but the other Enforcers had started to recover. Even though Otis and the soldiers had taken out a handful of them, there were still too many. They had to run.

They had reached the back of the shed when the lead soldier addressed them: "We can hold them off maybe for a minute, tops, but if they have grenades, we're done for. Hernandez, what's our escape route?"

"The other shed is across the clearing, through those Enforcers," Hernandez said. "It has a tunnel that leads directly outside the walls."

"They still outnumber us at least four to one," Otis said. "We can't fight our way through that."

We can't hold this position for more than another few seconds," Crane said. "We've gotta make a move."

Suddenly, they heard gunfire from the other side of the shed, but it was not being trained in their direction. The Enforcers were now shooting at something else.

"What in the —" Crane said, bewildered.

"QRF," Otis replied, an encouraged tone in his voice. "Gotta be."

"Let's give 'em some support, then," Crane said.

"Hernandez. Stay here with them," Crane ordered, gesturing to Enrique and Juanita. "Watch for any inbound threats."

"I can help you," Hernandez argued.

"We need you alive to get us out of here," Crane shot back.

Then, before another word was spoken, Otis and the soldiers quickly disappeared from view.

Enrique peered around the corner of the shed to see the three men beginning to fire at a large group of Enforcers whose backs were to them. The Enforcers themselves looked as if they were in disarray: they were firing their weapons in all directions, as if trying to get a bead on something that was moving too fast to hit.

Then he saw what that something was: it looked like a man, moving almost too quickly for the naked eye, jumping high into the air, bouncing off walls like a pinball, slamming into the Enforcers one by one. Each of them immediately fell to the ground the instant the blurry man came into contact with them, as if his touch alone was enough to put them down.

It was over in a matter of moments: the blurry man battering most of the Enforcers, Otis and the soldiers shooting the rest. The blurry man finally came to a stop, his short, bloodied frame standing amid the dead Enforcers.

It was the man who'd saved them in the firing range.

Moments earlier, he'd gotten to his feet, shaking off the effects of being thrown by the force of the blast. He turned, watching the flames burn brightly around the enormous hole in the drug lord's wall, the opening he'd created to get back into the compound and finish what he'd started.

He wasted no time, opening up into a full sprint toward the wall. Just before reaching the wall, he launched into a towering leap, clearing the burning debris strewn about the opening, feeling the intense heat of the flames on his feet and legs as he did so.

Once inside, he heard the sound of gunfire in the distance.

It had come from clear across the massive complex, but he reached its source in seconds. Several men – too many to count – were running toward a small building near the far wall. Some of the men were firing at the building.

He leaped high into the air, landing square in the middle of the pack, and immediately went to work. Before the first dead man hit the ground, he had already grasped two more, smashing their heads together with such force that both men's skulls were immediately crushed. He realized that attacking the group at its core put him in greater danger, but it would also take the gunfire away from whoever their current target was. As he'd expected, the gunmen quickly realized what was happening and turned their fire in his direction. He kept moving, using both ground and air, leaping over gunmen, bouncing off walls, using the most random attack patterns that were somehow coming to him to fend off the gunfire and keep pressing the attack. Was what he was doing instinctual, or was it something that he'd learned from his life before?

It was over in seconds. He stood among the bodies strewn across the ground beneath him, fists bloodied, heart racing, eyes glowing with fury.

The hunger – the *urge* – had welled inside him and was now boiling over. The fight had been over too quickly – he had counted on the enemy to serve as a feast, but he had consumed them like a rabid animal swallowing its prey whole.

He looked around hungrily for more – and saw the armed men ahead of him.

He was ready to charge ahead when recognition washed over him, laced with a heavy wave of disappointment. It was the group he'd encountered after escaping the Pit.

He clenched and unclenched his fists, wishing away the truth that he knew these men, searching his mind for any reason he could find, any logic upon which he could warrant an attack.

But there was nothing.

He began to calm himself as best he could: he continued clenching his fists, closed his eyes, let his heart rate begin to slow. He was fighting off the urge with all the will he could gather within himself.

But as he took a step toward the group, a bullet sliced through his chest. Then another.

The gunfire had come from behind.

There was no time for thought: as his consciousness wavered, he looked at the men ahead of him. He staggered to his left, just in time to feel the next several bullets punch through his midsection.

His vision blurred; blackness began to creep into the corners of his eyes. As he fell to his knees, he caught one last glimpse of the men ahead of him. His punctured lungs had left him just enough breath for one final word:

"Run!"

He collapsed to the ground and felt himself begin to slip away into darkness.

From behind the shed, Enrique looked on in horror as the man in black fell to the ground. Then he watched as Otis and the three soldiers began to dive for cover before quickly realizing that there was no cover to be had. They raised their weapons in the direction of the gunshots.

Then he saw him emerge from the shadows: his uncle Javier, smiling triumphantly. His semiautomatic rifle was pointed directly at Otis and the soldiers, with another thirty or so Enforcers flanking him, Alejandro in front with him.

"Come out, boy," he called out to Enrique. "Hernandez — you, too."

Hernandez held Enrique tightly by the arm. "Don't move," he urged him.

Enrique began to shake. It was in that moment that he knew: as long as his uncle lived, his family would always be in danger.

Twenty meters away, Otis surveyed the situation in which he, Crane, Wahler, and Baarton found themselves. They were out in the open, outgunned, and out of options.

The man in black — who'd saved their lives more times than Otis could count — lay dead on the ground before them, his face planted down in the blood that was slowly seeping from his body. Otis had seen his reaction to the gunshots: after taking the first two shots through the chest, he had lunged directly into the line of fire of Otis and the others, taking the bullets that had clearly been meant for them as well.

But there was no time to sift through the emotions that had begun to weigh on him: they had to find a way to get out of this predicament alive.

Their only advantage was that all four of them had their guns trained on the Jackal. And they weren't about to give that up.

"Drop your weapons," the Jackal ordered them.

"Now, why would we do that?" Crane responded.

"You are grossly outnumbered, for one," the Jackal said.

"We only need one shot to take you down," Crane replied sharply. "And we'll get that shot off before you can put all of us down. I guarantee it."

The Jackal laughed and lowered his weapon. "Then take it!" he exclaimed, opening his arms wide. "Certainly, there's nothing stopping you."

"I think we both know what'll happen after that," Crane said.

The Jackal shook his head, "That outcome is a certainty any way you look at it."

"Then why go down without a fight?" Crane said.

Suddenly, a voice boomed from above: "Javier Oropeza! You are surrounded. By order of the United States Navy, you are ordered to drop your weapons and stand down."

The Jackal looked up and around in all directions, trying to locate the source of the voice. "Show yourself, then," he challenged.

"We have you from multiple elevated positions," the voice returned. "You do not have a shot. Drop your weapons or we will begin firing."

At that moment, Otis noticed something about the dead man in black who lay between him and the Enforcers. A subtle movement.

The man's arm was slowly moving toward the body of an Enforcer that lay mere inches away from him.

Was he alive?

Everyone around him – the Jackal, Crane, Wahler, Baarton, the other Enforcers – was so entirely focused on this new voice from above that no one had seemed to notice this but him.

Then Otis saw what he was reaching for.

A grenade, clipped to the belt of the dead Enforcer.

Otis saw the man's fingers close around the grenade and tear it from the belt clip.

Then, in one blinding motion, he pulled the pin and, still face down on the ground, somehow flung it directly into the group of Enforcers with perfect accuracy.

Only the Jackal seemed to notice. He dove away from the throng of Enforcers just as the grenade exploded beneath the group. Many were killed instantly by the blast; yet more were badly injured. Only about a dozen remained, some of them scattering, others firing their guns up toward the source of the voice, clearly thinking that the grenade had come from that direction.

Otis and the others moved to open fire on them, but before they could, the remaining Enforcers were put down quickly by gunshots in rapid succession from above.

The Jackal had made it away from the immediate blast, but not far enough. The force of the explosion had thrown him in the air, flipping him over forward, landing him hard on his back.

Crane wasted no time. "Secure the target," he told Baarton.

That was when Otis spotted Alejandro. He had lost his gun but had somehow distanced himself from the blast and was running toward the shadows.

Aside from the Jackal himself, Otis knew that Alejandro presented the greatest threat to their escape.

Without a word to the others, Otis ran after him.

As he rounded the corner, Alejandro was waiting for him. He hit Otis in the face, knocking him backward. As he fell, the rifle flew from his reach. Through blurred vision, he saw Alejandro advance upon him.

He felt a fist smash against his face, then another on his nose. With every bit of remaining focus he had, Otis thrust a knee hard into Alejandro's groin, forcing him off of him. He quickly gathered himself up off the floor and dodged to his right just as the hunting knife swung within inches of his face. Otis fell backward again, this time atop the rifle. As Alejandro was about to strike again, Otis pulled the rifle in front of him and fired, again and again, connecting several times with Alejandro's chest, neck, and head.

Alejandro crumpled into a dead heap on top of him.

Otis threw the body off him and headed back toward the others.

As the scene came in view, his eyes widened in surprise as he saw Enrique straddled atop the Jackal's midsection, pointing a pistol right at the drug lord's face.

"Aw, hell," was all Otis could say.

Crane and the others stood near the Jackal and were clearly trying to convince Enrique to step away. Hernandez stood behind them, holding his shotgun low, his other arm around Juanita.

"Ha ... do it, boy," the Jackal struggled to laugh as he looked up at Enrique, who was shaking as he held the pistol. "Do you have it in you?"

"Enrique," Otis said as he came up next to him. "It's over. Don't do this."

"He will kill my family," Enrique said through tears. "My mother. My sister. The prisons won't hold him. He will come back and he will do it."

"You're either a killer or you ain't," Otis said. "All'o us around you — we've killed. An' I'll bet not one of us doesn't regret what we had to do. I think about it every day an' every night.

"Killin's a one-way ticket, son," Otis went on. "Once you've taken a man's life, you can't give it back. Doesn't matter who he is or what he's done. What matters is that life is gone — an' you're the one who took it. That's the part that never leaves."

"Please, Enrique," Otis heard Juanita say behind him. "Don't."

Enrique choked back tears. The gun was shaking violently in his hand, sweat pouring from his brow.

"I — I ..." he struggled, but no words came.

He put up a hand to wipe his tears.

His whole body trembling, he handed the gun to Otis.

"Good move, Son," Otis said.

In that instant, Oropeza popped up, grabbing Enrique around the throat with both hands, squeezing hard. Before anyone else could react, Hernandez stepped forward and smashed him in the forehead with the butt-end of his shotgun. The Jackal fell back, letting go of Enrique, but he recovered quickly and made to attack Hernandez, when Hernandez flipped the shotgun around and fired from point blank range, blowing a massive hole through Oropeza's chest.

The Jackal immediately fell back to the ground, dead.

"For my family," Hernandez said quietly as he stood over the Jackal's body.

Juanita ran to Enrique and held him tight.

"Let's get out of here and get a helo for extraction," Crane said.

At that moment, Otis saw someone arise from the ruins of one of the watchtowers. The figure threw a rope down the wall from his perch and immediately began rappelling down toward the ground. Once down, he began walking toward their position.

Otis raised his weapon, but Crane put a hand atop the rifle, lowering it.

"I'll be damned," Otis heard Crane say.

As the figure drew closer, Otis could see it was the C.O., Captain Johns.

"Captain Johns, Sir," Crane, Wahler, and Baarton said, saluting their superior officer as he approached them. Otis stood at attention as well, saluting.

"Figured you men could use some help," Johns said.

"How many are with you, Sir," Crane asked.

"I'm alone, Lieutenant," Johns answered. "But I had to make it seem like we had the enemy covered. Glad they didn't get a chance to call my bluff. What's our sit rep?"

"Target down," Crane said. "More enemy forces could be inbound. Suggest we take the nearest escape route, stat, and call for extraction."

"Let's move, then," Johns agreed. "I'll call in the helo."

"Hernandez there knows the way," Crane added.

"Follow me," Hernandez said, pointing toward the second shed.

"Wait," Otis cut in, pointing to the throng of dead bodies in the open area behind them. "We can't leave 'im — he could still be alive."

"Go," Johns said quickly, waving toward the bodies. "Baarton, help him carry. But hurry; we don't know how long before more enemy forces get here."

Otis quickly led Baarton to the spot where the man in black had been gunned down.

But the man had disappeared.

71

Morning had come over Biggs Airfield in El Paso.

Otis sat alone in a small room, the sun shining brightly through the high, narrow windows to his right. He was sitting on a grey metal chair that creaked intermittently beneath his large frame.

He glanced toward the clock on the wall; it was a few minutes past ten. He had been sitting alone in this room for well over an hour now, his patience worn thin, waiting for someone to come back in and release him, charge him, question him, anything but just leave him where he was, alone to stew with the many thoughts running through his head.

Those thoughts had focused mostly on what had happened just hours ago, but he also thought about what lay before him: what questions he would face by Navy officials, and whether he would be discharged by the Marines. But his main concern was his father: how would Silas would react upon finding out about Otis's involvement with the TIFF, and what that would mean for their relationship, as well as Silas's reputation as Sheriff.

He wondered what would happen to Enrique.

And what had happened to the man in black.

The man whose name Otis had never even learned, even when he'd rescued him from the Taliban prison camp months before.

What was his role in this? Why did he vanish?

Just as that thought settled on him, the door opened. In walked Captain Johns and a second man whom Otis didn't recognize. The second man was wearing Navy officer garb, his lapels lined with pins and medals for his various missions and achievements.

Otis rose from his chair, stood at attention, and saluted the two officers.

"At ease, soldier," Johns acknowledged him. "Please, have a seat."

"Good morning, Sergeant Brown," Johns said as they all sat. "This is Colonel Davidson, U.S. Navy. As you might imagine, we're here to discuss your involvement in the events that occurred across the U.S.-Mexican border earlier this morning."

"Yes, Sir," Otis responded.

"Now," Johns continued, "as I recall, my squadron crossed paths with you and the rest of your group at approximately 0200 hours this morning inside a drug lord's compound. The drug lord in question being Javier Oropeza."

"That's correct, Sir," Otis acknowledged.

"And as I understand it," Johns went on, "you found yourself at said compound as a result of pursuing an Enrique Castillo, who also happens to be related to the drug lord and is a prime suspect in the border crossing attack that occurred two weeks ago. The South Fitchburg crossing, at which you happened to be stationed while on leave, and were on shift at the exact time of the attack."

"Yes, Sir," Otis said.

"As you might imagine, Sergeant," Johns said, "we monitor chatter all over the globe, including within our very own borders. As our team pieced together the various communications throughout the region overnight, we came across some involving an organization called the TIFF, which stands for Texas Independent Freedom Fighters. Are you familiar?"

Otis hesitated. "… I am, Sir."

"We've learned that this organization has been rounding up border crossers of all kinds over the past week — human and drug traffickers alike — and bringing them in to the local police," Johns went on.

"Are you aware, Sergeant," Davidson cut in, "that the penalty for vigilantism is immediate dismissal from the Armed Services, along with applicable punishment decided by Federal law?"

"I am aware, Sir," Otis admitted, and then went on: "All due respect, Sirs, I understand what I've done. I had my reasons. And I understand the penalties that go along with it. I'm ready to accept whatever punishment comes my way."

Johns and Davidson exchanged a look.

"Well, then, Sergeant Brown," Davidson began, "today appears to be your lucky day. For reasons we are not at liberty to share, you have been granted a one-time exception for your involvement in the events of the previous evening."

Otis stared slack-jawed at Davidson, unsure of what he was hearing.

"This comes in the form of a full pardon, making you exempt from any further disciplinary action on this particular matter. You should know that this order is not coming from either of our branches of service, but from a higher authority in Washington. Your C.O. has been given this same information. That is all we are able to share at this time."

"Yes, Sir," Otis said, still processing everything that Davidson had just told him.

"That will be all, Sergeant," Johns said and then stood up.

Davidson joined him and added, "Captain Johns will escort you out."

Otis stood and saluted the two officers, who returned the salute. He stood at attention as Davidson strode from the room.

"At ease, soldier," Johns told him once Davidson had left. "Now, I'm sure you understand that you're not to speak of anything you saw over the past twelve hours."

"Loud and clear, Sir," Otis acknowledged.

"And you should know that we already have wire taps and surveillance measures in place to ensure that does not happen," Johns said. "I hope that's also understood."

"Understood, Sir," Otis replied. "But, Sir. I do have one question I hope you can answer."

"I doubt that I can," Johns said. "But you can certainly ask it."

"The one man," Otis said. "You called him the Specialist. He disappeared. Who was he? What happened to 'im?"

Johns sighed. "That's the one question, above all others," he said, "that I know I can't answer."

"Sir," Otis said. "I have a history with him. He rescued me from a Taliban prison camp months ago. An' there's ... *other* things about him. I saw him do things ... things that ain't human."

"Just a few of the reasons, Sergeant," Johns said heavily, "that I can't answer any of your questions."

"All right, Sir," Otis relented, then: "Then I have a request."

"And what's that, Sergeant?" Johns said.

"Can I have a moment with Enrique?"

Johns hesitated for a moment. "I think we can arrange that," he said, finally.

Moments earlier, Enrique and Juanita had been sitting in a similar small room down the hall from Otis, when a uniformed officer entered.

"Enrique Castillo?" the soldier addressed him.

"That's me, yes," Enrique said.

"Please come with me," the soldier said.

"What about my sister?" Enrique asked.

"She can remain here," the soldier responded. "We'll have you back with her momentarily."

Enrique glanced back at Juanita, who looked scared, but nodded in agreement.

"Okay," Enrique said and followed the soldier out.

Seconds later, he was entering another room, this one larger, with tiny windows along the back wall, which shared only a small amount of the bright sunlight outside. As he walked in, he first saw Hernandez sitting at a table. Sitting across from him was Captain Johns, who had joined them just before leaving the compound, and a second man, considerably older, appearing to be of Mexican descent. He had a moustache and slicked-back, salt-and-pepper hair, and he wore a dark suit. Somehow, he looked very familiar to Enrique.

"Mister Castillo," Johns addressed him, then gestured to the empty chair next to Hernandez. "Please have a seat."

Enrique sat down in the chair and glanced at the men around him at the table.

"First of all, on behalf of the United States government," Johns addressed both Enrique and Hernandez, "we would like to commend you for your assistance in the events that unfolded over the past several hours overnight. Especially you, Mr. Hernandez; while unexpected, your knowledge of the Jackal's operation was instrumental in enabling our men to get out of there alive.

"One thing I must first emphasize," Johns continued, "is that everything you witnessed is considered highly classified by both the U.S. and Mexican governments. Therefore, nothing you saw is to be shared with anyone, on any occasion, under any circumstances. We expect, Mister Castillo, that you will ensure that this remains the case with your family as well. Because of the sensitive nature of the events you've taken part in, you will both be under surveillance by the Mexican government – both for your protection and for that of our two governments. I hope that is understood."

Both Enrique and Hernandez nodded slowly.

"With me here is Mexico's Minister of Drug Enforcement, Hector Galvan," Johns gestured to the man in the suit. "Since you are both Mexican citizens, you fall under his jurisdiction, so he is here to tell you what will happen next. Minister Galvan, Sir."

Galvan nodded to Johns, then looked upon both Hernandez and Enrique. "Gentlemen," he began, "our American colleagues have kept the Ministry and President Vincennes himself notified of the events in which you were both involved over these past several hours.

"Thanks in part to your efforts," he went on, "Senor Javier Escondido Oropeza, known throughout Mexico as the Jackal, is dead. His assets have been seized by the Mexican government, and the majority of his top lieutenants are either dead or in the custody of the Mexican authorities.

"After your extraction, the Mexican army was brought in to finish the mission. As of this morning, the Jackal's compound is under our military's control.

"Now," Galvan continued, "what happens next for you two: because of your actions, the people of Mexico owe you a great debt. Therefore, the President has approved a small percentage of the assets seized to be apportioned to each of you. In the coming days, you will each receive a federal bank deposit equal to one-one-hundredth of a percent of Oropeza's total asset value."

Enrique didn't understand what the Minister meant; was he going to receive some of his uncle's fortune? He glanced over at Hernandez, who was clearly trying to hide his reaction to this news, but Enrique could tell that he understood the Minister.

Galvan must have read Enrique's puzzled expression, so he elaborated: "Oropeza's estimated wealth is equal to approximately 41 billion U.S. dollars, so this translates to the equivalent of about 4.1 million U.S. dollars, coming to each of you."

Enrique's eyebrows went up.

Galvan smiled at Enrique's speechless reaction, then added: "These funds will be yours, but I must warn you, they will be heavily tracked by our banking system. If we have reason to suspect any improper use of these funds, they will be removed from your accounts, and further punishment may apply. I'm sure that is clear."

Neither Enrique nor Hernandez spoke, both still absorbing what Galvan had said.

"Now," Johns said, "what questions do you have for us? Keep in mind, though, that we will not be at liberty to answer any involving our military presence in your country overnight."

"My mother," Enrique immediately cut in, "where is she? Is she safe?"

"Yes, she is," Galvan answered. "Once we learned of her situation, she was moved to a secure location. She has been under the care of our top military doctors. We understand she's expected to make a full recovery."

Enrique exhaled in relief. "Thank you," was all he could say.

"Now, if there aren't any further questions," Johns said, "we'll have you both on your way. Mister Hernandez, you'll be airlifted to your home city. Mister Castillo, you and your sister will be taken to your mother's current location."

Johns and Galvan stood up, and in walked two uniformed soldiers. "Nunez and Goode here will escort you both to your ride," Johns said. "Godspeed, gentlemen."

Enrique and Hernandez followed the soldiers down a long hallway to a large, open lobby right off the tarmac, where Juanita sat already waiting for them.

A few moments later, Johns entered the lobby. "Mister Castillo," Johns said, "may we have a word. Alone."

"Okay," Enrique said, glancing toward Juanita before getting up.

"Follow me," Johns said, and disappeared back into the long hallway.

Enrique followed Johns to a doorway about halfway down the hall, where Johns gestured for him to enter. Johns looked into the room and called, "Two minutes," to whomever was inside.

Enrique rounded into the doorway and saw Otis sitting at a table, an empty chair across from him. He saw Enrique and nodded.

"Sit with me for a minute, could ya," Otis said.

Enrique did so, taking a seat across from Otis.

"I hear your mama's gonna be fine," Otis said.

"Yes, she is," Enrique replied, unsure what else to say.

"We been through a lot together, past few hours," Otis said, sitting back in the chair. "Got shot at, beat up, knocked down. Coulda died a bunch o'times. Heck, you almost got eaten by a coupla dogs." He chuckled at this.

Enrique nodded, trying to smile back, shifting in his chair a bit.

"So listen. I need ya to promise me somethin'," he said.

"What?" Enrique asked.

"Remember when you were holdin' that gun to your uncle's head?" Otis said.

Enrique nodded.

"Remember how you felt in that moment," Otis said.

"I – I wanted to kill him," Enrique's voice cracked. "Just end it."

"Oh, it woulda been the end for him, yeah," Otis acknowledged. "But it woulda been only the beginnin' for you. An' that's the only part that matters.

"Nothin' good ever comes from killin' someone," Otis continued. "You either carry that regret for the rest o' your life, or you cross over to becomin' someone you don't ever wanna be. An' that second option is way worse than the first.

"You're no killer," Otis leaned forward, gazing directly at him. "An' you should never become one. Because once ya are, ya always will be. Ya can't ever take it back. I know – because I've tried.

"So promise me that, willya," he finally said. "Never become one."

"Okay," Enrique nodded.

"Thanks," Otis smiled. "An' if you ever need anythin', you can always call me. Take this." He slid a small slip of paper across the table, a phone number written on the front of it.

"Okay," Enrique said. "Thank – thank you."

"Now, we best be goin'," Otis said. "You got some folks waitin' for ya, as do I."

Otis stood up and extended his hand. Enrique shook it.

"Go take care o' your family, you hear?" Otis nodded to him.

"I will," Enrique replied.

And with that, Otis disappeared through the open doorway.

Moments later, Enrique was back to the lobby, where Juanita waited for him.

"Your vehicle is here now," the officer told him.

Enrique looked at Juanita, and they both followed the officer out to the waiting car outside.

At the other end of the hallway, Otis walked alongside Captain Johns, who had been silent up to this point.

"Sergeant Brown," he finally spoke. "Although the record will never show it, the Navy owes you a great debt. If there's anything you need, it would be my honor."

"Thank you, Sir," Otis said.

"Your ride home should be here by now," Johns said. "This way, please."

He was about to ask Johns exactly who his ride was when he turned the corner and saw his father standing there in police uniform, arms crossed expectantly.

His eyes met Otis's, and he strode forward, pulling his son into a tight embrace.

"Thank God," he said, his voice muffled against Otis' shoulder.

"Pa," Otis said, hugging Silas back, "how – how'd you know where –"

"Ferrell and Swank," Otis said. "Boys came into the station, outta breath and scared. Tol' me everythin'."

"Uh, everythin'?" Otis said.

"I know all about it," Silas pulled back and met Otis' eyes, a note of sternness coming to his voice. "The militia, Voorhees, the dead men, everything. An' you can bet we'll talk about it later."

"Yes, Sir," Otis said.

"But fer now," Silas said, "I'll just take ya alive."

He put his arm around Otis, and the two walked out of the base toward Silas's waiting cruiser.

72

The halls of the Pentagon were unusually busy for a Sunday afternoon, abuzz with teams working on various projects related to the overnight operation in Mexico.

Inside the War Room, General Jack Dunlap leaned back in his chair, a recount of the previous night's events in one hand, a cold cup of coffee in the other.

The mission had been deemed a success by the President, Homeland Security, State, and Defense: the target was dead, along with most of his top field lieutenants; his drug network was crippled, his assets and base of operations seized by the Mexican government.

But their victory had come at great cost.

They had lost four SEALs and two CIA agents in their first attempt on the target's compound, along with the sixty-two CBP agents and civilians killed in the initial attack.

Sixty-eight confirmed dead, most of whom were lost on American soil.

It would take the nation a long time to recover from such an attack.

And then, there was the only question mark remaining from the whole event.

The Specialist.

By the accounts of Captain Johns and the SEALs on the ground, he'd taken several hits to the midsection, presumably stepping into the line of fire to protect the SEALs and civilians in the target's sights. He immediately went down and was presumed dead. But when they went to recover the body, he had vanished.

His surviving the gunshots was of no surprise to Dunlap; he recalled video feeds and transcripts from several past missions where the Specialist had taken fire and lived through it. Certainly, on no previous occasion had he taken so much fire, but the man's durability and healing had enabled him to walk away on occasions where any other soldier would have been taken home in a body bag.

But why had he disappeared?

And where had he gone?

At that moment, Stewart approached him, Armstrong following closely behind.

"Sir, we have an update on the Specialist," Stewart said.

"Where is he?" Armstrong asked as he caught up to Stewart at the map table.

"No location as of yet, Sir," Stewart answered. "But we received more incoming data on him, some of which might explain his behavior."

"Such as?" Dunlap said, setting down the coffee.

"We gathered accounts of the SEALs and civilians on the ground, as well as audio transcripts of mobile-phone exchanges between cartel members who encountered him. The results led us to one likely conclusion."

"And that is?" Armstrong said impatiently.

"That the Specialist was suffering from some form of amnesia," Stewart said.

"Hmm," Dunlap sat back in his chair.

"How exactly could he have lost his memory?" Armstrong argued.

"Think about it, Edward," Dunlap said. "We don't know exactly how he survived the helo attack. But if he was anywhere near those birds when they were hit, the concussive force of the blast could easily have had that effect."

"All right," Armstrong said. "But he went back and finished the mission! How would he have known to do that?"

"A soldier's instinct," Dunlap said plainly. "It guides you more than you realize. The rest could be purely circumstantial. And I'll also bet that Stewart here is continuing to gather information to help piece things together. Isn't that correct?"

"We are, Sir," Stewart answered.

"Good work, son," Dunlap told him. "Keep working on his whereabouts."

"Yes, Sir," Stewart said, walking back toward his station.

Once they were alone, Armstrong sat down next to Dunlap and leaned in close.

"Jack," he began, "I don't like this one bit. We have to find him. Bring him in."

"Hmmm," Dunlap rubbed his chin. "If Stewart's intel rings true ... which my gut tells me it does ... that means he's out there somewhere ... with no idea of who he is, where he belongs, or what he's supposed to do."

"Or *what* he is," added Armstrong. "That's the part that concerns me."

"I think he has an idea of that by now," Dunlap said. "But what concerns *me* most is someone else finding out about him ... and finding him before *we* do."

"We absolutely can't allow that to happen," Armstrong agreed.

"Tell me something, Edward," Dunlap said, leaning back in the chair again. "Why do you think he left?"

"No idea," Armstrong said. "But I'm guessing you have a theory."

"I'm working a few through my mind," Dunlap answered.

"Care to share any?" Armstrong said.

"I'll share the one I think is right," Dunlap said.

"All right," Armstrong said.

'Think about this," Dunlap said. "If he had no memory of who he was ... he would have questions. Questions he'd be looking for answers to."

"Yes," Armstrong agreed.

"But what if he realized somewhere along the way ... that he wouldn't like what those answers were?"

"I suppose that's plausible," Armstrong began, "for most people. But not him."

"And why do you say that?" Dunlap asked.

"Because the man is a warrior at his very core," Armstrong said. "A killer. Capable of doing things most soldiers, most *men*, couldn't do. I don't think there's much that would deter him away from the chance to keep doing that."

"I see," Dunlap said. "But you've read the files on him almost as many times as I have. You know his history ... his ... imbalances."

"Yes," Armstrong said. "Exactly what are you suggesting?"

"What if," Dunlap began, "there was some kind of trigger that caused his mind to reverse course? That made him run."

"Like what?" Armstrong asked.

"No idea," Dunlap said. "Like I said ... it's only a theory."

"So that just leaves one question," Armstrong thought aloud. "Where is he?"

"We'll use everything we've got to find him," Dunlap said. "Satellite, wiretaps, drones, boots on the ground. But we'll find him. We won't stop until we do."

EPILOGUE

The sun had nearly set over the high hills and valleys that stretched across the barren desert landscape; off in the distance, the night creatures had begun their evening song.

Along the lone, dust-swept dirt road that ran through the empty town, everything remained still, as it had done for decades. The desert breeze whispered between ancient stone, clay, and wood structures that stood silently against the fading sky, immobile silhouettes harboring countless stories of an era gone by, bereft of a single soul to tell them.

Small creatures scurried amid the worn, faded buildings; there were rodents and lizards alike, darting in and out of tiny openings, in search of their evening meal. The sound of crickets began to stream throughout the tiny town, the nightly elements of twilight in full bloom.

But as the sound of slow, scuffling footsteps began to draw near the village, the tiny creatures stopped scurrying, darting into the nearest holes they could find. The crickets ceased their singing, falling as silent as the still desert air.

The footsteps grew more audible. Amid each footfall was the sound of something being dragged along, like an enormous, heavy tail, slithering across the dirt and sand.

He came into the town bearing the fruit of his latest hunt, a black bear that would serve as his dinner, dragging it by its hind leg.

He passed the same old, worn buildings along the main thoroughfare: the general store, saloon, bank, and sheriff's lockup, before finally reaching the hotel that had served as his home these past several weeks. Across the street from the hotel, the one-story clay structure, which had presumably once served as the town's post office, displayed the words FULLERTON, N.M. in iron letters above its front doorway.

He set the carcass on the rickety wooden walkway that led into the building and plunked down next to it. He sat still for a moment, looking out over the remnants of the town in the fading light.

He had been here for thirty-five days and nights now, each day marked by a small notch carved into the hotel's stone wall.

He had come across this town after several days of traversing countless miles of desert, scavenging for food and water wherever he could along the way. When he'd discovered a well at the edge of this town, he decided to stay until he could figure out what to do next. He had not moved on since.

The surrounding land did not offer an abundance of food choices, but there was easily enough desert flora, fauna, and wildlife to sustain him. Tonight's catch was unusually large; he would be able to eat from it for days. His usual catches had consisted of jackrabbits, foxes, and the occasional weasel. He'd also caught a few coyotes, but their flesh was too gristly and thin for his liking. He'd even caught a silver-haired bat during one desperate hunt early on. That would be the only bat he would ever eat.

He had also learned which desert plants were edible and which were not: certain kinds of cacti and desert brush — which he now knew by appearance — had given him a bad enough stomachache that he knew to avoid them. He assumed that some of those plants would likely have killed him if not for his healing abilities. But now that he recognized the five or six that he knew were safe to consume, he no longer ventured to try out any new ones.

Behind the hotel, he'd built a large fire pit complete with a spit in order to cook his dinner every night. And, to his surprise, whoever had abandoned this town had left behind many useful tools: knives, a machete, even an axe, enabling him to carve up each nightly catch.

The hotel itself was constructed mostly of stone and clay, which he figured was largely the reason it was still standing after a hundred-plus years. Most of the wood structures in the town had sagged inward or collapsed altogether.

The sleeping rooms were located upstairs, the wood stairwell leading up to them at the rear of the lobby. The stairs did not look sturdy enough to support any weight, but for him, the second floor was only one quick leap away.

He'd chosen a room near the back of the short hallway, the third door on the left. Inside was a straw bed, which he'd covered with old burlap sacks in order to sleep on it each night.

His thoughts trailed back to the sequence of events that had led him here.

Waking up in the desert, with no memory of who he was.

Being chased and shot at everywhere he turned.

Discovering his unique abilities. Using them to survive.

The vicious, overpowering, unbearable urges.

Getting trapped by the drug lord in his compound. Surviving that.

Encountering the soldier who had known him from before.

The child. That one, terrible memory returning to him.

Stopping the bomb. Then the drug lord.

Leaving the soldiers, their orders, their questions behind.

Not knowing who he was. But knowing what he had done.

The one memory staying in his mind.

The child. Killed by his own hand.

The image hanging before him. As if from a noose he had fashioned himself.

This. This was the reason he had left all other questions unanswered.

If this was all he knew about himself ... he did not want to know any more.

He closed his eyes, then opened them again, washing the thoughts from his mind.

His eyes moved along the still desert street.

It was the end of another day.

He rose to his feet and ventured inside the hotel lobby.

Once inside, he noticed something unfamiliar on the stairwell. Something new; something very out of place.

A tablet computer.

He looked at is more closely, making sure he wasn't seeing things.

His heart began to race.

They had found him.

He turned from the stairs, scanning the lobby, then the windows that opened to the street outside.

No one in view.

"Who's there?" he growled quietly.

He moved to the staircase and leapt up to the second floor. He charged into the bedroom, slamming open the door with his shoulder.

His eyes darted about the room.

There was no one.

He went to the window, looking out at the landscape in the dim light.

No signs of movement; nothing.

He made his way back to the front of the hotel, stepping outside and into the street. Again, he could see no one, nor any sign of anything being disturbed.

"WHO'S THERE?" he roared into the prevailing darkness, his booming voice echoing off buttes and foothills alike, sending creatures large and small into their holes and hiding places for miles around.

He waited. Still nothing.

From everything he could see, he was alone.

Cautiously, he strode back inside and took the tablet in his hands, staring at it for a long moment.

He looked around again. *Who could have left this here?*

They had brought it while he was out on his hunt; that much was certain.

Which meant that they had been watching him for longer than just today.

He slowly lifted the cover.

As the screen lit up before him, a low beeping sound emitted from the tablet's small speaker. Almost as if his opening the tablet was calling someone on the other end.

A second later, the screen changed, and a man's face appeared. It was an older man with thin graying hair and mustache, a stern expression gazing directly at him; one that projected undeniable authority. He was wearing a blue military uniform with several stars and decorations on his shoulders and lapels, a clear indication that he was of high rank.

The stern face spoke: "It's good to see you alive, soldier."

He said nothing in return.

The face stared at him for a long moment, then continued.

"Do you recognize me?" the face said.

"No," he said.

"Do you have any questions for me?"

"How did you find me?"

"Yes. Let's start there," the man said. "That was no simple task. But between satellite imaging and spy drones, no one can stay out of our view for long.

"As to who I am," he continued, "I am Army Brigadier General Jack Dunlap. I serve on the Joint Chiefs of Staff for the President of the United

States. I am your commanding officer, ultimately responsible for you and your role with the United States Armed Forces."

The face named Dunlap let this information settle for a moment.

"Does that mean anything to you?" Dunlap finally asked him.

"No," was all he said.

"So you have no recollection of who you are. Nothing at all," Dunlap said.

"No," he repeated.

"It's what we'd suspected, based on everything we'd seen," Dunlap admitted. "You had an event during your last mission. Your unit was ambushed, and you were the only survivor. That event must have taken your memory."

He said nothing in return, just continued to stare blankly at the screen.

"But now, it's time for you to come home. You must have many questions. Many to which we can provide answers. As well as ensure that you get back to good health, re-trained, and ready to serve your country once again."

"I'm doing just fine here," he said flatly.

"Nonsense," Dunlap said dismissively. "You have no idea of the life you have waiting for you. You're a national hero."

"I have an idea of it," he said, "and I'm not going anywhere."

Dunlap stared at him, puzzled. "And what idea is that?" he questioned.

"I remember one thing," he said, casting his eyes downward, away from Dunlap's gaze. "And that's all I need."

"And what one thing is that?" Dunlap asked.

He looked back up at him accusingly. "The child," was all he said.

Dunlap's face showed confusion for a moment, then recognition.

"So you know about it, too," he said.

"So, of all your memories, that's the only one that you recall," Dunlap said.

'Yes," he said.

"Your condition must have triggered it somehow," Dunlap surmised. "Or something that happened to you recently. Or a combination of both."

"It doesn't matter," he said. "If I did that, I must have done other things like it. Worse things."

"No," Dunlap replied matter-of-factly. "You did not. That one instance was an anomaly. And an accident. At worst it was collateral damage. It happens every day in war. You can't stop it."

"I can," he retorted, "by not being a part of it."

"You have no idea what you've done for your country," Dunlap said. "How many calamities you've stopped, lives you've saved."

"I killed a child. Why should I believe that I didn't do other terrible things."

Dunlap hesitated. "Because," he finally said, "that's the one memory we took from you."

"What?" he said, a look of confusion coming across his face. "Why?"

"After that mission," Dunlap explained, "you returned home feeling much like you are right now: distraught. Full of doubt. Unwilling to go on.

"So," he continued after a pause, "we had to do something about it."

"So you — brainwashed me," he concluded.

"No," Dunlap corrected him. "We merely suppressed that one memory — or more specifically, that single element of the memory — from your conscious mind."

"I don't believe you," he said.

"From where you're sitting, I probably wouldn't either," Dunlap admitted. "But we can help you. If we could take a memory away, then we can put them back."

"I'm not going back," he maintained.

"One thousand, six hundred and fifty-one," Dunlap called out. "Do you know what that number means?"

"No," he said.

"It's the number of lives you've saved," Dunlap said. "Both civilian and military. By everything you've done on your missions. Those lives would unquestionably have been lost if not for your actions. And I have no question that you'll save thousands more."

"If you know me as well as you say you do," he said, "then you know what ... happens to me. That ... once it starts ... I can't stop it."

Dunlap nodded slowly. "Yes, I do," Dunlap acknowledged. "But we've found a solution for that. We can help you control it."

"The only way I know how to control it," he replied. "Is by avoiding it altogether. And you would have me go right back into it. Every day."

"No," Dunlap argued. "It won't be like that. It never has. We only deploy you on highly critical missions. You're not a blunt instrument."

At that moment, he noticed something in the doorway of the post office across the street. A subtle movement.

He kept his eyes on the tablet.

"Just come home," Dunlap added. "We'll help you get back to where you were — *who* you were — and you can continue doing good for the world."

He stayed silent for a moment, staring at the tablet.

"And if I agree?" he finally asked.

"Like I said, you'll return to your old life," Dunlap explained. "With all the benefits. You can continue to help make the world a safer place."

"And if I don't?"

"Then, I'm afraid," Dunlap said somberly, "we'd have no choice but to bring you in."

"Why?" he questioned.

"To protect you, and our nation," Dunlap said matter-of-factly. "You are our most valuable soldier in the war on terror. And if we don't take you in – if somehow you were to end up in the wrong hands – our national security would be at risk."

He stayed silent for a moment, then: "So in the end, I don't have a choice."

"You always have a choice," Dunlap said. "I just hope you'll make the right one."

"Just answer me one question first," he said.

"Anything," Dunlap replied.

"What's my name?"

He could see Dunlap straighten in his seat. "The only name we have on record for you," he said, "is Rage."

"Rage," he repeated it deliberately, as if pondering whether to keep it.

"But there is much for you to re-learn, to rediscover," Dunlap added.

"We can begin as soon as you're ready."

He said nothing, merely nodding at Dunlap's statement.

"Good," Dunlap nodded back. "Very good. I have a helo en route to pick you up; ETA ten minutes."

Moments later, he was outside and could see the Black Hawk helicopter approaching above the horizon to the southeast. The tablet was still in his hand, with Dunlap's image showing on the screen.

The Black Hawk landed at the very center of the street, the rotors kicking up a swirling dust storm in their wake. He stepped back and shielded his eyes, then cautiously approached the helicopter.

As he got closer, he saw the two pilots through the front windshield, as well as two soldiers in full mission gear, who stepped out to greet him. He glanced around the aircraft but saw no one else in the immediate vicinity.

"Sir," the first soldier said as he came before him. "Sergeant First-Class Simonson, USMC. This is Sergeant Second-Class Abramson, USMC. It's an honor, Sir."

He said nothing in return, merely nodding to both soldiers before looking around again, and again seeing no sign of anyone.

The soldier gestured to the Black Hawk. "This way, please, Sir —"

Before the tablet hit the ground, he'd struck both soldiers in the head, immediately knocking them unconscious. As they crumpled to either side of him, he leapt into the helo's cockpit, quickly knocking both pilots out cold as well. He scanned the control panel, locating the ignition switch and flipping it to the off position, cutting the engine. He then gripped the control stick and pulled hard, tearing it straight out of its mounting. The helo was now disabled.

He knelt down in the cockpit for a moment, gripping the pilot's seat with both hands, taking deep breaths. He needed to calm himself. The urge was trying to force its way in; he needed to curb it for what would happen next.

He removed the co-pilot's helmet and put it on, lowering the night-vision scope to his field of view. Darkness had prevailed outside, and he knew what was waiting for him in the street beyond. He would need to see what he was up against.

At that moment, a small silver canister landed in the cockpit, rolling for a split second before coming to a stop against his foot.

Tear gas.

He catapulted into the street, tackling the soldier in his line of sight, barreling with him over his shoulder into the saloon while shots fired all around him. He leapt over the long, ancient wooden bar, using the soldier as a human cushion as they landed hard on the floor behind the bar. He then pulled him up face to face.

"How many are there?" he snarled.

The dazed soldier glanced back up at him. "More than ... you can handle," he struggled to say.

He grunted in disgust, pushing the soldier back to the floor before knocking him cold.

He'd known that Dunlap had hedged his bets the moment he saw movement in the post office: if he wouldn't come willingly, they would take him by any means necessary. They *had* been watching him, waiting for him to go out on a hunt, when they moved the soldiers into position in his town.

And if they knew him as well as they claimed to, then he had no doubt that they'd sent a large enough force of highly-trained soldiers to overwhelm even him. And they were more than likely everywhere in this little town, hidden in every crack and crevice, including snipers on the rooftops. He had no question that he was surrounded.

He couldn't just fight his way out. Either they would take him down, or he would be pulled down by the urge, driven to maim and murder every single soldier who had been sent to retrieve him.

No. His only option was to run.

He heard the voices outside; they were assembling around the saloon, no doubt at the front and rear entrances, and every window in between.

Without hesitation, he jumped straight upward, grabbing hold of one of the cross-beams along the ceiling. Keeping hold of the beam with one hand, he smashed through the ceiling with his other, sending splinters and shards of old, dried wood down to the floor below, just as the soldiers began to storm the saloon. He pulled himself up onto the roof and sprinted across it, feeling the century-old surface buckle beneath his every step, before leaping across the wide street to the bank, whose stone-and-clay rooftop easily supported his landing.

He quickly scanned the street and rooftops; many of the soldiers had stormed the saloon, but there were more at each end of the street, and he noticed two snipers, one perched up on the hotel, the second on the sheriff's lockup. He ducked as they both fired upon him, his reflexes barely enabling him to evade both shots. He caught a quick glance at one of the rounds as it stuck to a rooftop post next to him: they were using tranquilizer darts. They wanted him alive.

There was no time to plan; he'd bought himself a few seconds with his escape, but the bulk of the soldiers had begun pouring out of the saloon, some taking positions in the street, some already moving toward the rear of the bank to surround him.

Now or never, he realized.

He sprinted toward the rear of the bank, taking a towering leap as he reached the roof's edge, soaring into the night sky. As he hit the ground, he could hear a buzzing noise. He looked up to see a small drone, a quad-copter about the size of a shoebox, pacing about fifteen feet above him. He leapt straight upward and grabbed hold of the drone, pulling it down as he came back to earth. He quickly smashed it against the ground, not taking more than a second before he began running again.

He knew that there would be more soldiers, more helicopters, more drones, on the hunt for him, so he had to move faster; he had to stretch his abilities beyond even their knowledge of what he could do.

He leapt again, hitting the ground in a full sprint, moving as fast as his legs would carry him, before launching into another long leap, then another, then another still, before continuing to run, finally vanishing into the darkness of the night beyond.

Chris Lindberg lives in the Chicago suburbs with his wife and two children. Besides writing, he enjoys bicycling, running, grilling, any kind of vintage music, college football, and just about any activity with his kids.

Devil in the Dark is the follow-up to his first novel, *Code of Darkness*, available at Amazon, Barnes & Noble.com, and many other online retailers.

Chris wrote both novels while riding a commuter train into the city. You might find him there some morning, working away on his next project.

Chris would love to hear from you; you can contact him at chris@codeofdarkness.com